PRAISE FOR SIMON BRETT
AND THE FETHERING MYSTERIES

'A skilful and entertaining cosy mystery which oozes clues, red herrings and flights, or perhaps hops, of deductive reasoning . . . Thank heaven, he reminds us, part of England remains forever Fethering'
Andrew Taylor, *Spectator*

'It's hard to resist a title like *Death Under the Dryer*, especially when the author is that king of the witty village mystery, Simon Brett . . . an enjoyable read'
Sunday Telegraph

'A feast of red herrings, broadly drawn characters and gentle thrills and spills litter the witty plot'
Guardian

'Simon Brett writes the that could have been w he has a sly
The

'An irresistibly old-time mystery'
Daily Mail

'This is lovely stuff, as comforting – and as unputdownable – as a Sussex cream tea.

BLOOD AT THE BOOKIES

Simon Brett worked as a producer in radio and television before taking up writing full-time. As well as the much-loved Fethering series, the Mrs Pargeter novels and the Charles Paris detective series, he is the author of the radio and television series *After Henry*, the radio series *No Commitments* and *Smelling of Roses* and the bestselling *How to Be a Little Sod*. His novel *A Shock to the System* was filmed, starring Michael Caine.

Married with three grown-up children, he lives in an Agatha Christie-style village on the South Downs.

Blood at the Bookies is the ninth novel in the Fethering Mysteries series. The tenth, *The Poisoning in the Pub*, is available now.

SIMON BRETT

BLOOD AT THE BOOKIES

A FETHERING MYSTERY

PAN BOOKS

First published 2008 by Macmillan

First published in paperback 2009 by Pan Books
an imprint of Pan Macmillan
20 New Wharf Road, London N1 9RR
Associated companies throughout the world
www.panmacmillan.com

ISBN 978-1-5098-0751-2

Copyright © Simon Brett 2008

The right of Simon Brett to be identified as the
author of this work has been asserted by him in accordance
with the Copyright, Designs and Patents Act 1988.

All rights reserved. No part of this publication may be
reproduced, stored in or introduced into a retrieval system, or
transmitted, in any form, or by any means (electronic, mechanical,
photocopying, recording or otherwise) without the prior written
permission of the publisher. Any person who does any unauthorized
act in relation to this publication may be liable to criminal
prosecution and civil claims for damages.

1 3 5 7 9 8 6 4 2

A CIP catalogue record for this book is available from
the British Library.

Typeset by Intype Libra Ltd
Printed in the UK by CPI Group (UK) Ltd, Croydon, CR0 4YY

This book is sold subject to the condition that it shall not,
by way of trade or otherwise, be lent, re-sold, hired out,
or otherwise circulated without the publisher's prior consent
in any form of binding or cover other than that in which
it is published and without a similar condition including this
condition being imposed on the subsequent purchaser.

Visit www.panmacmillan.com to read more about all our books
and to buy them. You will also find features, author interviews and
news of any author events, and you can sign up for e-newsletters
so that you're always first to hear about our new releases.

To Jake,

hoping he gets lucky on the horses

Chapter One

'Come on, everyone likes a bet,' said Jude.

'Well, I don't,' sniffed Carole.

The response was so characteristic and instinctive that her friend couldn't help smiling. In a world where everyone was encouraged to be 'hands-on' and 'touchy-feely', Carole Seddon's approach to life was always going to be 'hands-off' and 'keep-your-distance'. But those idiosyncrasies didn't diminish Jude's affection for her. And that February morning the affection was increased by the diminished state her neighbour was in. The response to the idea of betting would always have been sniffy, but on this occasion it had been accompanied by a genuine sniff. Carole was drowned by a virulent winter flu bug, and Jude felt the last emotion her neighbour would ever wish to inspire in anyone – pity.

'Anyway, I've promised Harold I'll go to the betting shop and put his bets on, so I can't not do it.'

'Huh,' was Carole's predictable response. Her pinched face looked even thinner behind her rimless glasses. The pale blue eyes were bleary and the short grey hair hung lank.

'Come on, it's one of the few pleasures Harold Peskett has at his age. And he's got this wretched flu just like you. It's the least I can do for him. I can't see that there's anything wrong with it.'

'It's encouraging bad habits,' came the prissy reply.

'Carole, Harold is ninety-two, for God's sake! I don't think I'm going to make his habits any worse at this stage of his life. And it's no hardship – I've got to go to the shops anyway, to get my stuff . . . and yours.'

'What do you mean – mine?'

'You're in no state to go out shopping.'

'Oh, I'm sure I will be later. I've got a touch of flu, that's all.'

'You look ghastly. You should go straight back to bed. I don't know why you bothered to get dressed this morning.'

Carole looked shocked. 'What, are you suggesting I should be lolling round the house in my dressing-gown?'

'No. As I say, I'm suggesting you should go back to bed and give yourself a chance of getting rid of this bug. Have you got an electric blanket?'

'Of course not!' Carole was appalled by the idea of such self-indulgence.

'Hot water-bottle?'

With some shame, Carole admitted that she did possess one of those luxury items. Jude picked the kettle up off the Aga and moved to fill it at the sink. 'Tell me where the hot water-bottle is and I'll—'

'Jude!' The name was spoken with considerable

2

asperity. 'This is my house, and I'll thank you to let me manage it in my own way.'

'I'm not stopping you from doing that. But you're ill, and there are some things you can't do at the minute.'

'I am not ill!' Carole Seddon rose assertively from her chair. But she was taken aback by the wave of giddiness that assailed her. She tottered, reached for the support of the kitchen table and slowly subsided back down.

A grin spread across Jude's plump face. Her brown eyes sparkled and the stacked-up blonde hair swayed as she shook her head in the most benign of I-told-you-so gestures. 'See. You can't even stand up. There's no way you could make it down Fethering High Street even as far as Allinstore. I will do your shopping for you, and you will go to bed.'

'There's nothing I want,' Carole mumbled with bad grace. 'I'm well stocked up with everything.'

'Not the kind of things you need. You need nice warming soups and things like that. Lucozade, whisky . . . When you're ill, you need to feel pampered.'

'What nonsense you do talk, Jude.' But the resistance was already diminishing. Carole felt so rotten that even her opposition to the idea of pampering, built up over more than fifty years, was beginning to erode.

What defeated her residual contrariness was the issue of her dog. Gulliver, slumped by the Aga in his usual state of Labrador passivity, was going to need walking very soon or there might be a nasty accident on the kitchen floor. What was more, the house was completely out of dog food. And Carole was just not strong enough to complete either of these tasks. Much as it went against her every instinct, she was going to need help. And getting that help from Jude, who had already witnessed her parlous state, was preferable to involving anyone else, letting a stranger into her life. Grudgingly, Carole Seddon bit the bullet and agreed that her neighbour should add to her own errands the task of walking Gulliver out to buy some of his favourite Pedigree Chum.

She still showed token resistance to the idea of pampering. She certainly wouldn't contemplate the idea of Jude helping her undress and get back to bed. But she did let slip where the hot water-bottle was to be found.

Jude was discreet enough to tap on the bedroom door before she entered with the filled bottle and a steaming drink. She looked at the drained face peering miserably over the edge of the duvet. 'There. At least you look a bit more comfortable.'

'I'll be all right,' said Carole, who hated the notion of being ill.

'Don't worry. We'll soon get you better.'

'What do you mean – "we"?' A spark of disgust came into the pale blue eyes. 'You're not going to try and *heal* me, are you?'

Again Jude had difficulty suppressing a grin. Nothing would ever shift her neighbour's antipathy to the idea of healing . . . or indeed any other alternative therapy.

'I promise I am not going to try and heal you. It

4

wouldn't work, anyway. Bugs like this just sort them-selves out in their own time.'

'Then who's this "we"?' Carole persisted suspi-ciously.

'For heaven's sake, it's just a figure of speech. "*We*'ll get you better" – it doesn't mean anything more than the fact that I'll keep an eye on you, see you've got everything you need.'

'Oh, but I don't want you to . . .' The words trickled away as Carole realized just how ghastly she did actu-ally feel. She had no more resistance left.

'Anyway,' said Jude cheerily, 'we – or "I" if you prefer – have got to see you're all right by Sunday.'

'Why?'

'I thought you said that's when Stephen and Gaby are bringing Lily down to see you.'

But this reminder of her status as a grandmother didn't bring any warmth of Carole's manner. 'No,' she said, 'I've put them off.'

'What?'

'I don't want to breathe germs over the baby, do I?' replied Carole piously.

It was in a way the correct answer, but it stimulated an anxiety within Jude about how Carole was adjusting to her new role as a grandmother. Still, this was not the appropriate moment to follow up on that. She handed the hot drink across to her patient.

Carole sniffed. 'It's got whisky in it,' she said accus-ingly.

'Of course it has,' said Jude.

*

5

Jude was unused to walking a dog, but Gulliver's equable temper did not make the task difficult. His benevolence was more or less universal. When he barked it was from excitement, and his encounters with other dogs were playful rather than combative. Most important, he was never aware that Carole, not a natural dog person, had only bought one so that she wouldn't be thought to be lonely as she was seen walking with him around Fethering.

After her divorce and what she still thought of as her premature retirement from the Home Office, Carole Seddon had planned her life in Fethering so that she would be completely self-sufficient. She didn't want other people in her life, and Gulliver had been just one of the defence mechanisms she had carefully constructed to prevent such intrusions.

But then Jude had moved into Woodside Cottage next door, and even Carole found her resistance weakened by the charm of her new neighbour's personality. Jude rarely spoke about her past, but the details she did let slip led Carole to deduce that it had been a varied – not to say chequered – one. There was something of the former hippy about Jude. She was a healer and had introduced into the bourgeois fastness of Woodside Cottage such exotic items as crystals and wind-chimes. It would have been hard to imagine a more unlikely friend for Carole Seddon, but, though Carole would never have admitted it out loud, she valued the friendship more than almost anything else in her life.

Jude took Gulliver on to the beach and let him scamper around off the lead, playing elaborate war games with weed-fringed plastic bottles and lumps of polystyrene. She allowed him twenty minutes of this, while she scrunched to and fro on the shingle. Then she let out a hopeful whistle, and was gratified that Gulliver came obediently to heel and let her reattach the lead.

It was a typical early February day. Though the people of West Sussex bemoaned the lack of winter snow and spoke ominously of global warming, the weather proved itself able still to come up with good old-fashioned coldness. Jude's face, the only part of her not wrapped in a swathe of coats and scarves, was stung by the air, and underfoot the pebbles were joined by links of ice.

She did her shopping at Allinstore, the town's only supermarket (though many Fethering residents reckoned the prefix 'super' in that context was an offence under the Trades Descriptions Act). Jude bought organically when it came to meat and fresh vegetables, but she was not proscriptive about it. There were also baked beans on her shelves and hamburgers in her fridge. She knew her own body and, though she generally ate healthily, she would occasionally indulge in a massive fry-up or a fish supper in one of the local cafés. Jude believed that in all things well-being came from variety.

As well as the Pedigree Chum and a couple of other items her neighbour had asked for, Jude bought some of the things she thought Carole *needed*. As she had said, warming soups, Lucozade and whisky. Jude was very definite about the style in which one should be ill.

Illness made you feel miserable, so there was no point in making yourself feel even more miserable. Pampering was the answer. Oh yes, and of course, magazines. *Country Life* and *Marie-Claire*. She bought them, already relishing Carole's reaction to such frivolous extravagance.

As she emerged from Allinstore the heavens opened, vindictively spitting down a fusillade of hailstones. The parade was suddenly evacuated, as the denizens of Fethering rushed for shelter. So fierce was the blizzard that Jude, scuttling to her destination, could hardly see a foot in front of her face. Fortunately, the betting shop had a projecting canopy over its frontage, and she was able to tie Gulliver's lead to a metal ring which would keep him out of the weather.

Fethering High Street still had an old-fashioned parade of shops. Although this meant there weren't many of them, it did ensure that they were all close together. But the choice was limited. You could still get your hair styled at what used to be Connie's Cuts but had now been made-over and rebranded as 'Marnie'. You could still investigate house purchase at Urquhart & Pease or one of the other estate agents. But in the previous ten years the independent butcher and greengrocer had both closed and been replaced by charity shops.

And Sonny Frank's, the former independent bookmaker's, had been taken over by one of the major national chains. This Jude knew from no less an authority than Sonny Frank himself, who had been unable to cut his links with the business completely and was still a fixture on the premises. Sonny, who in his days as a bookie had been known as 'Perfectly' Frank, always sat on a tall stool near the betting shop's central pillar, from where he could command a good view of the wall of television screens, as well as the enclosed counter where bets were taken and winnings paid.

And, sure enough, there he was at one-thirty that Thursday afternoon, when Jude hurried in from the sleet to put on Harold Peskett's bets. Sonny Frank was a small man, whose arms and legs seemed almost irrelevant appendages to the round ball of his body. On top of this was another ball, his head, across which dyed black hair had been combed over so tight that it looked as though it had been painted on. He wore a frayed suit in subdued colours but large checks, and he greeted Jude cheerfully. Sonny Frank greeted everyone who went into the shop cheerfully, as though he were still its owner, but he held back an extra ration of cheerfulness for attractive women.

Though Jude had popped in sporadically since she'd been a Fethering resident, during the fortnight of Harold Peskett's flu she had become a regular, so Sonny knew her name. 'Hello, Jude darling. You look like you just come out of the fridge.'

Sure enough, in the short dash from Allinstore to the betting shop, her head and shoulders had taken on an encrustation of ice.

'Yes, look at it out there. It's quite revolting.'

'I would look at it, but I can't see a thing.' It was

true. The opposite side of the road was invisible through the icy downpour.

'So we're all much snugger in here, Jude. So . . . got a hot tip for me today, have you . . . as the actress said to the bishop?'

'You're much more likely to know something than I am, Sonny,' Jude replied, as she brushed the ice off her shoulders. 'You're the one with the inside knowledge.'

'Don't you believe it, darling. What you've got and I haven't is women's intuition.'

'A fat lot of good that's ever done me.'

'What, with the men or the horses?'

'Either. Both totally unreliable.'

'What's old Harold up for today then?'

'Heaven knows.' She reached into her pocket and flourished a sheaf of closely written betting slips. 'All his usual trebles and Yankees and goodness knows what. I don't understand what he does – I just put the bets on.'

It was true. Harold Peskett's betting system was arcane and deeply personal. Every morning he spent two hours religiously scouring the *Racing Post* and checking the tips given in the *Sun*, *Daily Express* and *Daily Mirror* before coming up with his recipe for 'the big win'. This involved a complex combination of horses at meetings across the country in formulations which, to the untrained eye, made Fermat's Last Theorem look straightforward. The total sum invested never exceeded two pounds, so it didn't make too many inroads into his pension. And at least his betting habit kept the ninety-two-year-old off the streets.

Jude handed over the betting slips to the vacuously beautiful blonde behind the counter, whose name badge proclaimed her to be 'Nikki'. She got an automatic 'Thank you', but not the automatic smile she would have received had she been a man. Behind the girl, the shop's manager, Ryan, fiddled on the keyboard of a computer. He was an edgy and uncommunicative man in his mid-thirties, thin with nervous dark eyes and with spiky black hair that could never quite be flattened by comb or brush. He always seemed to be sucking a peppermint. Both he and Nikki were dressed in the blue and black livery of their employers. Supported by other part-time staff, Ryan and Nikki provided the continuity of the betting shop. Though there was a lot of banter flying about the place, they never really joined in. They produced the manufactured smiles they had been taught during their training, but neither gave much impression of enjoying the job.

'So . . .' asked Sonny Frank, as Jude passed him on the way to the door, 'know anything?'

It was another of his regular lines. And anyone incautious enough to ask what he meant – as Jude had been when he first said it to her – would be treated to the full explanation. As a young man Sonny had actually met Edgar Wallace, who, as well as being a prolific writing phenomenon, was also an obsessive gambler. And Wallace's opening gambit to betting friends had always been the punter's eternal search for the life-changing tip: 'Know anything?'

'You've already asked me, Sonny, and I've already said you're the one with the inside knowledge.'

The ex-bookie looked elaborately furtive, then leaned forward on his stool till his cracked lips were very close to Jude's ear and his purple cheek brushed against the hanging tendrils of her hair. 'Well, as it happens . . . I do know a good thing.'

'Oh?'

'1.40 at Wincanton. Hasn't raced for over two hundred days. Gonna romp home.'

Jude looked out of the window. Still the sleet fell relentlessly. But Gulliver, under his sheltering roof, had lain down with his front paws forward and looked perfectly content. Maybe she could leave him out there a little longer. 'Which horse are you talking about?' she whispered, knowing that Sonny wouldn't broadcast his tip to the entire room.

He pointed up to the screen displaying the odds for the Wincanton race. 'Seven down,' he murmured. 'Number Four.'

The horse's name was Nature's Vacuum.

'If you're going to bet, do it quickly. That twenty to one won't last.'

Jude looked at the central screen, where the horses were ambling their way towards the start. Down in Wincanton the weather looked almost springlike. She wished she were there rather than Fethering.

'Go on, are you going to have a punt?'

She took one more dutiful look out of the window. In spite of the ice bouncing off the pavement only feet away from him, Gulliver's tail was actually wagging. He really did have a very nice nature.

'Why not?' replied Jude.

Chapter Two

As she sat down and looked around her at the punters trying to read the runes of the racing pages spread over the walls, Jude reflected on the unique egalitarianism of betting shops. She had encountered a few that had been silent and dour, but she'd never been in one where she'd felt uncomfortable. True, a less secure soul might have objected to the casual sexism that was the norm in such places, but she had never found the remarks flung at her less than good-natured. With an inward giggle, she wondered whether Carole would feel equally at ease in the environment.

Her bet was placed. Five pounds on Nature's Vacuum. And she had managed to get the twenty to one – Nikki had written the price on her slip. As Sonny predicted, the odds on the horse had come down in the minutes before the off. Somebody knew something. The twenty to one gave way to sixteen to one. Fourteen to one. The starting price might even be twelves.

With the instinctive reaction of all punters, Jude was already beginning to feel that she was in profit. At fourteen to one, a fiver on the win would only bring in seventy pounds. Whereas the fiver she'd put on at twenty to one would bring in a hundred. She was thirty quid up even before the race started. That there was a hot odds-on favourite called Girton Girl and that Nature's Vacuum remained a rank outsider were irrelevant details. In the mind of a punter the law of probability never carries as much weight as the law of possibility. And in the extraordinarily unlikely event of Nature's Vacuum not winning, Jude reckoned the rush of excitement she was feeling at that moment was well worth a fiver.

She looked around at the betting shop's other occupants and recognized plenty. There was a pair of decorators whose names she knew from overhearing their conversation to be Wes and Vic. The spatters of fresh paint on their overalls suggested that they were actually working, but the frequency with which they rushed in and out of the betting shop made Jude glad they weren't working for her. Over the years she'd seen them almost every time she had been in, which prompted the bizarre idea that they only took on decorating commissions within walking distance of the place. Wes and Vic were not men who kept their emotions to themselves. Every hope and disappointment was vocalized. Horses and greyhounds, subjects of veneration and hope before their races, were quickly and loudly vilified when they lost.

The other infallible attendees were the waiters from Fethering's only Chinese restaurant, the Golden Palace. There were never less than two and sometimes as many as five, all young, dressed in their uniform of black shirts and trousers, constantly chattering to each other in high chopped tones.

Another regular was a grey-haired man, dressed unfailingly in a suit and sober tie and carrying a brief-case. He looked like an accountant, who in retirement had chosen to continue working in a variation of his former profession, turf accountancy. And, according to Sonny Frank, that's what he was. He noted his bets, successes and failures in an old-fashioned ledger, and his face remained impassive, regardless of the out-come. Though he had never spoken directly to her, Jude had overheard him placing bets at the counter. His accent was extremely cultured.

There was also a female regular, whose presence might have reassured a less confident woman than Jude about entering such a predominantly male enclave. A dumpy, white-haired woman, whom again Jude had seen whenever she'd been in. Every day the woman sat in the same chair and, without being par-ticularly outgoing, seemed to be perfectly friendly with everyone. Her name was Pauline, and she was habitu-ally surrounded by scraps of racing pages torn out of newspapers. In the early days Jude had always seen her with a fag in her mouth and a full ashtray in front of her, but now the woman was obedient to the smok-ing ban. The attraction of betting was apparently stronger than that of tobacco.

Sonny Frank, who always spoke nostalgically of the past history of bookmaking, and thought things had gone downhill since the days when his father and he took illegal bets in the back rooms of pubs, reckoned the smoking ban was another nail in the coffin of the industry he loved. 'Punters just won't come in,' he'd say. 'And now they can do it all at home online, anyway. Soon won't be any high street betting shops left.'

While his prognostication might be true in the long term, Jude reckoned the Fethering business still looked fairly healthy. And, from her own point of view, she thought the smoking ban was an inestimable improvement. It was now possible to spend five minutes in a betting shop without emerging reeking of tobacco.

As the horses on the screen lined up for the 1.40, a change came over the room. Even with the number of races scheduled – at least three meetings for the horses, interspersed with the greyhounds, not to mention computer-generated virtual racing – there was still a moment of intense concentration before the 'off' of each one.

'Come on, Girton Girl, you can do it,' said the decorator Wes.

'No way,' said Sonny Frank. 'Iffy jumper if ever I saw one. Came down three out last time out at Uttoxeter.'

'But that was the jockey,' Vic, the other decorator, countered. 'Useless apprentice. She's got McCoy up today.'

'Which is why she's down to eleven to eight,' Wes contributed.

'Still an iffy jumper.'

'What you on then, Sonny?'

'The winner.'

'Oh yeah? So you're on Girton Girl too, are you?'

The globular old man chuckled. 'No, no, I recognize rubbish when I see it. Remember – bookies never lose.'

'*Ex*-bookies do,' said Wes.

'Ssh, they're away,' said Vic.

There was an animated exchange between the Chinese waiters and then a moment of relative silence – interrupted only by the endless jingles from the slot machines and the hiss of the sleet-storm outside – descended on the room as the punters listened to the race commentary. One horse had got left at the start and, by the time it got into its running, was some seven lengths away from its nearest rival. The horse was Nature's Vacuum. Oh dear, thought Jude.

The odds-on favourite, Girton Girl, meanwhile, seemed contemptuous of her opposition and swept over the first fence four lengths ahead of the rest of the field.

'Gone too soon,' shouted Sonny Frank.

'Cobblers,' came the riposte from Wes. 'That horse stays like the mother-in-law.'

'Others never going to catch her,' Vic agreed.

'Don't you believe it,' said Sonny.

Amongst the desultory cries of 'Yes, yes!' and 'Move it, you lump of cat's meat!' Jude was vaguely aware that a new customer had come into the betting shop. He was a man in his twenties, his face pale and pinched. The reddish hair was cut very short and he was muffled up in a dark blue overcoat that looked almost naval. His head and shoulders were frosted with ice. He stood by the doorway, as though looking for someone. He swayed slightly. Perhaps he'd had too good a lunch at the Crown and Anchor. Jude was too preoccupied with the race to take much notice of him. And a shout from Sonny Frank of 'What did I tell you, Jude?' brought her attention firmly back to the screen.

And yes, after that pathetic start, Nature's Vacuum was slowly picking his way through the field. First past the exhausted stragglers, then the one-paced hopefuls, till he'd got himself up to fourth place.

Jude found herself instinctively joining in the shouts of encouragement. 'Come on, Nature's Vacuum!' she yelled.

Three fences to go. Nature's Vacuum looked full of running. But then so did the favourite. The distance between Girton Girl and the second horse was increasing rather than diminishing. She avoided the fate that had ended her hopes at Uttoxeter, and sailed over the third from last like a gazelle.

'Hang on in there, Nature's Vacuum!' shouted Jude. But for the first time she was assailed by doubt. Sonny's tip had been right in a sense. Nature's Vacuum was a good prospect, certainly much better than the odds suggested, and maybe he'd soon win a race. But it didn't look like being this one at Wincanton.

The contest wasn't over yet, though. With an effort of will she clamped down on her negative thoughts. Her horse remained upright, she was still in with the chance of a hundred quid. 'Come on, Nature's Vacuum! You can do it!'

At the penultimate fence the horse came up alongside the long-time second, and put in a flying leap which gave him a length advantage. But he still had five lengths to make up on the leading filly, who looked to be coasting home.

'That's the way, Gertie!' shouted Wes.

'Go on, my son!' roared Vic. (People in racing have never been too specific about the names and genders of horses.)

Sonny Frank and Jude just sat and watched.

Running up to the last, Nature's Vacuum maybe picked up half a length, but it looked like being too little, too late. Wes and Vic's beams threatened to split their faces. 'Come on, my son!' they roared together. There was no way Girton Girl could lose.

National Hunt racing, though, is an unpredictable sport. The favourite approached the last at a slight angle, cleared it fine, but then veered alarmingly off towards the rail. Nature's Vacuum took a dead straight line and put in a superb jump. That, together with Girton Girl's detour, meant that by the time the two horses were again together on the run-in, the second was less than a length behind. Both jockeys flashed away with their whips and used every ounce of their own energy to drive their horses forward. Nature's Vacuum drew alongside, then Girton Girl seemed to find a new reservoir of strength and regained the lead. But neither wanted to come second, and Nature's Vacuum surged again.

They crossed the line together and the photograph was called.

'Which one was it?' shrieked Jude.

'Gertie got there,' declared Wes with dispiriting certainty.

'I wouldn't be so sure,' said Sonny. 'The angle's deceptive at Wincanton. I think the other one's the winner.' Still he didn't declare an interest in either horse.

'And I think the result's coming . . .' the commentator announced.

'Number Four,' boomed over the racecourse's PA system. 'The winner was Number Four. Second, Number Seven. Third, Number Two. The distances were a short head and seven lengths.'

Jude turned with glee to look at Sonny Frank. The old bookie winked at her.

'Always knew it was a crap horse,' said Wes, crumpling up his betting slip.

'Iffy jumper,' Vic agreed, doing the same.

And the two of them went off to do a few minutes' decorating before the next race. Outside, the sleet had stopped as suddenly as it had started.

In a state of euphoria Jude rushed towards the counter. The young man in the naval overcoat was still swaying by the doorway. She grinned at him, feeling benevolent towards the entire world, and was rewarded by a weak but rather charming smile which revealed discoloured teeth.

Jude went to collect her hundred and five pounds (a hundred winnings, five pound stake) from an impassive Nikki and once again turned to thank Sonny.

'Going to have a flutter on the next?' he asked, as he folded a large pile of winnings into his back pocket.

Like all punters, she was tempted. Maybe this wasn't

just a one-off win . . .? Maybe it was the beginning of a winning streak . . .? Maybe her luck was in . . .?

But a glimpse of Gulliver outside reminded her of her priorities. The hailstorm might have ended, but the poor dog must be feeling pretty cold. No, she wouldn't bet again. She would do what all gamblers intend – and almost always fail – to do: stop after a big win. She thanked Sonny Frank profusely for the tip and, picking up her Allinstore carriers, made for the door.

The young man in the blue naval overcoat was no longer there. Off to lie down somewhere, sleep off the booze, Jude conjectured.

And then she saw it. A circle of dark fluid seeping into the carpet tiles by the door. Against the blue the red turned almost purple. She didn't have to touch it to recognize it was blood.

More drips had stained coin-sized marks, tracing the man's exit from the betting shop. Without a word to anyone, Jude followed them.

Outside, she freed Gulliver from the ring he'd been tied to and held his lead tightly. As she pulled him in the direction the red spots on the pavement indicated, the Labrador sniffed at one and then almost pulled her arm out of its socket as he followed the track. His first experience of being a bloodhound, and Gulliver liked it.

The trail of blood, though diluted by the melting sleet, was still easy to follow.

They didn't have far to go. Alongside the betting shop was a narrow alley which led round the back of the building to a small area of scrub that gave access to Fethering Beach.

He hadn't made it all the way down the alley. The bloodspots grew bigger and bigger until they coalesced into a widening stream.

At the end of which lay the man in the navy overcoat.

He hardly breathed and his eyes were glazing over. As Jude knelt down beside him, he murmured something in a heavily accented voice. It sounded like 'Fifi . . .'

A moment later the man was dead.

Chapter Three

Jude had rung Carole on the mobile to say she would be delayed in bringing her shopping back, though she didn't specify the reason. And when she finally got back to Woodside Cottage after being questioned by the police, she rang again on the landline. They had long ago exchanged spare keys, but Jude knew that her neighbour never liked being surprised by an unannounced visit, even from her. Carole Seddon endeavoured to organize her life so that it involved the minimum of surprises. The slipping in and out of people's houses in which some people indulged was anathema to her. It was one of those habits for which Carole reserved one of her adjectives expressing major disapprobation: northern.

Inside High Tor, Jude, having served Gulliver a large helping of his long-wished-for Pedigree Chum, went upstairs to see the invalid.

It was a measure of the severity of Carole's flu that, having granted permission for the visit, she hadn't got out of bed to greet her guest. And in her reduced state even the news of a suspicious death in Fethering High Street didn't bring the animation it usually would have done. The questions she asked were listless, and Jude almost had to insist on telling her the known details of what had happened.

'As ever, the police didn't volunteer much information, but then I don't think they had much information to volunteer. Until they've established the identity of the dead man, they haven't really got anything to go on. I can tell you, though, that he wasn't a regular at the betting shop.'

Jude waited to be asked how she knew that, but with no question forthcoming, continued her monologue. 'The detectives took me back into the shop after I'd shown them the body, and they asked general questions to everyone who was there. Most of the punters hadn't even noticed the guy, but Ryan the Manager – who I guess makes it his business to clock everyone who comes in – said he'd never seen him before.'

She waited for a further prompt, but didn't get one. 'Obviously, having only seen him in the overcoat, I don't know which part of his body the blood was coming from, and it could be something natural . . . a haemorrhage of some kind . . . but I'm afraid my first thought was murder.'

This word did bring a small spark to Carole's pale blue eyes. Probably the activity she'd most enjoyed since her retirement to Fethering had been the investigation of murders with Jude.

'If it was murder,' her neighbour went on, 'then the most obvious thought would be that it was a stabbing. I suppose it could also be a gunshot wound . . . Either way, the actual attack didn't happen in the betting shop.'

'Are you sure?' asked Carole, intrigued in spite of herself.

'Positive. He came in through the front door.'

'Is it just the one room?' asked Carole, who prided herself on never having been inside a betting shop.

'Well, there are offices behind the counter . . . and there are the toilets . . . and presumably there is a back entrance,' Jude added thoughtfully. 'But he definitely came in at the front. It was as if he was looking for something . . . Or maybe someone.' The skin around her brown eyes tightened as she tried to work it out. 'And I'm pretty sure he must have put the overcoat on after he was stabbed – or shot or whatever it was.'

'What makes you think that?'

'The lack of visible blood. It was a thick coat. If he'd put it on after he'd been wounded, then it would have taken a while for the blood to seep through.'

'There's one odd thing . . .' mused Carole, now firmly hooked in spite of her illness.

'What?'

'Why didn't he ask for help?'

'Sorry?'

'Here's this man, seriously wounded – mortally wounded, as it turned out – and he must know that he's hurt . . . and he staggers into a public place, the betting shop, surrounded by people . . . and he doesn't say a thing. You'd have thought, in those circumstances, almost anyone would have said something . . . would have asked for a doctor to be called, or an ambulance . . .

But he didn't say anything. Or did he, Jude? Did he say anything to you?'

'Not in the betting shop, no. He just smiled.' And the image of that weak smile brought home to her the horror of what she had witnessed. An involuntary shiver ran through her plump body.

'Well,' Carole continued, joining the links in her chain of logic, 'the fact that he didn't say anything . . . didn't draw attention to himself, even though he was dying . . . suggests, wouldn't you say, that the man had something to hide?'

'Yes,' said Jude, 'I suppose it could.'

'And if we find out what he was trying to hide, then we'll probably be a good way to finding out why he was killed.'

Jude wasn't really convinced by that line of enquiry. But it was the only one they had.

Both women realized that they had been letting their imaginations run away with them. They didn't even know that the death had been unnatural, and already they were building up pictures of a man with a guilty secret. Both were sheepish, feeling that the wildness of their conjectures was about to be shown up, as they waited for the early evening television news. Carole had roused her aching limbs and come down to the sitting room to watch. Jude had offered to bring the television upstairs, but her neighbour had been appalled by the idea. For Carole having a television in a bedroom was an unpardonable offence against decency, on the level with actually watching the thing during the daytime (though there was an afternoon chat show to which she was becoming almost addicted, but that was a secret vice).

The killing in Fethering was deemed sufficiently important to make the national news, and the bulletin did at least provide them with some solid information. The dead man had been identified as Tadeusz Jankowski, aged twenty-four. He was a Polish immigrant who had been in Britain less than six months. He had died of stab wounds and the police were launching a murder investigation.

Though it was an awful thing to think, both Carole and Jude would have been terribly disappointed if he'd turned out to have died a natural death.

That evening Jude, still more shaken than she liked to admit to herself, decided that she'd have supper at Fethering's only pub, the Crown and Anchor. Before she left High Tor she heated up some soup, but the invalid didn't seem interested in eating. Carole just sipped a little Lucozade and looked with affronted fascination at the magazines she had been given. Jude had a feeling that the minute she was alone in the house, Carole would pounce on them and start reading. The offer of a hot toddy was refused, but Jude said she'd come in later and maybe make one then. After her surge of excitement over the murder, Carole had now slumped back into total lethargy and voiced no objections to the idea of another visit from her neighbour.

In the Crown and Anchor it didn't take long for the subject to get round to Fethering's latest murder. After his usual pleasantries to Jude and the quick provision of her customary large Chilean Chardonnay, the landlord Ted Crisp was on to it straight away. 'Nasty business down by the betting shop this afternoon.'

'Tell me about it. I was the one who found the poor soul.'

'Were you? Blimey, you and your mate Carole certainly have a knack of being in the wrong place at the wrong time. Where is she, by the way?'

'Laid up with flu.'

'Poor thing. Give her my best.'

'Will do.' It was still at times incongruous to Jude that her fastidious neighbour had once had a brief fling with the scruffy bearded landlord of the Crown and Anchor. That evening he was in his habitual faded jeans, though in deference to the cold weather he was wearing a faded zip-up hoodie over his customary faded sweatshirt.

'Immigrant, I gather from the news,' he said darkly. In spite of his background as a stand-up comedian, Ted Crisp was capable of being, to Jude's mind, distressingly right-wing.

His point was quickly taken up by another customer, a man in his fifties, dressed in tweed jacket, salmon pink corduroy trousers and a tie that looked as if it should have been regimental but probably wasn't. He was thick-set, but in quite good condition. His receding hair was sandy, freckled with grey. He was accompanied by a younger, similarly dressed version of himself, who had to be his son. The boy was probably mid-twenties, large and slightly ungainly, with a thick crest of auburn hair. What might once have been a well-muscled body was on the verge of giving way to fat.

Jude knew the older man by sight. He worked in one of Fethering's estate agencies on the parade (however small the town in West Sussex, there always seemed to be business for more than one estate agent). The agency was called Urquhart & Pease, though whether the man had one of those as his surname Jude didn't know.

'Been only a matter of time before something like this happened,' he announced in a voice that had been to all the right schools. 'Ever since the wretched EU opened up our boundaries to all and sundry, it's been an accident waiting to happen. I mean, I'm the last person to be racist . . .' Wasn't it strange, Jude reflected, how people who started sentences like that always ended up being exactly what they denied they were '. . . but I do think we ought to have a bit of a say in who we let into our country. We are islanders, after all, with everything that goes with that . . . and we have a long history of doing things our way. And I'm not saying all immigration is bad. I'm as tolerant as the next man . . .' Which in West Sussex, thought Jude, wasn't saying a lot '. . . and I've got friends and colleagues who . . . What are you allowed to say now? Have different ethnic backgrounds . . .? Pakistani chap works as our accountant, and he fits in, you'd never know . . . Doesn't he, Hamish?'

The younger man agreed that their Pakistani

accountant did fit in, and listened dutifully as the estate agent pontificated on. 'But I still do think you have to draw the line somewhere . . . or we'll see more things happening like we did today.'

Jude didn't want to get drawn into the conversation – she knew she'd be on a hiding to nothing – but she couldn't help asking, 'So you think this man was murdered because he was an immigrant?'

'Obviously.' He flashed her an urbane and slightly patronizing smile. 'I'm sorry, we don't know each other. Ewan Urquhart.' So he was one of the partners in the agency. 'And my son Hamish.'

'This is Jude,' said Ted Crisp, as though he'd been remiss in not making the introduction before.

'I've seen you walking along the High Street,' said the estate agent. 'Never fail to notice an attractive woman, you know.' It was a knee-jerk compliment, a little too smoothly delivered. Jude decided she would not buy a house from this man.

'But, Mr Urquhart, you were saying—'

'Ewan, please.'

'Ewan. You seemed to be making the assumption that this man's death must have happened because he was an immigrant . . .?'

'Well, my dear, in a situation like this the law of probability kicks in, doesn't it? Get the country full of foreigners and they bring their own ways with them. So you get welfare scroungers, gangs, people traffickers . . .' He seemed to be picking randomly at *Daily Mail* headlines. 'And then with the ones from the Indian subcontinent you get these so-called "honour killings". Bumping your sister off because you don't like her choice of boyfriend. I mean, what kind of behaviour is that?'

'Barbaric,' his son supplied.

'You're right, Hamish. It's barbaric. A culture of violence. We never used to have a culture of violence in this country.'

'No? What about our good old traditional soccer hooligans . . .?' Jude was tempted to add, 'or our good old traditional public schools . . .?', but didn't.

Ewan Urquhart smiled blandly. He was clearly a man who thought he had a way with women and knew how to deal with their little foibles. 'Ah, now I think you're just being perverse, Jude. Much as we'd all like to believe there's no connection between increased immigration and the crime statistics, I'm afraid the facts don't leave much room for doubt. If you leave your borders open, it's inevitable that you're going to get a lot of riff-raff coming in. For me, I'm afraid, it all goes back to joining the Common Market. Worst move this country ever made.'

He was clearly preaching to the converted as far as Ted Crisp was concerned. 'Couldn't agree with you more, Ewan. I don't want to be ordered about by bloody Brussels.'

'Nor me,' Hamish managed to slip in before his father continued. 'Being British used to be a cause for pride. Not showing-off pride like some other countries are so fond of. Not standing up and saying "Aren't I wonderful?" pride. But that quiet British pride that just does the right thing without crowing about it. And where's that gone, I ask you? God knows. Now our bloody politicians seem to be apologizing all the time . . . desperate not to offend anyone "of a different ethnic background". Margaret Thatcher never used to apologize for being British.'

Surely Ted was going to take issue with that? In his stand-up days Thatcher-bashing had been a major ingredient of his material. But he said nothing, as Ewan Urquhart steamrollered on. 'Things like this murder should be a wake-up call, you know. Get people to stop and think what we're actually doing to this country by allowing uncontrolled immigration. As I say, I'm not a racist, but I do think there comes a point when you have to recognize that enough is enough.'

'You're too right, Dad,' said Hamish.

Jude had intended to have supper in the Crown and Anchor. But as Ewan Urquhart continued his tub-thumping, and as Ted Crisp and Hamish continued to agree with him, the prospect became less attractive. When she'd finished the one Chilean Chardonnay, she went back to Woodside Cottage. She'd find something in the fridge.

Chapter Four

Carole Seddon's flu was slow to shift, but after the weekend the prospect of life continuing in some form did once again seem a possibility. She was pleased to feel better, but also guiltily relieved that it had lasted as long as it did. The weekend had been one she was dreading, and she was glad that the flu had prevented her from participating in it. Being Carole Seddon, she was also worried about the extent to which she had used the illness as an excuse.

The event she had avoided was a meeting with her son Stephen, his wife Gaby and their four-month-old daughter Lily. But it wasn't them Carole didn't want to see. Since the baby's birth she had actually bonded more with the young couple, happy on occasions to go and help her daughter-in-law out at their Fulham house. And she found Lily a miracle. That something so tiny and so perfect could suddenly exist was a source of constant amazement to her. Though she was the last person to go all gooey in public about babies, Carole did find she was suffering from considerable internal gooeyness. Of course she didn't vocalize such self-indulgent thoughts, but they did give her a warm glow.

It was all so different from when she'd had Stephen. Then she'd been in such turmoil, finding herself in the one state she had tried to avoid all her life – out of control. The strange things that had happened to her body, the demanding new presence in her life, the realignment of her relationship with her husband . . . everything conspired to make her feel threatened and useless. Had she gone to a doctor about her feelings, there might have been a diagnosis of mild post-natal depression, but Carole Seddon had always believed that doctors were there to deal with physical problems, not feelings. And depression was something that happened to other people.

So she hadn't been worried about seeing Lily and her parents at the weekend. In fact she longed to witness her granddaughter's every tiny development. But Stephen had included another person in the proposed visit to Fethering.

His father. Carole's ex-husband David. Stephen was still under the illusion that, because he'd seen his estranged parents together at social events – like his wedding – when they hadn't actually come to blows, a new rapprochement between them was possible. With a wistful innocence that made Carole feel even guiltier, her son was desperate to be part of a happy family. And, now Lily was on the scene, of a happy extended family.

It was an ambition that Carole couldn't share. Getting over the divorce had taken a good few years and at times it still felt like an open wound. But one of the important components of rehabilitation into her new single life had been not seeing David. Even the sound of his voice on the phone could upset her hard-won equilibrium for days on end.

As a result of this, she had bought a new telephone with a Caller Display facility. If David were to ring her, she could then identify his number and choose whether or not to take the call. So far he hadn't called – and in fact David's was the one set of digits where Carole's usual facility for remembering phone numbers failed (a psychological block no doubt, though she would never have recognized it as such). But the Caller Display did give her a sense of security.

The thought of seeing David in Fethering made Carole feel even more unsettled. High Tor had been bought as a weekend retreat for both of them in hap-pier times, when the marriage was still more or less ticking over. Under the terms of the divorce settlement, Carole had taken sole possession, and had managed over the years to expunge all memories of their shared occupation. Seeing David back on the premises would stir up a hornets' nest of unwanted recollection.

As soon as she'd made the arrangement for the weekend, Carole had regretted it. Stephen had caught her in an unguarded moment, when she had been cud-dling Lily, and at such times all the world seemed benign and she hadn't been able to refuse him. So the fated weekend had continued to loom ever larger on her horizon until the threat was removed by the mercy of her flu.

She felt deeply relieved that the encounter hadn't happened. But she was sorry not to have seen Lily.

Still, now she was feeling better, she could begin to focus her mind on the death of Tadeusz Jankowski. With the return of her health came a prurient wistfulness, almost a jealousy, prompted by the fact that Jude had witnessed the young man's dying moments. If there was to be an investigation, Carole wanted to be part of it. So she sought through the weekend papers and cut out all the coverage of the murder, anything that might have relevance to the case. She found quite a lot of material. Immigration, particularly from Poland, was a topical issue, and the murder had unleashed pages and pages of ill-informed speculation.

Jude was surprised it took till the Monday for the police to contact her again. They'd taken all her details when they'd questioned her on the Thursday, saying they'd be in touch. And on the old principle that the first suspect in a murder investigation tends to be the person who finds the body, she had expected them to show more interest in her.

But the two young detectives who came to Woodside Cottage seemed very relaxed. They certainly didn't give her the impression that she was a suspect and, given her previous experience of dealing with the police, were surprisingly generous with information.

'We're pretty sure,' said the one who was called Detective Sergeant Baines, 'that the victim had nothing to do with anyone in the betting shop that afternoon.'

'No one in there knew him?'

'No. We took statements from them all, you know,

after you'd gone. None of them knew him from Adam. The manager, who makes it his business to see who comes in and out, had never seen him before.'

'So why did he go into the betting shop?'

'No idea. Maybe he was walking past and, feeling weak after being stabbed, just went in there to sit down. Or to get some shelter from the hailstorm.'

'Don't you think it's odd he didn't ask for help?' asked Jude, reiterating Carole's point.

Baines shrugged. 'Perhaps he didn't know how badly injured he was. Perhaps he was already too weak to speak. Or he could have been in shock. I don't know.'

'And do you know where he actually was when he was stabbed?'

The other one, Detective Sergeant Yelland, exchanged a grin with Baines and said, 'If we knew that, we'd be well on the way to solving the case, wouldn't we?'

'But it can't have been far away, can it? Or there would have been more blood at the bookie's, wouldn't there?'

Unlike previous detectives Jude had met, these two didn't seem to object to her working out her own theories. 'Maybe,' said Baines. 'They won't really know till they get the detailed post-mortem report. It could have been an injury that didn't bleed much at first, but then got worse. In fact, that must have been the case, because there was no trail of blood leading towards the betting shop, only away from it.'

Jude found his use of the personal pronoun inter-esting. 'They' would get the post-mortem report, not 'we'. The main part of the investigation was going on elsewhere. Baines and Yelland were juniors, minor players in the game. Realizing this encouraged her to ask more questions.

'I just heard the man's name on the television. And they said he was Polish. Have you been able to find out much more about him?'

Baines showed no reticence in answering. 'He was from Warsaw. Finished at university there last year. Been doing casual bar work over here.'

'Do you know where he lived?'

'Rented room in Littlehampton.'

'Not far away . . .' Jude looked thoughtful. 'Have his family in Poland been contacted?'

Detective Sergeant Yelland seemed suddenly aware of the incongruity of the situation. 'Just a minute. Aren't we the ones who're meant to be asking you the questions?' But he sounded amused rather than resentful.

'I agree that's traditional,' said Jude with a winning smile. 'But you haven't asked many, and we don't want to sit here in silence, do we?'

Both men grinned. 'Yes, his family have been told,' Baines replied. 'And there's been contact with the Polish police authorities.'

'Oh?'

'Well, makes sense. Most likely the reason he was attacked is something to do with his own community. Probably goes back to some rivalry back home.'

'Can you be sure of that?'

'Can't be sure of much in our business,' said Yelland.

Jude now understood the explanation for their relaxed demeanour. Neither Baines nor Yelland was particularly interested in the case. They were underlings who did as they were told. They had been told to interview her and they were following their instructions. But they had no expectations that anything she might say would be useful to the investigation. They regarded the murder as a foreign case, which just happened to have taken place on their patch.

Jude decided to test the limits of their goodwill and persist in her questioning. 'I just wondered . . . whether it might be more local . . .?' Remembering Ewan Urquhart's pontificating in the Crown and Anchor the previous week, she went on, 'There does seem to be quite a lot of resentment of immigrants round here.'

'Not that much,' said Baines. 'In some of the inner city areas, yes, there are problems. But down here, it's not as if they're taking people's jobs or anything like that. Maybe a bit of trouble in the bigger cities . . . Brighton, Portsmouth, Southampton. Get a bit of racial conflict at chucking-out time, you know, the odd fight. But not somewhere as small as Fethering. We don't get called out much on disputes with immigrants, do we?'

Yelland agreed that they didn't.

'I would just have thought—'

'I can assure you that they are investigating every possibility.' Again Baines's tell-tale use of 'they'. 'And if there is someone local involved, I'm sure they'll find out about it. But the initial enquiries will be focusing on the Polish community.'

'Right.'

'So . . .' asked Yelland ironically, 'is there anything else you want to ask us?'

'Not at the moment. But if there are any further questions, I'll be in touch.'

Yelland grinned at his colleague. 'Stealing all our lines, isn't she?'

'Yes,' said Baines. 'And if you remember anything else you might think is relevant, you be in touch too.'

'Will do.'

'Or if there's anything you want to add to the statement you made on Thursday . . .?'

'I can't think of anything at the moment.'

'Fine. Well, if there's an arrest, you'll hear about it on the telly.'

But Detective Sergeant Baines didn't sound optimistic. Jude got the firm impression that neither he nor Yelland expected an early solution to the case. And that they weren't that bothered.

Chapter Five

After the murder the betting shop had been closed while the police made their forensic examination of the premises, but it was allowed to reopen on the Monday. Which, Jude extrapolated, meant that they had been expecting to receive little information there. It wasn't exactly a crime scene; the crime had happened elsewhere. Apparently detectives had made enquiries at other premises along the parade, but did not seem to have identified where the stabbing had taken place. Or if they had, they were keeping quiet about it.

No unsuspecting punter entering the betting shop on the Monday would have been aware that anything untoward had taken place there. But when she arrived that afternoon, Jude noticed that new, brighter blue carpet tiles had replaced the ones on to which the dying man's blood had dripped. The originals were presumably under scrutiny in a police laboratory.

She had come in again to place Harold Peskett's bets. The old man's flu seemed to be hanging on. He felt lousy, but he still wanted to keep up with what he insisted on calling his 'investments'. This had obviously been a problem over the weekend, with the betting shop closed, but Jude had found a solution. Using a laptop which she had inherited from a deceased lover, Laurence Hawker, she had opened up an online account.

The process had been so seductively easy that it gave her something of a shock. She had discovered that in a matter of moments anyone, armed only with an internet connection and a credit card, could have the capacity to lose money at will in the privacy of their own home. Jude was glad she didn't have an addictive personality. Bankruptcy had never been so readily available.

But she only used her new account to put on Harold Peskett's bets that weekend. Once the betting shop reopened, she thought it quite possible that she'd never log on again. She felt comforted to have the account, though. It was a convenience. If she fancied the name of a horse she saw in the paper or suddenly wanted to have a punt on the Grand National . . . well, the facility was there.

The regulars were in their allotted places when she arrived that Monday afternoon shortly before one. And they greeted her as one of their own. Nor was there any tasteful reticence about bringing up the subject uppermost in all their minds.

'So, who're you going to murder this afternoon, Jude?' asked Wes.

'Surprised they've allowed you out,' said Vic. 'On bail, are you?'

Sonny Frank came to her rescue. 'Leave the lady alone. She might still be in a state of shock.'

'I'm not, actually. But thanks for the thought, Sonny.'

'Well, from what I see on telly, with all those Poirots and Morses and what-have-you,' Wes went on, 'the one the police always go for is the one who found the body.'

'So I'm supposed to have stabbed the poor bloke outside, am I? Before I came in here?'

'You could have done,' said Vic wisely. 'You're the only one of us who's a suspect, Jude. You found the body.'

'All right.' Jude held up her arms in mock-surrender. 'I did it. What are you going to do – call the cops again?'

'No, we'll let you get away with this one,' Wes conceded generously. 'But you murder someone else and you're in trouble.'

All of this dialogue was lightly conducted, humour as ever diluting the awkwardness of an unpleasant situation. None of them was unaffected by the stranger's death; they were just finding ways of coping with it.

'Have any of you had follow-up calls from the police?'

None of them had. 'Thank goodness,' said Pauline. 'My old man always told me to keep clear of the police. If you don't talk to them, they can't twist your words in court, he always said.'

'But I heard you speaking to them on Thursday,' said Jude.

'Hadn't got much choice, had I? They come in here and asked us all to stay. If I'd legged it right then, they'd have thought I was well dodgy.'

'Suppose so. Well, I must do these bets for old Harold.' Jude moved across to the counter. Nikki was seated at a table checking through sheaves of betting slips. Ryan came to serve her. 'Presumably they asked you if you recognized the dead man?'

'Yes,' the manager replied.

Characteristically, he didn't volunteer any other information, so Jude prompted him. 'And you said you'd never seen him?'

'That's right.'

He turned away, wanting the conversation to end there, but Jude persisted. 'But you do normally check out everyone who comes through the door?'

'Yes. Part of the job. There are some villains about. Head Office sends us photos of the ones we got to watch out for. So I look at everyone.'

'And you didn't recognize him either, did you, Nikki?'

The girl looked up at Jude from her betting slips, her beautiful eyes blank. 'Wossat?'

'I was asking if you'd ever seen the dead man before?'

'Nah,' she replied. 'I never.'

'But do you normally check who comes in and out of the betting shop?'

Jude received one of those curious looks that the young reserve for the old and mad. 'Nah. Not my job, is it? Ryan does that. I just do what I have to do. Take the punters' bets. I don't have to notice who they are.'

Jude was inclined to believe her. She noticed the girl sported an engagement ring. And no doubt she made some young man very happy . . . so long as his demands didn't stretch to the intellectual.

'Know anything?' asked Sonny Frank, as Jude returned from the counter.

'About the murder or the horses?'

'Let's stick with the horses. A murder's a nine-day wonder, but horse racing is forever.'

'Well, I'd give you the same answer if you were talking about the murder or the horses. No, I don't know anything. How about you? And I am talking about horses. Know anything?'

He screwed up his round face into an expression of dubiety. 'Dunno.'

'Come on, Sonny, you won me a hundred quid on Thursday. You've got a reputation to keep up. Give me another tip.'

'All right. Here's a good 'un.' He beckoned her forward and whispered into her ear. '"A successful gambler doesn't bet more than he bets."'

'Meaning?'

'The successful ones know when to stop. When they have a big win, they leave it for a while, wait to see how things go, ignore all the nearly-good ones, wait for the really-good one. They don't bet on every race.'

Jude shook her head ruefully. 'Then I'm afraid I'll never make a successful gambler. In spite of what happened afterwards, I'm still flushed with the thought of that hundred quid I won last week. I'm sure my luck's on a roll.'

'That's another thing you'll never hear a successful gambler say. No such thing as luck. Graft, application, weighing up the variables – that's how you make money.'

'I'm never going to make much then.'

'No, darling, I'm afraid you're not. And I'm not going to make any today either.'

'What do you mean, Sonny?'

'I been through all the cards. There isn't a single nag I fancy.'

'So you won't have a bet?' He shook his head. 'Then why are you here?'

'Because I like racing, Jude. Can't get round to the courses like I used to do these days, but I can sit in here and see the lot. Coo, what my old man would have thought of a place like this, where you can sit in comfort and have all the racing come to you. He spent his entire life dragging from one racecourse to another, lugging his boards and boxes about. Setting up in the rain, standing there all afternoon, shouting the odds. He'd have thought he was in heaven in a place like this.'

Jude didn't think she could do what Sonny did, just watch the races. So far as she was concerned, take away the gambling and the whole exercise became a bit dull.

She looked up at the screen displaying the runners and prices for the next race, the 1.20 at Fontwell Park, the nearest racecourse to Fethering. She had been there once or twice, so that already gave her a sense of special interest. And then she saw there was a horse in the race called Carol's Duty. 'I'm going to do that,' she said to Sonny.

'Why?'

'I've got a friend called Carole – spelt differently but

near enough, and she's got an overdeveloped sense of duty, so it was clearly meant.'

'What was clearly meant?'

'That the horse is going to win the race.'

Sonny Frank shook his head in exasperated pity. 'That is no way to pick a horse. You could make up some kind of personal reference to any one of those names, if you put your mind to it.'

'I've just got a feeling it's going to win.'

'Oh dear.' The ex-bookmaker's expression clearly demonstrated his views on 'feelings'.

The odds on Carol's Duty were eight to one. Jude was going to put on a fiver but then, remembering that you have to speculate to accumulate, she wrote out a new slip and gave Nikki ten pounds. Horse was still at eight to one – she asked to take the price. The girl scribbled on the slip, ran it through the till and handed over the copy.

By the time Jude had sat down, the price of Carol's Duty had gone out to ten to one. Damn, thought Jude, that means I'll win less.

'Nothing's going to touch this favourite,' said Wes.

'Though eight to thirteen on is a stinking price,' said Vic.

'Not if you compare it to other investments. You don't get that kind of return from the building society.'

'No, but then you don't stand a chance of losing every ten minutes with the building society, do you?'

'Anyway,' said Wes with satisfaction, 'this favourite's going to romp home like there's no other horses in the race.'

Jude glowed inwardly. Let them crow, they'd done the same before the race on Thursday. A fat lot of good it had done them. And the same thing would happen again. Carol's Duty would romp home. She looked up at the screen. Annoyingly, her horse had gone out to twelve to one. Never mind, eighty quid profit was still worth having.

The race was run to the customary barracking from Wes, Vic and Sonny. The favourite won. Carol's Duty pulled up after three fences. Jude gave Sonny a rueful smile. He responded with an I-told-you-so pursing of his lips.

'Most of 'em lose,' said a voice beside her. Jude realized she had unwittingly sat herself right next to Pauline, who was at her usual post, surrounded by shreds of racing newspapers.

'You're right,' Jude agreed. 'Did you have anything on the last race?'

The dumpy elderly woman shook her head. 'No, I don't often bet. Just once or twice a week.'

'But you just like horse racing?'

'Not that bothered really.'

'Then why . . .?'

A knowing grin came across the woman's powdered features. 'Nice and warm in here, isn't it? If I was at home, what'd I be doing? Sitting in a chair in front of the telly, paying God knows what on my central heating. Here I can do just the same, but someone else is paying.'

'But you do like it in here?'

'Oh yes, there's people around. Better than just sitting on my tod.'

'Have you been coming here a long time?'

'Since after my old man died, yes. And that was back before the place got taken over. When Sonny used to run it.'

The ex-bookie grinned acknowledgement of his name. Jude lowered her voice. 'And nobody minds you just coming in every day?'

'Why should they? I have a bet every now and then. I buy myself the odd cup of tea. I don't cause trouble. And I keep my eyes open.'

'What do you mean by that?'

Pauline grinned sagely. 'Neither more nor less than what I said.'

'Would you like a cup of tea now?' asked Jude.

'Wouldn't say no. Four sugars, please.'

Tea was dispensed by Nikki from behind the counter. It came in plastic cups and wasn't very nice. Still, it might prove a useful bridge to Pauline.

When Jude sat down again, another race was in progress. A couple of Chinese waiters had come in – Monday lunchtime business was clearly slack at the Golden Palace – and they added their incomprehensible comments to the raucous exhortations of Wes, Vic and Sonny. It was a good time for an intimate conversation.

'So tell me . . .' Jude began, 'Thursday afternoon, when Tadeusz Jankowski came in to the shop, you saw him?'

'Oh yes,' said Pauline, emptying sachet after sachet of sugar into her cup.

'Did you notice anything odd about him?'

'I thought he looked pale. At least I think he did. But that's the kind of thing you can think after the event. You know, since I've known he died, now maybe I've made myself remember that he looked pale. Memories are pretty unreliable things.'

The shrewdness of the comment seemed at odds with the old woman's vague manner. 'And when he went out of here, did you notice anything about him then?'

'No, not really. No more than I'm sure you did. He did seem to sway a bit, and it crossed my mind he might have had a few too many at lunchtime, but that was all.'

'Yes, I thought that too.' Jude's full lips formed a moue of frustration. 'It would be nice to know more about him, wouldn't it? But since he'd never been in the betting shop before . . .'

'Oh, he'd been in.'

'What?'

'I'd seen him in here.'

'When?'

'Last autumn.'

'Did you tell the police that?'

Pauline let out a derisive laugh. ''Course I didn't.'

'Why not?'

'My old man taught me to be very wary so far as the police are concerned. If they once start nosing into your life, you never get rid of them. "Never tell the cops anything they don't already know, Pauline," my old man used to say to me. And I've stuck to his advice on that . . . as well as on a lot of other things.'

'Ah.' The latest race came to its climax. Wes and Vic's shouts of confidence subsided into moans of disappointment. 'What did your husband do?' asked Jude.

Pauline gave her a little, mischievous smile.

'A bit of this . . . a bit of that . . .'

Jude looked across to the counter. Behind the glass Ryan was impassively counting through piles of banknotes. The Ryan who had assured everyone he had never seen Tadeusz Jankowski before the day of his death.

Maybe there was more connection between the murder victim and the betting shop than everyone had so far assumed.

Chapter Six

Fethering boasted two cafés. On the beach was the
Seaview, open around the year, welcoming in the summer but a rather dispiriting venue in February. Much
more appealing was Polly's Cake Shop, which was on
the main parade, just a few doors away from the
bookie's. And Pauline was more than happy when Jude
suggested they adjourn there for a proper pot of tea. So
long as she wasn't increasing her own heating bills,
Pauline didn't seem to mind where she went.

Polly's Cake Shop restored an image which at one
stage had almost vanished from the British high street.
It had oak beams hung with horse brasses and warming
pans, red and white gingham tablecloths and little
lamps with white shades over candle bulbs. The waitresses wore black dresses and white frilly aprons. And
they served such delicacies as toasted teacakes, cinna-
mon toast, cucumber sandwiches, 'homemade' coconut
kisses, sponge fancies, éclairs and fairy cakes.

It was of course all an exercise in retro marketing.
The beams had been affixed to the bare nineteen-
thirties walls in the late nineteen-nineties, and the
'homemade' delicacies were delivered daily from a

specialist manufacturer in Brighton. Those who liked to use pretentious terms could have described Polly's Cake Shop as a post-modernist gloss on the traditional cake shop. But the residents of Fethering were not bothered about such niceties, and the older ones relaxed into the environment as if it had been unchanged since their childhoods. The only difference was in the prices. Nostalgia never did come cheap.

Pauline wasn't a regular customer at Polly's Cake Shop, but, offered the chance of a free meal, wasn't going to waste it. From the variety of teas proposed she asked for 'ordinary tea', then added a toasted teacake and the 'selection of cakes' to her order. Jude went for the same tea, together with a huge (and hugely sinful) éclair.

'Nice place,' said Pauline, looking around. 'I used to be called Polly, you know.'

'Oh yes?'

'That's what my old man used to call me. Kind of pet name, I suppose.'

'How long ago did he . . .?'

'Twelve years now. Women live longer, don't they?'

'But have you got used to—?'

'You never get used to it. You just learn to live with it.'

Anonymous in the betting shop, on her own Pauline seemed a much stronger personality. Her little-old-lady looks, white permed hair and heavily powdered pinkish face presented an image that was perhaps more benign than the reality. The grey coat she wore over a flowered print dress also fostered the ideal of a cosy little grandmother, but Jude was beginning to think that Pauline might have a bit of the wolf in her too.

'Yes,' she said sympathetically. 'But you manage OK?'

Pauline shrugged. 'OK. Moved into a smaller place after he passed on. Got the pension and he left me a bit. Not much, considering how much'd been through his hands over the years, but . . . yes, I manage.'

'And your husband . . . you didn't say exactly what he did . . .?'

'No, I didn't.' Pauline did another of her mischievous grins. 'Let's just say that what my old man earned . . . well, the taxman didn't know much about it.'

'Right. I think I get your message.'

Jude might have asked more about the dubious past of Pauline's late husband, but their teas were delivered then, and the moment passed.

When the pouring was done and they'd both taken a comforting sip, Jude got straight to the point. 'You said you'd seen Tadeusz Jankowski in the betting shop before.'

The old woman looked her straight in the eye. 'Before I answer your questions, there's something I want to get clear.'

'What?'

'Why you're asking them.'

'There's been a murder. It's natural to be curious, isn't it?'

'Is it? It's natural to be curious if you're a police officer, yes.'

'I can assure you I'm not a police officer.'

'No? Because they use the most unlikely people in plain clothes.'

A beam spread across Jude's chubby face. 'Not as unlikely as me, I promise.'

The moment of levity seemed to have allayed some of Pauline's suspicion. 'So what's your interest in all this then? You another of Fethering's self-appointed amateur detectives?'

Jude found herself blushing as she admitted that she was.

Pauline chuckled. 'I don't know, place like this, a bit of crime gets all the old biddies excited.'

Jude wasn't bothered about being categorized as an old biddy. So long as Pauline would talk to her. Which now the old woman seemed prepared to do. 'All right,' she said. 'So yes, I had seen the Polish boy in the betting shop before.'

'Often?'

'Just the once.'

'When was it?'

'Last year. Late September, maybe early October, I'd say. He come in the shop in the middle of the afternoon.'

'You have a very good memory.'

The little old lady smiled complacently. 'It's a matter of training, you know. Everyone could have a good memory if they trained it. These old biddies who go senile . . . what do they call it now – Alzheimer's? If they'd trained their memories when they was younger, they wouldn't have no problems. My old man, he used to get me to train my memory. "Focus on things," he used to say. "Concentrate. Every face you see, clock it. Use your mind like a camera, store the image." And since he taught me how, that's what I've always done.'

'Why was he so keen for you to do that?' asked Jude, knowing that the question was slightly mischievous.

Pauline instantly picked up the nuance, and winked as she replied, 'Let's just say my old man had a well-developed sense of self-preservation. He was always watching his back, so he liked me to keep my eyes peeled in case there was anyone dodgy about.'

'With faces then, for you it's "once seen, never forgotten".'

'That is exactly right, Jude. For faces I got this photographic memory.'

'So the minute that young man walked into the betting shop last Thursday, you knew who he was?'

'Well, you're overstating things a bit there. I never knew who he was . . . not till I heard on the telly like you did. But the minute he come in the betting shop on Thursday I knew I'd seen him before. Mind you, I didn't know it was going to be important. I didn't know he was just about to die, did I?'

'Of course you didn't.' Jude took a huge bite of her éclair and felt the cream squirting. She wiped her mouth before asking, 'You didn't speak to him then?'

'No. He was just another punter coming into the betting shop.'

'You say a punter. The first time he came in, did you actually see him put on a bet?'

'Oh, come on, Jude. We're talking last October. I

may have a photographic memory for faces. I can't do an instant replay of my whole blooming life.'

'Sorry. Thought it was worth asking. So, so far as you remember, you didn't see him put on a bet?'

'I don't recall seeing him do that. But I'm not saying he didn't.'

'You didn't hear him speak? You didn't notice that he had an accent?'

'I don't recall hearing him speak either. I just remember that I seen him in the betting shop last October.'

'Right. Thank you.' Jude didn't think she was going to get a lot more information out of the canny old woman, but it might be worth trying a slight change of direction. 'It's confusing, isn't it, all the different ideas that are buzzing around the grapevine? So far as I can see, everyone in Fethering seems to have their own theory about the murder.'

'Everyone in Fethering has their own theory about everything,' said Pauline with some asperity. 'People here have too much time on their hands, so they spend it snooping into other people's business. Load of blabbermouths they are.'

'But have you heard any of the blabbermouths saying anything that might have any relevance to the case?'

'Some, maybe.'

'So, what theories have you heard?'

Pauline focused on another fairy cake and slowly bit the tiny slice of angelica off the top. 'Well, I've heard theories ranging from Russian hit men to Mafia gang wars. The only sensible theory I've heard is that no one has a clue why the poor bugger was stabbed.'

'And do you have any theories of your own?'

Pauline looked at Jude shrewdly and said, 'What my old man always used to say was, "If a crime of violence happens, the first question to ask is why the issue couldn't have been sorted out without violence." And the answer to that might be because the people you're dealing with are psychopaths or people of a highly nervous temperament, or there could be any number of other reasons. Moving on to the matter of murder, my old man used to say, "The only reason for murdering someone is to keep them quiet. If you just want to put the frighteners on them, you don't have to go as far as murder. So you only murder someone when the consequences of what they might tell another party constitute a bigger risk than the risk of actually committing a murder." That's what he always said, and my old man knew what he was talking about.'

Jude nodded. 'That makes very good sense.'

But then Pauline added, rather mischievously, 'Though, of course, the reason for this murder could be something else entirely.'

'Yes, but going along for a moment with your husband's theory . . . the question we should be asking is: what did Tadeusz Jankowski know that represented a threat to someone else?'

'That's the question. Mind you, finding the answer might be more difficult, since we don't know anything about the poor bugger except for his unpronounceable name.'

Jude nodded ruefully. It always came back to the same thing for amateur detectives; they suffered from a dearth of information.

'And there's nothing else,' she asked without much hope, 'that you can remember about when you saw him in October? Presumably he wasn't wearing the big overcoat?'

'No, T-shirt and jeans, as far as I remember.'

'And you've said you don't recall him going up to the counter to place a bet . . . You didn't see him speak to anyone, did you?'

To her surprise, Jude's last despairing question brought a response. 'Oh yes, he did talk to someone.'

'Really? Who?'

'A woman who's often in there.'

A spark of excitement had rekindled in Jude. 'One of the regulars?'

'She used to be in there a lot. Well-dressed woman, early forties maybe.'

'What's her name?'

'Ah, I never found that out. Kept herself to herself. Put on a lot of bets, but never joined in any of the backchat.'

'But you could point her out to me if she came into the betting shop?'

'Oh yes, of course I could.'

Jude's pulse quickened. At least she'd got the beginnings of a lead.

'Mind you,' Pauline went on, 'she hasn't been in for some months.'

'Oh? Since when?'

'I suppose I stopped seeing her . . .' The old lady screwed up her face with the effort of memory '. . . quite a few months back . . . October probably.'

'Just after you'd seen her talking to Tadeusz Jankowski?'

'Yes, that's right,' replied Pauline, before cramming a whole coconut kiss into her mouth.

'I went back to the betting shop and asked around,' Jude told Carole. 'Most of them remembered the woman all right, but none of them had ever seen her off the premises.'

'Did you get a name?'

'No.'

'Well, couldn't you have asked the manager?'

'I did ask the manager, Carole.'

'Without giving away why you were interested?'

'Of course without giving away why I was interested. I said something about a woman matching the description of a friend of mine having been seen in the betting shop and described her as Pauline had to me.'

'You do seem to find lying easy, Jude.'

'Yes, never been a problem for me. Except in certain relationship situations.'

'Ah.' Though intrigued, Carole didn't feel moved to pursue that subject.

'Anyway, what did the manager say to you?'

'Like everyone else, Ryan remembered the woman, but didn't have a name for her.'

'Surely they keep records?'

'Placing a bet is an anonymous exercise. Generally speaking, you pay in cash and, unless you have an account, no one has a clue who you are.'

'Hm.' Carole still looked a bit pale, but she was a lot better than she had been at the end of the previous week. Her hands were wrapped round a cup of coffee in the kitchen at High Tor. By the Aga Gulliver snuffled comfortably. His mistress was taking him out for walks again and all was even more serene in his comfortable doggy world.

'So this woman,' she went on, 'used to be a regular at the betting shop . . .?'

'Semi-regular, it seems. She didn't go absolutely every afternoon, and she never stayed for long.'

'All right. So she was a semi-regular till round October . . . and then suddenly she disappeared?'

'I think that's over-dramatic, Carole. She stopped going into the betting shop, that's all. We have no evidence that she disappeared from the rest of her life . . . chiefly because we know absolutely nothing about the rest of her life. Anything might have happened. Most likely she moved out of the area. Or maybe she lost interest in the horses . . . or she underwent a religious conversion and decided that gambling was sinful . . . There are so many possibilities that, quite honestly, any of them could be viable.'

Carole looked thoughtful. Though she was still physically weakened by the flu, her brain was once again firing on all cylinders. 'So this unknown woman was in the betting shop one day last October . . . and

Tadeusz Jankowski came into the place and spoke to her?'

'That's what Pauline told me.'

'And did he speak to her as though he knew her?'

'Apparently, yes.'

'So we have got something to go on.'

'Not much. A man about whom we know nothing except his name met a woman whose name we don't even know . . . I think it'd be a while before we could get that case to court.'

'But it's interesting. Did any of the other regulars see Tadeusz Jankowski last October?'

'I asked them. They all said no. But although they're regulars, they're not there every single day. Or it's quite possible he did go in when they were there and they didn't notice. Not everyone has Pauline's photographic memory for faces.'

'But the manager . . .'

'Yes, there's something funny there. He told me it's part of his job to clock everyone who goes in and out of the place. And he also told me he'd never seen the dead man before last Thursday.'

'So something doesn't quite ring true, does it?'

'Well, unless Pauline's lying and, although I'm sure she's quite capable of it in the right circumstances, I can't imagine why she'd do so in this instance.'

'So what can we do?'

'I think, given our current lack of information, the only thing we can do is to try and get a quiet word with Ryan.'

Chapter Seven

Jude went into the betting shop the following morning, the Tuesday, at around eleven, thinking it would be a good time to talk to the manager before the main racing fixtures started. But Ryan wasn't there. His place had been taken by an older man of uncongenial appearance. Jude's immediate thought was that the police had spotted the same inconsistency in Ryan's statements that she had, and he was 'helping them with their enquiries'. But a question to the vacuous Nikki provided a much less dramatic explanation. Ryan was laid up with the 'nasty flu' that had been going round.

At a loose end, Jude decided that she and Carole should have lunch at the Crown and Anchor. Her neighbour initially opposed the idea – she opposed anything that smacked of self-indulgence – but was persuaded. She was, after all, in a convalescent state after her own bout of flu. She wasn't yet up to cooking for herself. A meal out would be a necessary part of her recovery.

Carole was secretly pleased at the plan. All morning she'd been putting off ringing her daughter-in-law. After the postponement of the weekend, she needed to fix another date to meet up with Lily and her parents. But Carole didn't feel up to the challenge of such a call. She was always shy of Gaby, and she knew that any discussion of rescheduling their meeting would also involve mention of David. She wasn't sure she felt strong enough to state the truth: that she didn't want to see her granddaughter with her ex-husband present.

So going off to the Crown and Anchor gave her the perfect excuse to put off her difficult phone call till the afternoon.

'Heard you'd been out of sorts,' said Ted Crisp when they arrived at the pub. 'Still looking a bit peaky, aren't you?'

Carole had to think about her response. Every fibre of her being revolted against the idea of ever 'making a fuss', but then again she didn't want anyone to under-estimate how ghastly she had felt for the previous few days. So she contented herself with a brave, 'Getting better, but it's been a really nasty bug.'

'Tell me about it. Everyone in the pub seems to have had it. Can't hear yourself speak in here for all the coughing and spluttering. And my latest barmaid's using it as an excuse for not turning up.'

'Poor kid,' said Jude.

'I'm not so sure about that. Quite capable of "taking a sickie". She's a right little skiver, that one. Most of them seem to be these days, certainly the youngsters. Whatever happened to the concept of "taking pride in your work"? This lot all seem to want to get paid for doing the absolute minimum. Bloody work ethic's gone out the window in this country, you know.'

Jude was once again struck by how right-wing Ted was becoming. Ironic how almost all of those who had derided the establishment in their youth came round later in life to endorsing its continued existence.

'The younger generation are all hopeless,' he went on. 'But round here older people are too well-heeled to bother with bar work. Hey, you wouldn't like to be a barmaid, would you, Jude? You'd bring lots of custom in, someone like you.'

She grinned. 'I have a sneaking feeling the word "buxom" is about to be mentioned.'

'I wasn't going to say it.'

'But you were thinking it, Ted.'

'Well, maybe.'

'I'll consider your offer. If I run out of clients for my healing services. It's not as if I haven't done it before.'

Carole, reminded of this detail from her neighbour's past, shuddered to the core of her middle-class heart.

Ted Crisp grinned at her discomfiture. 'Anyway, I'm the one in charge of the bar for the time being. So, what are you ladies drinking? Is it the old Chilean Chards again?'

'I should probably have something soft,' said Carole. 'You know, I'm not a hundred per cent yet.'

'All the more reason why you need a proper drink,' Jude assured her. 'You should probably be having a quadruple brandy.'

'Oh, I think that would be excessive. But all right, a small Chilean Chardonnay, if you insist.'

'I insist,' said Ted Crisp, 'that it should be a large one.'

'But—'

'You pay for a small one. I'll top it up to a large one. Landlord's privilege.' Carole didn't argue. 'And I assume a large one for you, Jude . . .?'

'Please. And what's good to eat? Healthy nutritious fare to help restore Carole to her old self?'

'You won't go wrong with the Local Game Pie. Served with Special Gravy.'

'Two of those then, please.'

'Though I don't actually think I've got much of an appetite,' said Carole. 'I probably won't be able to eat it all, given the size of your usual portions.'

'You'll manage,' said Ted, writing down the order.

'By the way,' Carole asked, 'what is the Local Game today?'

Deliberately misunderstanding, Ted replied, 'The Local Game in Fethering is still trying to work out who killed that poor Polish bloke. Tell you, I've heard more theories in this pub than you've had hot lunches here.'

'Any that sound convincing?'

The landlord shook his shaggy head. 'Not unless you're a big fan of Cold War spy fiction, no. I think the trouble is, nobody knows what the poor bloke was doing in this country, anyway.'

'Bar work, I gather.'

'Yes, Jude, that's what he was doing, but surely that wasn't why he was here. As I know all too well, it's a crap job, bar work. That's why I can't get any decent staff. The pay's not good enough.'

'No, but for him it was still probably more than he'd get paid in Poland,' said Carole.

'He was living in Littlehampton,' said Jude. 'You know most of the pubs and bars around, Ted. You haven't heard where he was working, have you?'

'No. I could ask around, though.'

'Be grateful if you did.'

'All right,' said the landlord. 'But we're rather starved of information, aren't we? Nobody really knows anything about the bloke, what he was like, what he wanted from life. Those are the kind of things you want to know if you're going to find out why someone was murdered.'

Carole and Jude were already far too aware of the truth in Ted's words. After a little more desultory banter, they adjourned to one of the pub's alcoves with their drinks.

'What about the girl?' Carole asked suddenly.

'What girl?'

'You said there's also a girl who works regularly in the betting shop.'

'Oh yes, Nikki.'

'Well, maybe she's seen the mysterious woman Tadeusz Jankowski spoke to. Maybe she knows who it is.'

'Possible. Nikki doesn't come across as the most observant of people – or indeed the most intelligent – but I suppose it's worth asking her. She can't be as dim as she appears.'

The Local Game Pie lived up to Ted Crisp's recommendation. And the Special Gravy was delicious. In spite of her prognostications, Carole finished every last morsel, but the food – and a second glass of wine –

left her feeling very sleepy. 'But I can't sleep during the daytime,' she told Jude. Sleeping in the daytime – like watching daytime television – was a slippery slope for retired people, so far as Carole was concerned. Go too far down that route and you'll stop bothering to get up or get dressed in the morning. Then you'll start to smell and 'become a burden'. Carole's mind was full of imagined slippery slopes to cause her anxiety.

'You go straight back to bed,' said Jude, 'and have a nice long sleep. You're still washed out. Sleep's nature's way of making you better.'

Carole didn't argue any more. Sleeping during the day for health reasons was quite acceptable. But such indulgence must stop the minute she was fully fit again.

Before she took to her bed, she felt sufficiently buoyed up by the Chilean Chardonnay to ring Gaby. And, to her delight, her daughter-in-law suggested coming down to Fethering that Friday. Just her and Lily. The perfect configuration, and no mention of David. Exactly what Carole would have wished for. Heartened by the conversation, she was quickly nestled under her duvet and asleep.

Jude felt restless when she returned from the pub. Although she had a presence that spread serenity, inside her mind all was not always serene. She had had a varied life in many different places. Sometimes the quietness of Fethering soothed her, but at others it rankled and she felt a surge of wanderlust. There was so much world out there, so much yet to be seen. Maybe it was time that her wings were once again spread.

Normally she would ease such moods by yoga. The familiarity of the movements, the relinquishing of her thoughts to a stronger imperative, could usually be relied on to settle her. But that afternoon she'd had two large glasses of wine and she knew her concentration would not be adequate to the demands of yoga.

So she lit a fire and then sat down to read the manuscript of a book written by one of her healer friends. It was about control, not controlling others, but taking control of one's own life, developing one's own potentialities. Jude, who had read and been disappointed by more than her fair share of self-help books, thought this one was rather good.

But her mind kept straying. The pale image of the dying Tadeusz Jankowski recurred like an old reproach. What had happened to him? Why did he have to die? She hoped she would soon have answers to those questions.

The phone rang. Jude answered it.

'Hello. Is this, Jude, please?' The voice was female, young, heavily accented.

'Yes, it is.'

'It was you who found the body of Tadeusz Jankowski?'

'Yes.'

'Please, I like to meet you.'

'I'm sorry, who am I talking to?'

'My name is Zofia Jankowska. I am the sister of Tadeusz.'

Chapter Eight

The girl was in her early twenties, with hazel eyes and blonded hair divided into two pigtails. She wore jeans and a blue waterproof jacket. There were silver rings on her fingers and in her pierced ears. She had a feeling of energy about her, as if all inactive time was wasted, as if she couldn't wait to be getting on with something.

Zofia had come straight from the police, having rung Jude from the Major Crime Centre at Hollingbury near Brighton. And Jude had invited her straight over.

'They were helpful to me, the police, but not very helpful, if you understand.'

'Yes, I think I do,' said Jude. 'Can I get you something to drink? Or have you eaten?'

'I have a sort of plastic breakfast on the plane.'

'And how long ago was that?'

'The flight left at 6.20 from Warsaw.'

'You must be starving. Come through to the kitchen and I'll get you something.'

Bacon and eggs were the most obvious emergency rations and while Jude rustled them up, the two women continued their conversation. 'When you say the police were helpful and unhelpful, what exactly did you mean?'

'They were helpful in the way how they were polite to me and answering my questions, but they did not give me a lot information.'

'They gave you my number, though.'

'They give me your name. I find your number in phonebook. I don't think the police were keeping information from me. I think they just don't have a lot information to give.'

'No, that was the impression I got.' Jude sat the girl down at her kitchen table and dished up the bacon and eggs. 'What would you like to drink? Tea – or something stronger?'

'You have coffee?'

Jude had coffee. While she made it, Zofia wolfed down the food as if she hadn't eaten for months. Whatever her reaction had been to the news of her brother's death, it hadn't affected her appetite.

Jude sat down and waited till the plate was empty. 'Can I get you anything else?'

'No, I . . . You are very kind. You give me much.'

'I bought a rather self-indulgent ginger cake yesterday. Let's have some of that by the fire, and you can tell me everything you know.'

'I prefer you tell me what you know. You are the one who find Tadek.'

'Tadek?'

'I'm sorry – Tadeusz. Tadek is short name for him. In family and friends, we all say Tadek.'

'Right.'

They sat down in a heavily draped sofa. Jude hadn't put any lights on yet, though the February evening was encroaching and soon they would be needed. The flickering of the fire illuminated the clutter of Woodside Cottage's sitting room, its shrouded furniture, its every surface crowded with memorabilia from the varied lives of its owner.

'Were you close to your brother?' asked Jude.

'When we live together as children with my mother, very close. Then he go to university, we do not see so much of each other. Still we stay close . . . from a distance, can you say?'

'Yes. You said your mother . . . are your parents not together?'

'My father he died when Tadek and I are small children. There is just my mother.'

'She must have been devastated when she heard the news about your brother.'

'Yes, I suppose. We do not get on, she and I. But, in her way, she is upset. She do not understand. I do not understand. That is why I know I must come here. I stop everything, get a flight, come here.'

'How much did you have to stop? Do you have a job?'

'I do not. Not yet. Not permanent job. I was student. At university in Warsaw.'

'Studying English? You speak it very well.'

'No, not English. Not major in English, though I try to get it better, because it is important. But I studied journalism. I wanted to be reporter.'

'"Studied"? "Wanted"? Why the past tense? What went wrong?'

'I did not like the course, not good. I drop out. Wait tables, work in bars till I decide what I really want to do.'

'Maybe you've got enough reporter's skills to get to the bottom of what happened to your brother.'

'This I hope. This is why I come.' She pulled a small notebook out of the back pocket of her jeans. 'In this I write down my notes, everything I find out. I have to know something, have to know why Tadek was killed.'

'It must be terrible for you.'

'I think it will be. Now I am too full of . . . unbelieving . . . and angriness. Now I just want to know what happened. When I have found this out, then I think there will be time for sadness.'

'I'm sure there will.'

'So I must know everything that is known. This is why I need see you. Please, tell me about how you saw Tadek . . . my brother.'

As simply and sympathetically as she could, Jude re-created the events of the previous Thursday afternoon. It didn't take long. She could only say what happened. She had no explanations, nothing that might assuage Zofia's thirst for detail. Meanwhile the girl scribbled down notes in her little blue book.

When Jude had finished her narration, there was a long silence. Then Zofia spoke slowly. 'It is terrible. That you should see Tadek like that. That I did not see him. That I will not see him again. That is the thing that is hard to understand. That he is not there any more, not anywhere any more.'

'When did you last see him, Zofia?'

'Please do not call me "Zofia". That is very formal. My friends have a special name for me.'

A sudden thought came to Jude. 'It isn't "Fifi", is it?'

The girl looked at her in bewilderment. 'No. "Fifi" I think is a name for a dog.'

Jude didn't think the time was right to elaborate the reasoning behind her question. 'I just thought . . . "Zofia" . . . it might be shortened to—'

'No, "Zosia". That is the name everyone calls me. Please, you call me "Zosia".'

'Very well. Zosia,' said Jude.

'Why you think I am "Fifi"?'

Jude explained about her brother's dying word, hoping that now she might get some explanation for it. But Zofia was as puzzled as she was. So far as the girl knew, Tadek had not known a "Fifi". He'd certainly never mentioned one. And no Polish word that he might have been trying to get out seemed to have any relevance.

'You ask me when I last see Tadek . . . Of course I did not know it was the last time I would see him, but it was in Warsaw in September. Just before he come to England.'

'Why did he come to England?'

'I do not know. He would not tell me.'

'What was he doing in Warsaw?'

'He finish a year ago a degree in music. He want make a career in music. He write songs, play piano, guitar. He love playing his guitar. Now he will not do that any more.' These reminders of her brother's absence did not seem yet to cause sadness to Zofia. Her reaction was more one of bewilderment, an inability to take in the sheer scale of what had happened.

'So did Tadek have a job?'

'Small jobs. Temporary work. Like me. He wanted to buy time to write his songs.'

'Do you think he came to England because he thought there would be better opportunities in the English music scene?'

The girl shrugged. 'Maybe. But I don't think so. He was enjoying his music in Warsaw. He was in a band with some friends, it all seemed to be going well. Then suddenly he tell us all he is going to England.'

'And you've no idea why he might have done that?'

'No. Tadek was not very . . . I don't know the word . . . not good at details of life, doing things that needed to be done every day.'

'You mean he wasn't practical?'

'I think this is the word, yes. He lived in the clouds. He had wild ideas which were not easy to make happen.'

'He was a romantic?'

'Yes. And an optimist. He think everything will come good some time. But of course he was wrong.'

'When you say he was a romantic,' asked Jude, 'does that extend to his emotional life? Was he romantic about women?'

Zofia nodded vigorously. 'Yes, even after growing

up with me and our mother, Tadek still put women . . .
up high . . . I don't know . . .'

'On a pedestal?'

'That is good word. Often he want to be with
women who are not right for him. Too old for him
sometimes. But he still . . . yes, put them on a pedestal.'

'So do you think it might have been a woman who
brought him to England?'

'It is possible. But he did not say anything to me
about a woman. Usually he tell me who is the new one
he has fallen in love with. And tell me when it has broken up – as they all did.'

'Did your brother have any friends in England? Was
there someone he could have stayed with when he first
arrived?'

'I do not know of many. Tadek had not been to
England before. I do not know of any English friends of
him. But it is possible he meet people. He travelled a
lot in Europe. To music festivals and such events, with
his band. But again it is unusual for him not to tell me
about people he meet.'

'Did the police ask you about his friends?'

'Of course. I cannot help them much – like I cannot
help you much. But they do tell me where he was living.'

'Littlehampton, I gather.'

'Yes, they give me address. I will go there. After seeing you, this must be the next place I go. Maybe I find
out something.'

'Well, if you do, please let me know.'

The girl's hazel eyes sought out Jude's brown ones. 'You also are wanting to find out how Tadek died?'

'Yes,' Jude replied simply.

After Zofia had left, Jude was tidying up in the kitchen when she heard the rattle of something coming through her letterbox. Too late for the post (even though that did seem to be getting later and later). She managed to get to the front window just in time to see the person who'd made the delivery moving on next door to High Tor.

Through the encroaching dusk, she recognized him from the previous week in the Crown and Anchor. Dressed in a Drizabone coat and tweed cap, it was Hamish Urquhart. Running errands for his father. Jude looked down at the mat to see what he had delivered.

The envelope was addressed to 'The Occupier'. From, as she might have guessed, Urquhart & Pease, the estate agents. They were always looking for new properties in the 'much sought-after' location of Fethering. Anyone looking to sell could not do better than engage the services of the long-established, efficient and courteous firm of Urquhart & Pease, who would be happy to offer a free valuation.

Normally Jude would have shoved such a letter straight into the bin. But that day, given her earlier restlessness, it had a pertinence for her. Maybe it was a psychic nudge, telling her she should be moving out of Fethering. The timing was interesting. And Jude was a great believer in synchronicity.

Chapter Nine

Shortly after Carole had put her flyer from Urquhart & Pease straight in the recycling bin, she had a phone call from Ted Crisp. He wasn't good at remembering numbers, but hers had stayed stuck in his head from the time of their brief affair, so he rang her rather than Jude.

'Been doing my bit on the old Licensed Victuallers grapevine,' he announced. 'Found out where the dead man did his bar work.'

'Oh, really? Well done.'

'Pub on the Fedborough road out of Littlehampton. Just by the river bridge. Cat and Fiddle. Do you know it?'

'No,' said Carole unsurprisingly. The Crown and Anchor was about the only pub she did know. Carole Seddon still didn't think of herself as a 'pub person'.

'Run by a woman called Shona Nuttall. Known in the trade as "The Cat On The Fiddle". One of those self-appointed "characters", of whom there are so many in the pub business.'

'Your tone of voice suggests that she's not your favourite person.'

'Does it?' He neither confirmed nor denied the impression.

'And what about the pub? How does she run that?'

'Not the way I would,' Ted Crisp replied eloquently.

The Cat and Fiddle's perfect riverside position ensured continuous trade throughout the summer, but it wasn't so busy on a cold Tuesday evening in February. Even before Carole and Jude entered, they were aware of why it wasn't the sort of pub Ted Crisp would have liked. The inn sign was a Disneyfied version of a cute cat with bulbous eyes playing the fiddle to a group of goofy-toothed square-dancing rabbits. Notices in the vast car park bore the same motif, as did the signs on the children's play area. Whether the Cat and Fiddle was a one-off business or not, it gave the impression of being part of a franchise.

This was intensified by the interior, open-plan with lots of pine divisions which were reminiscent of some immaculate stable-yard, an image encouraged by the romantic country music that filled the air. Pointless rosettes were pinned to pillars; halters and unused riding tack hung from hooks. The narrow awning over the bar was thatched, and the bar staff, male and female, wore dungarees over red gingham shirts. On the wall-mounted menus another incarnation of the goggle-eyed cat pointed down to a sign reading 'Good Ol' Country Cookin''.

The few customers did not sit on their show-home pine stools with the ease that identifies the true pub regular. Suited businessmen at single tables worked silently through meals piled high with orange chips. An unspeaking couple in a stable-like booth looked as if they were mentally checking through the final details of their suicide pact.

Behind the bar stood a large woman whose lack of dungaree livery meant she must be the landlady. Tight cream trousers outlined the contours of her substantial bottom and thighs, while a spangly black and gold top gave a generous view of her vertiginously deep cleavage. She had a tan that looked as if it had just returned from the Canary Islands and wore a lot of chunky gold. Earrings, necklaces, bracelets and a jeweller's windowful of rings. When she flashed a greeting to the two women, a gold tooth was exposed at the corner of her smile.

'Good evening. Welcome to the Cat and Fiddle.' Her voice was brash and slightly nasal. 'What can I get you? We do have a Special Winter Warmer Mulled Wine for these winter evenings.'

Carole and Jude, who shared the view that nothing spoiled wine so much as heating it up and shoving in herbs and sugar, both opted for a Chilean Chardonnay. Carole had intended not to drink alcohol on this rare second visit to a pub in the same day, but the atmosphere of the place seemed to require some form of anaesthetic.

They had wondered in the car how they were going to get round to the subject of Tadeusz Jankowski, but they needn't have worried. The landlady, who must be the Shona Nuttall Ted had referred to, brought it up almost immediately.

'You local, are you?' she began.

'Fethering.'

'Oh, very close. I haven't seen you in here before, though.' She beamed so far that the gold tooth glinted again. 'Well, now you've found us, I hope you'll get the Cat and Fiddle habit.'

Both women, while mentally forswearing the place for ever, made some polite reaction.

'It's a real old-fashioned friendly pub. Got lots of atmosphere,' said Shona Nuttall, in the teeth of the evidence. The many photographs pinned behind the bar all featured the landlady grinning hugely and crushing some hapless customer in her flabby arms.

'Mind you, though,' she went on, saving them the effort of even the most basic probing, 'we have had our sadnesses here recently . . .'

'Oh?' asked Carole, providing a prompt which probably wasn't needed.

'I don't know if you heard on the telly about that poor young man who was stabbed . . .?'

'Yes, we did,' said Jude.

"Course you would have done, living right there in Fethering. Well, do you know . . .' She gathered up her bosom in her arms as she prepared to make the revelation '. . .that boy only worked in here.'

'Really?' Jude sounded suitably surprised. 'Tadeusz Jankowski?'

'Yes, him. Mind you, I could never pronounce his name, so I just called him Teddy.'

'What did he actually do for you . . .? Sorry, I don't know your name . . .?' Carole lied.

First names were exchanged, then the landlady went on with what was clearly becoming her party piece. 'I'd got an ad in the *Littlehampton Gazette* for staff. I always need extra bodies running up to Christmas and New Year, then it slackens off, but some of my real stalwarts tend to take their holidays this time of year, so I'm still a bit short. Well, Teddy saw the ad and came along.'

'When would this have been?'

'Middle of October. That's when I have to start thinking about Christmas. Anyway, Teddy seemed a nice enough lad . . . well, considering he was Polish . . . so I thought I'd give him a try.'

'Was he working behind the bar?' Jude tried with difficulty to visualize the young man she'd seen in dungarees and red gingham.

'No, no. His English wasn't good enough for that. And, you know, handling the money . . . you can't be too careful . . . particularly with foreigners.' As she had been with Ewan Urquhart, Jude was struck by the endemic mild racism of West Sussex. 'My staff do a kind of probation period before I let them behind the bar.'

'What work did he do then?' asked Carole.

'Washing up mostly. You know, clearing the rubbish from the kitchen, helping the chef. No cooking, mind. Kitchen porter kind of thing.'

'But not mixing with the customers?'

'No.'

'Was he friendly with the other staff?'

'Oh yes, yes, he was a nice boy. Such a tragedy, somebody so young,' Shona said automatically. 'Look, that's how friendly he was.' She pointed to one of the photographs behind the bar. Out of deference to the deceased, somebody had pinned a black ribbon bow over it. Tadeusz Jankowski looked very small and embarrassed in his employer's all-consuming embrace. The photograph may have shown how friendly Shona Nuttall was; it didn't look as though the boy had had much choice in the matter.

'Any particular friends amongst the other staff?' Carole persisted.

'No, not really. Not that I noticed. He only did two-hour shifts, and he was kept pretty busy, so he didn't have much time to socialize.'

'Did he ever mention having a girlfriend? Or did you see him with one?'

The landlady shook her head. 'I was asked all these questions by the police, you know.' This was not said to make them desist in their interrogation; it was spoken with pride. The death of Tadeusz Jankowski had given Shona Nuttall a starring role in her own drama and she was going to enjoy every moment of it.

'Did he say anything about other friends?' asked Jude. 'Or why he had come to England?'

'The police asked me that too, but I wasn't able to help them, you know. I mean, I'm very good to all the people who work for me, but I do have a business to run, so that has to be my first priority. Not too much time for idle chatter with the kitchen staff, particularly when they don't speak much English.'

'Did the police question you for long?'

'Oh, quite a while. Half an hour, probably. And . . .'

Shona Nuttall slowed down as she prepared to produce her biggest bombshell '. . . I was actually on the television.'

'Were you?'

'Yes. You may have seen me. Friday I was on the news.'

Carole looked puzzled. 'I'm fairly sure I did see the news on Friday evening. I had flu, but I got out of bed specially to watch it. I don't remember seeing you, though.'

'Ah, well, I was just on the local news.' The landlady seemed put out to have to make this admission. 'Six-thirty in the evening.'

'No, then I wouldn't have seen that.'

'I do have the video.' Not only did she have it, she had it set up in the VCR on the bar. She pressed the relevant controls and told them to look up at the big screen. The practised ease with which she went through these motions suggested that Carole and Jude weren't the first Cat and Fiddle customers who had been shown the recording.

Shona Nuttall's moment of television fame was very short. A brief shot of the exterior of the pub was shown, followed by a close-up of her behind the bar saying, 'He seemed a nice boy. I can't imagine why anyone would want to hurt him.' Then, with one of those bad edits so beloved of local television news, they cut back to the studio and the presenter talking about the increase of the rat population in Worthing.

'You came across very well,' said Jude, and Shona Nuttall glowed with the compliment. What a sycophantic remark, thought Carole, but she was still envious of the way her neighbour could always say the right thing to put people at their ease.

'And did Tad . . . Teddy ever talk to you about his music?'

'Sorry?'

'He was a very keen musician. He wrote songs and played guitar.'

'I didn't know that. He wasn't into country music, was he?'

'I don't think so. More sort of folk.'

'Oh. Because we do have regular Country Evenings here at the Cat and Fiddle. Line Dancing too. I don't know if that's your sort of thing . . .?'

'Not really,' said Carole, suppressing a shudder.

They continued their conversation with Shona a little longer. Relishing her moment in the spotlight, she was happy to talk for as long as they wanted. But it soon became obvious that she had almost nothing to tell them. 'Teddy' had been employed as cheap labour in the kitchen of the Cat and Fiddle. She had had no interest in him apart from that. Though happy after his death to project the image of the big-hearted employer struck by tragedy, Shona Nuttall actually knew nothing about the young man.

And when in the course of conversation Jude revealed that she was the one who had been present at his death, the landlady could not hide her annoyance. She didn't want anyone else muscling in on her fifteen minutes of fame.

Chapter Ten

'You want me to go into a betting shop?' said Carole, appalled.

'The betting shop is, if not the Scene of the Crime, at least the only place we know related to the crime. It's going to be rather hard to find out anything about the case if we don't go back there. Shona Nuttall proved to be something of a dead end – not to say a dead loss – so the betting shop must be our next port of call.'

'But, Jude, what on earth will people think I'm doing?'

'They'll think you're going into the betting shop, that's all. People wander in and out all the time. Nobody'll take any notice of you.'

'But supposing there was someone I knew in there? Or someone I knew saw me going in there?'

'So?'

'What would they think?'

'They would think that you were going into the betting shop. Full stop. It's only a betting shop, Carole. It's not an opium den in Limehouse.'

'No, but—'

'I'm going there right now. Picking up Harold Peskett's bets on the way. Are you coming?'

'Yes,' Carole replied meekly. But not without misgiving.

As it turned out, Carole and Jude went to the betting shop that Wednesday morning before seeing Harold Peskett. They didn't go inside, but to the small alley where Jude had witnessed the young man's death. She'd had the thought as they were walking along Fethering High Street that revisiting the scene might spark some recollection, might set her mind going in a different direction.

Though the day was dry, the alley looked drab and uninviting, littered with burger wrappers and plastic bottles. A smell of urine hung in the air. It had been used as a comfort station by many beerful customers taking a short cut back from the Crown and Anchor.

Tied to a drainpipe near where Tadeusz Jankowski had died was a bunch of flowers. Though not yet wilting, they looked infinitely pathetic. Attached to the stalks was a card with words in a language that neither woman understood.

'Zofia's tribute to her brother,' said Jude softly.

Carole was silent. Though not as sensitive to atmospheres as her neighbour, she could still feel the piercing melancholy of the location.

'So why did he come down here?' asked Jude, as if thinking out loud. 'Why did he go into the betting shop? What was he looking for?'

'Maybe he was going to meet someone on the beach? Or round the back of one of the shops?' The alley led to a little service road behind the parade.

'We could look.' Jude tried unsuccessfully to banish the sadness from her face. 'Maybe we'll see something obvious that he was making for?'

But no. There was nothing obvious. Nothing unusual at all. A lorry was delivering what was undoubtedly the wrong stock to the loading bay behind Allinstore. There was no other sign of human activity. Towards the sea was an area of scrubland, rough grass snaking its way over sandy soil, too flat to be called a dune.

'Nothing springs to mind,' said Carole dispiritedly.

'No.' Jude turned away from the beach to face the overgrown back yard of the betting shop. Through wire-netting gates, she found herself looking straight at Ryan the Manager. He looked as shocked to see her as she did him.

Jude raised her hand in a little half-wave of acknowledgement, but the young man did not respond. Instead, shoving the bulky contents of a brown paper bag into his pocket, he turned on his heel and disappeared through the back door of the shop.

Harold Peskett lived in sheltered accommodation, a tiny flat in a purpose-built block with views over Fethering Beach. Though still suffering from the flu, he was up and dressed by the time Jude and Carole arrived.

A small, birdlike man, ninety-two years had whittled away at him, so that now there seemed to be only one layer of skin on his prominent bones. There was no hair on the blotched cranium, and he peered at the world through thick-lensed tortoiseshell glasses. In spite of the considerable warmth of central heating turned up high, he wore two jumpers under a tweed jacket whose elbows and cuffs had been reinforced with leather. His shoes were polished to a high gloss and he wore a thin, greasy dark tie with some insignia on it.

His room was meticulously tidy, the bed neatly squared off and lots of box files regimented on shelves. Only on the table in the window facing the sea was there disarray, an untidy spread of the day's racing papers, from which he had been working out his latest foolproof fortune-bringing strategy.

He was very glad to see Carole. Any friend of Jude's was a friend of his. And he was sick of the wretched flu. 'I still wake up every morning as weak as a kitten. Mind you, even when I'm a hundred per cent, I'm not much stronger than a kitten these days.' He chuckled, and through the lenses there was a sparkle in his clouded eyes.

'Carole's just recovered from the flu too.'

'Oh, have you, love?' Carole didn't really like being called 'love', but the ninety-two-year-old's charm enabled him to get away with it. 'Then you have my sympathy. Rotten one, this is. Hangs on like the smell of damp in an empty house. Nasty.'

'Yes, it certainly took it out of me.'

'Well, I'm glad to see you're on the mend. Hope I

will be soon. Then you won't have to come collecting my bets every day, Jude.'

'It's no hardship. I really don't mind.'

'That's very kind of you to say so, but I hope it won't be for much longer. Anyway, I like putting the bets on myself. Then I can say my own special little prayer to Lady Luck. "Come on, love, today you're going to give me the big win, aren't you?"'

'And does she usually oblige?' asked Carole.

'Oh, no. Never. Well, I'll get the odd little double, but never the big one I'm really after. Still . . .' He chuckled again '. . . at ninety-two, what would I do with all the money if I did have a big win? No, no, it's not the money that's really the attraction for me. It's pitting myself against the system, against the whole random universe, trying to impose order on total chaos.'

'You're a bit of a philosopher in your quiet way, aren't you?' said Jude.

'Guilty as charged.' The little man placed his frail hands on his chest in a gesture of submission. 'Now, can I offer you ladies a cup of tea or something?'

'No, really, we've just had some coffee. Anyway, Harold, you're not fit enough to be doing that sort of thing. Can I get you a cup of tea?'

'Well, Jude, if you don't mind . . .' This exchange had become a part of their morning ritual. Harold would make the offer of tea, Jude would refuse and offer to make some for him, and he'd accept.

While she busied herself in the tiny kitchen, Carole said to the old man, 'So you're normally a regular at the betting shop?'

'Never miss a day. Been doing the horses all my life. Back when I started the bookie's were on the street corners with their clock bags.'

'I'm sorry?'

'Clock bags. They had to be closed at a certain time before the race started, so's no one could cheat by knowing the result. While now . . . well, very plush all the stuff they got in those betting shops these days. Comfy chairs, get a cup of tea, everything.'

'But over the years, Harold . . . you know, the years you've been betting, do you think you're up or down?'

'In financial terms?'

'Yes.'

'Oh, down. Definitely down.'

An expression of puzzlement settled on Carole's face. But rather than actually vocalizing the thought, 'Then why on earth do you do it?' she moved the subject on. 'So, if you're in the betting shop every day, Harold, maybe you saw the poor man who was killed?'

'No. Didn't Jude say? I was ill last week.'

'I know that. I just thought you might have seen him before.'

'No idea. I don't know what he looks like.'

'Haven't you seen the pictures on the news?'

He gestured around the room. 'Don't have a telly, do I? There's one downstairs in what they call one of the "communal rooms". But I'm not going to spend my time sitting with those old biddies. They never put the racing on, anyway. Just watch these endless soaps and chat shows with everyone spilling their guts about everything. No one's got any shame any more. I don't need the television.'

'And you don't get a local paper?'

'No, nothing much happens in Fethering, and what there does I usually hear along the grapevine.'

At that moment Jude reappeared with a steaming cup of tea.

'I was just asking Harold whether he'd seen Tadeusz Jankowski in the betting shop . . . you know, before last Thursday. But Harold doesn't know what he looked like. Fortunately, though . . .' Carole reached triumphantly into her handbag '. . . I've brought along all the cuttings I've collected about the murder.'

Harold Peskett was shown a photograph of the dead man and immediately responded, 'Oh yes, I seen him all right.'

'In the betting shop?'

'Yes.'

'When?'

'While back. Late summer, I think.'

'End of September, early October?'

'Could have been.'

'Did you see him speak to a woman?'

The parchment-like skin wrinkled around the old man's eyes. 'Hard to remember that far back. Maybe he did . . .'

'The woman we're talking about,' Jude said gently, 'was a regular in the betting shop . . .'

'Do you mean old Pauline?'

'No. Another one. Apparently used to be a regular and then suddenly stopped coming.'

Again the thin skin was stretched with the strain of recollection. 'Doesn't ring any bells.'

'Younger woman . . . smartly dressed . . .'

'Ooh, just a minute. Yes, there was this lady used to come in, now you come to mention it. Yeah, looked like she had a few bob. Nice clothes, like you say.'

'Did you ever talk to her?' asked Carole.

'Well, only to, like, pass the time of day. You know, say "bad luck" when she had a loser, that kind of thing.'

'Did she have a lot of losers?'

He shrugged. 'All punters have a lot of losers.'

'Yes, but I mean – did she bet a lot?'

'Mm, think she did. Put something on every race, she would.'

'Big stakes?'

'Dunno. You never really know what other punters are putting on, unless they draw attention to themselves. And she was a quiet one, that woman. That's why I had trouble remembering her.'

'Do you know her name?'

He shook his head. 'Like I say, she was quiet. Almost, like, a bit secretive. And people who come in on their own, well, you never hear their names. Different with those decorators, Wes and Vic, a right double act they are. And Sonny "Perfectly" Frank, everyone knows him. But that woman . . . haven't a clue.'

'Did you see her talking to Tadek . . . to the man in the photograph?' asked Jude.

The wizened old man shook his head. 'Don't recall. She might have done, but, you know, there's a lot of comings and goings in a betting shop. You don't notice all of them.'

'Of course not.' Jude looked at Carole, as if to indicate that they weren't going to get much more information from this source, and said, 'Have you got all your bets done, Harold?'

'Been ready for an hour,' the old man replied, producing a pile of closely scribbled betting slips from the table. 'Ooh, and could you bring me some more of these, Jude love? I'm running out. I mean, hope I'll be better tomorrow and be able to go down there under my own steam, but just in case . . .'

'Yes, of course. I'll pick them up and drop them in tomorrow morning.'

'That's very good of you.' He looked at his watch. 'The first bet's on a twelve-thirty race.'

'Don't worry, we're on our way.'

'Well, good to see you. And nice to meet you, Carole love. You going down to sort out your day's investments, are you?'

'I beg your pardon?'

'You going down the betting shop to have a bit of a punt, are you?'

'Good heavens, no,' said Carole.

Jude smiled. 'Don't bother to get up, Harold.'

But he was on his feet before she had finished the words. 'No, no, I may be old and decrepit and full of flu, but I'm still capable of seeing ladies to the door of my own home.'

Harold Peskett moved stiffly across to the door and

opened it for them. 'And that poor geezer with the funny name got stabbed, did he?'

'So it seems, yes.'

'Rotten luck. He didn't seem the sort to get on the wrong side of anybody.'

Carole stopped in her tracks. 'You speak as if you know him.'

'Well, don't *know*, but I chatted to him a bit when he come into the betting shop in the autumn.'

'When he spoke to the mystery woman?' asked Jude.

'Maybe. Come to think of it, yes, I did only see him in bookie's just the once.'

'And when you spoke to him, what did you talk about?'

'Oh, nothing important. Just like passed the time of day.' He screwed up his face with the effort of squeezing out more detail. 'Ooh, and I remember . . . I did give him some directions.'

'Where to?'

'Well, as I recollect it, that's why he come in the betting shop, to ask the way. That's probably why he talked to the woman . . . you know, the one you were asking about.'

'Where did he want to go to?' Carole insisted.

'He was looking for Clincham College,' replied Harold Peskett.

Chapter Eleven

'I've heard of Clincham College, but I don't know much about it,' said Jude, as they walked briskly along the front towards Fethering High Street. 'Presumably it's in Clincham?'

Carole affirmed that it was. Clincham was a largish coastal town some ten miles west of Fethering. It had a well-heeled retired community, and a matching set of boutiques and knick-knack shops to cater for them. It also had a growing population of students, a lot of them foreigners studying at the town's many language schools.

'The place has been around for a long time. As a college, or it may even have been a poly. Not very academic, did courses in estate management, animal husbandry, catering, that sort of thing. Most of the students there were local, and I gather they still are. I always think that's the difference between a college and a university. A university is a place where young people go to get away from home, to spread their wings a little, start to find their own personalities, whereas a college . . . Anyway, in recent years, *following government policy . . .*' Distaste steeped Carole's words as she spoke them '. . . Clincham College has been accorded university status. So, rather than dishing out diplomas and certificates, Clincham College is now dishing out degrees. Which, I would imagine, are about as valuable from the academic point of view as the diplomas and certificates they replaced.'

'Does it take a lot of foreign students?'

'That I wouldn't know. I don't think more than the average so-called university.'

'Well, it'd be fairly easy to check if Tadek was enrolled there.'

'But how could he have been, Jude? If he was, surely the police would have described him as a "student", not a "bar worker"?'

'He could have been doing a part-time course. Or maybe he started something and dropped out. A lot of students do.' Her neighbour didn't seem particularly impressed by this new area of potential investigation. 'Look, Carole, we do now have at least one connection for Tadek and the Fethering area. Apart from Madame Ego at the Cat and Fiddle. He was looking for Clincham College. It's a lead.'

'About the only one we've got,' said Carole frostily.

Silence reigned between them until they reached the High Street. The cold wind off the sea stung their cheeks. Jude noticed with amusement how, the closer they got to the betting shop, the more the anxiety in Carole's face grew. At last, when they were only yards away, she burst out, 'Is there anything I ought to know? I don't want to look a fool. I don't want people staring at me. I don't want to do the wrong thing.'

'Carole, it's a betting shop we're going into, not the temple of some obscure religious sect. Nobody will take any notice of you. And if you do feel self-conscious, just study the sheets from the newspapers stuck up on the walls. They'll show all the runners and riders.'

'And nobody will think it odd if I don't bet?'

'Nobody will think anything about you.'

'Oh.' But she didn't sound reassured.

'Know anything?' asked Sonny Frank, the minute the two women entered the betting shop.

'Sorry. Nothing,' Jude replied.

'How's about your friend?'

'Sonny, this is Carole. Sonny Frank – Carole Seddon.'

'Good afternoon.'

'How do? And what about you – know anything?'

'Well,' Carole replied, primly mystified, 'I know quite a lot of things, I suppose. In which particular area were you interested?'

'Horses,' said Sonny. 'Wondered if you knew a good thing on today's cards?'

Carole looked to Jude for help, which was readily supplied. 'Sonny was wondering if you had a tip for any of today's races.'

'Oh, good heavens, no. I'm afraid I don't know anything about horses.'

'Join the club,' said Sonny Frank. 'The great international conspiracy of mug punters.'

'Ah.' Carole still looked confused.

'You know anything, Sonny?' asked Jude.

'Might be something in the 3.20 at Exeter.'

'Oh?'

'From a yard in the north. Long way to travel if the trainer reckons it's a no-hoper.'

'So you're saying it's a cert?'

'No such thing, darling.'

'Are you going to tell me the name?'

The round head shook, its plastered-down hair unstirred by the movement. 'Maybe later. See what form the jockey's in first.'

Jude nodded acceptance of his reticence and crossed to the counter to hand in Harold Peskett's bets. Carole felt stranded. Sonny Frank had returned to his *Racing Post*, three Chinese waiters chattered incomprehensibly, the gambling machines recycled their interminable jingles. She didn't know whether to follow her neighbour or just sit down as if her presence in the betting shop had some purpose. Then she remembered Jude's advice and drifted across to look at the newspaper sheets pinned to the wall. The lists of runners and riders from Exeter and Lingfield meant nothing to her, but she stared at them with the concentration of an aficionado.

'The ground hasn't really thawed out after the frost,' said a cultured voice behind her. 'The going shouldn't be too heavy.'

'Oh. Really?' Carole turned to see a smartly suited mature man with an impeccably knotted tie. He was the former accountant whom Jude knew as a regular, but to whom she had never spoken.

'I don't believe I've seen you in here before.'

'No, I am not an habituée.' Why on earth had she

said that? Was it some form of inverted snobbery that put her gentility into overdrive in a common place like a betting shop?

'Well, I am, I'm afraid. Gerald Hume.' He stretched out a hand and formally took hers.

'Carole Seddon.'

At the counter, Jude had had Harold Peskett's bets scanned by the manager, but lingered. Ryan looked sweaty and ill at ease. Once again Jude was aware of the strong peppermint smell that was always around him. 'I was wondering if my friend and I could talk to you about something . . .?'

'What's that?'

'About Tadeusz Jankowski . . . you know, the person who died.'

The young man was instantly suspicious. His dark eyes darted from side to side as he said, 'I only saw him the once, that afternoon. I told you that. I've already told you everything I know.'

'Yes, but we'd like to talk to you a bit more about it. Amongst other things . . .'

'Why, what do you know?' There was a note of panic in his voice.

'Oh, this and that,' Jude replied, casually – and mendaciously. 'We thought it'd be nice to have a chat and bring you up to date on what we do know. And you're the person who knows everything that goes on in this betting shop. You, as it were, know where the bodies are buried.'

His pupils flickered like trapped tadpoles. 'I can't talk now,' he said.

'What time do you finish?'

'Five-thirty this time of year.'

'Meet in the Crown and Anchor?'

'OK,' he grunted reluctantly.

Someone's got a guilty secret, thought Jude. She wondered if Ryan's manner towards her had something to do with their encounter earlier that morning. Had he been doing something he shouldn't have been in the betting shop's back yard? And did he think she was a witness to his wrong-doing? Had her random talk of knowing 'where the bodies are buried' triggered some guilt in the manager?

These were her thoughts as she crossed back towards her neighbour, who she was surprised to see was in earnest conversation with the man whom Sonny Frank had once identified as a retired accountant. Animated by talking, he didn't look quite as old as he had before. Probably only early sixties, steel-grey hair and a lean face with unexpectedly blue eyes. When he smiled, he was almost good-looking.

'Oh, Gerald, this is my friend Jude,' said Carole in a manner which was, by her standards, fulsome.

The introductions were duly made. 'Yes, I've seen you in here before, but never known your name,' said Gerald.

'Same for me with you. And indeed with a lot of other Fethering residents.'

'You're certainly right there. Isn't that typical of England – everyone knows who everyone else is, but they never speak to each other?' He seemed slightly embarrassed by his own seriousness. 'Carole was just giving me her views on the first race at Lingfield.'

'Was she?' asked Jude, with some surprise.

'She fancies Deirdre's Cup, and I can see the way her mind's working, but I just wonder whether he can produce his turf form on the all-weather.'

'That's obviously the big question,' said Carole, trying to avoid her friend's eye. Out of Gerald Hume's sightline, Jude let her jaw drop in a parody of stunned surprise.

'Well, I might be swayed by your opinion,' said the retired accountant. 'I'll wait till just before the off, see how the market rates Deirdre's Cup.'

'Good idea,' said Carole.

'We can actually go now,' said Jude. 'Our meeting's going to be later in the day.'

'Oh,' said Carole. 'Well, may as well just stay and see this first race at Exeter.'

'Yes, wait and see if Deirdre's Cup floweth over,' said Gerald Hume, rather pleased with this verbal felicity.

'Very well,' said Jude, still bemused.

In the few minutes before the race, the odds on Deirdre's Cup grew shorter and shorter till he was see-sawing for favouritism with the horse which had started the day odds-on.

'Someone knows something,' observed Gerald Hume. 'Where do you get your information from, Carole?'

'Oh, here and there,' she replied airily. 'One keeps one's ear to the ground.' Again she looked studiously away from Jude, on whose face was a pop-eyed expression of disbelief.

'Right, I'm going to grab that eleven to four while stocks last,' said Gerald Hume and hurried up to the counter with open wallet.

'Are you not betting?'

'No.' Carole still avoided Jude's eye.

'Well, I'm going to do something. I can't watch a race without having a financial interest in it.'

Jude went each way on a wild outsider called Lumsreek, which she got at thirty-three to one. Already planning how she'd spend her winnings, she rejoined Carole and Gerald, who seemed as relaxed as if they'd known each other since schooldays.

Before the race started, Wes and Vic rushed in from some other abandoned decorating job and just managed to get their bets on in time, so the actual running was accompanied by their raucous shouts of encouragement.

Not that they did much good. In both cases, the horses whose praises they had been singing before the 'off' were condemned at the end as hopeless nags. Deirdre's Cup did better, though. Never out of the first four, he put in a big challenge in the last furlong, actually leading for a few strides before the favourite reasserted its class and got home by a short head.

'Worth watching, that horse,' said Gerald Hume. 'Going to win a race soon.'

'Yes,' Carole agreed sagely.

'So how much did you lose?' he asked.

'Oh, I didn't bet on it.'

'Canny. You fancied it, but you knew something . . .?'

'Well . . .'

'Thought he needed the race?'

Carole wasn't quite sure what the question meant, but it seemed to invite agreement, so, ignoring the flabbergasted look on Jude's face, she agreed.

'Yes, I should have thought it through,' said Gerald Hume. 'Are you going to do something on the next?'

'Oh no, I think Jude and I had better be off. Things to do, haven't we?'

Jude, still mystified by Carole's behaviour, agreed that they did indeed have things to do. 'Also,' she said, 'if the way my luck's going is characterized by the running of Lumsreek . . .' Her fancy had come a very distant last '. . . I think I should keep out of betting shops for the next few days.'

'Still, maybe I'll see you in here again?' asked Gerald Hume, directing the enquiry very firmly towards Carole rather than Jude.

'Oh, I don't think so. As I said, I'm not an habituée.' This time she didn't feel so stupid saying the word. In fact, she felt rather classy. Confident even.

'Well, I hope we will meet again somewhere,' said Gerald.

'I'm sure we will. Fethering's a very small place, and I only live in the High Street.'

'Good heavens, I'm in River Road.'

'Very close then.'

'I'm sure we'll meet up.'

The two women were nearly back at their respective homes before Jude asked, 'So what was all that about, Carole?'

Her friend looked all innocent. 'What?'

'Gerald Hume. Had you met him before?'

'Never.'

'Well, you behaved as if you knew each other very well.'

'Yes. Strange, that, isn't it . . .?' Carole mused.

'Any explanation . . .?'

'No, it's just . . . there are some people one meets, with whom one just . . . clicks. Do you know what I mean?'

'Oh, definitely,' said Jude, suppressing a smile. 'I've fixed to meet Ryan in the Crown and Anchor soon after five-thirty. Are you coming?'

'I certainly am,' Carole replied.

'Very well. See you then.' And Jude went into Woodside Cottage, her bewilderment by no means reduced.

Carole went into High Tor, feeling really rather good. She really had clicked with Gerald. For a moment she toyed with the unfamiliar sensation of being a bit of a femme fatale.

Chapter Twelve

'I speak to Tadek's landlord. Nothing,' said Zofia. Her voice down the phone was cold and disappointed.

'What do you mean – nothing?' asked Jude.

'It is like he do not know who he rents his rooms to. So long as they pay, he doesn't care who they are. Tadek was just another student for him. If the police had not questioned him, he would have forgotten my brother's name.'

'So you didn't get any idea of how Tadek spent his time?'

'The landlord does not live near the house with the rooms in. It is just for money. He might as well be taking profits from slot machines.'

'Did you go to the house?'

'Yes.'

'And did you manage to speak to any of the other residents?'

'Not many are in. Two I speak to. They also only remember Tadek because the police have been round asking questions. How can people live so close and not know each other?' the girl asked plaintively.

'They can do it because they're English,' Jude

replied. 'I'm afraid there's a strong tradition in this country of "keeping oneself to oneself". Have you heard the expression: "An Englishman's home is his castle"?'

'No. And certainly where Tadek was living was not a castle. It was very bare, not a nice place.'

'So what you're saying, Zosia, is that you've drawn a blank? You haven't met anyone who knew your brother?'

'I meet the woman at the pub he work. Cat and Fiddle. But she no use. She did not seem to know him at all.'

'Shona Nuttall. A friend and I met her too, and that was the impression we got. I think your brother was just cheap labour to her. She seemed to be a bit of a slave-driver.'

'She not even know Tadek was interested in music. That means she did not know him at all.'

'No.'

'It is strange, Jude. Tadek is a warm person, he always have friends. But no one in the house at Littlehampton know him. And that woman in the pub, she not interested in him.'

'I don't think Shona Nuttall's interested in anyone but herself.'

'No. But, Tadek . . . how can he come somewhere and make no friends?'

'He may not have made friends where he lived, but perhaps he had some somewhere else.'

'Where?'

'At college?'

107

'Tadek was at university in Warsaw. I tell you. He finish there last year.'

'Yes, I know. But we've got a lead that he might have had some connection with a college near here. Clincham College. Now called the University of Clincham.' Jude briefly outlined the information they had got from Harold Peskett. 'Tadek didn't say anything to you about going to college here?'

'No.'

'I mean, he was in touch with you, was he?'

'Tadek was never very good at keeping in touch. Oh, he always meant to, but other things would take his attention. He was a dreamer. So, since he leave for England, maybe he send one letter to our mother.'

'Was he close to her?'

'No. Like me, he did not get on with her.'

'But was he in touch with you?'

'More. But not a lot. A few texts on the mobile phone.'

'When was the last one you had from him?'

'I do not remember. Not since Christmas perhaps.'

'Well,' said Jude, 'I'm planning to make contact with Clincham College. Just see if anyone there knows anything about your brother.'

'Yes. You will tell me, please, if you find out something.'

'Of course.'

'You will keep in touch, Jude?' The appeal in Zofia's voice was naked. She sounded much younger than the nineteen or twenty that she must be. Jude felt a sudden rush of pity for the girl. Already shaken by bereavement, she had rushed to a country where she had no contacts, and had just experienced encounters with the English at their most aloof. She must have been feeling very alone.

'Zosia, have you got somewhere to stay while you're here?' Jude asked gently. 'Where did you spend last night?'

'Last night I was fine.' She clearly didn't want to give details. Jude wondered if the girl had slept rough. Not very pleasant when the weather was cold.

'And what about tonight?'

'I will find somewhere.' The girl dismissed the question as if it wasn't a problem. 'Somewhere cheap. A *pension*, a . . . what is it called in England? A Bed and Breakfast?'

'That's what it's called, yes. But if you'd like to, Zosia, you could stay here with me.'

'Oh, but I couldn't. No, I don't want to be trouble to anyone. I can do on my own.'

It took a bit of cajoling; not much, though. The girl's pride obliged her to put up some resistance, but Jude's arguments soon blew it away. There was a spare bedroom in Woodside Cottage; it made sense that it should be used. Jude didn't mention money, but she couldn't imagine that Zofia had much with her. The cost of living in Poland was a lot lower than in England, and even in the off-season B and Bs along the South Coast could be quite pricey. She was pleased when the girl gratefully accepted her offer, and suggested she should come straight from Littlehampton to Woodside Cottage.

By the time she arrived, the spare room would be made up for her.

As she put the phone down, Jude felt a double glow of satisfaction. Part came from the altruism of doing something that would be of help to someone in need. The other part was more selfish. Having the victim's sister on the premises might well prove very useful in the murder enquiry on which she and Carole had embarked.

Her recapitulation of what Harold Peskett had said about Clincham College prompted a new question. Had the old boy told the police what he had overheard Tadek say in the betting shop? Were they aware of the Clincham College connection?

She rang through to Harold. No, he hadn't been contacted by the police. Why should he have been, Jude reflected. He hadn't been in the betting shop on the relevant afternoon.

Jude was now faced with a moral dilemma. She had information which the police might not have. And her sense of duty told her that she should immediately share it with them. She felt certain that was the course Carole, with her Home Office background, would have recommended. An immediate call to the police was required, to alert them to Tadek's connection with Clincham College.

On the other hand . . . The police might have heard about the young man's enquiry from another of the betting shop regulars . . . There was a very strong temptation to leave them in ignorance . . .

No, she should do the right thing. Unfair though it

was – because she knew there was no chance of the police reciprocating by sharing their findings with an amateur detective – she should let them know what she'd heard.

Reluctantly, Jude rang the number Detective Sergeant Baines had given her. She got his voicemail. She didn't give details of what she knew, merely said that there was another regular of the betting shop whom it might be worth their contacting for information in connection with the case of Tadeusz Jankowski. And gave Harold Peskett's number.

She put the phone down with mixed feelings. Her sense of virtue at having done the right thing was transient. Stronger was the hope that the police might classify her message as just the witterings of a middle-aged woman, over-excited by her proximity to a criminal investigation. That, in fact, they would ignore it.

Zofia Jankowska had very few belongings with her, and the clothes she unpacked looked pitifully cheap. But she was extremely grateful to her hostess. 'Please, I pay you money . . .?'

'No need,' said Jude.

'But for food? Already you cook me one meal.'

'All right. If that happens more often, you can make a contribution.'

'Please. You not ask how long I stay?'

'It's not a problem.'

'No, but I not be trouble you long. I go when I find

111

out all I can find out. I just want to know why my brother died.'

'Which is exactly what I want to know,' said Jude.

Ryan the betting shop manager looked more nervous than ever when he appeared in the Crown and Anchor very soon after five-thirty that evening. He wore a fur-hooded anorak over his uniform, but made no attempt to remove or even unzip it when he sat down in the booth opposite Carole and Jude. The latter introduced the former. He told Carole his name was Ryan Masterson and accepted Jude's offer of a drink, asking for 'A double Smirnoff, please, just with some ice.'

The two women had planned the way they wanted the conversation to go. From her snatched exchange with him in the morning, Jude had concluded that Ryan thought she knew something discreditable about him. She reckoned that was probably the fact that he had denied ever seeing Tadek in the betting shop before the afternoon of his death, but it might be something else, possibly something he thought she'd witnessed that morning. So she and Carole had decided to keep the one bit of information they did have on hold, and see if the manager had anything else to reveal.

'Busy day?' asked Carole uncontroversially.

'All right. Not too frantic this time of year.' The answer was automatic; there was tension in his voice.

'Do you know,' said Carole, uncharacteristically winsome, 'today was the first day I'd ever been into a betting shop.'

'Yes, I saw you come in.'

'You take note of everyone who enters the premises, do you?'

'Have to. There are a lot of villains around.'

'What, they're likely to cause fights, are they?'

'Not that. Some shops, maybe. Not in Fethering.'

'So what kind of villains are they?'

'Crooked punters. There are some who've got systems going. Multiple bets on fixed races, gangs of them going into a lot of different betting shops. We have to watch out for them.'

'Ah.' There was a silence. The question about his taking note of everyone who came into the shop had brought Carole the perfect cue to ask Ryan about Tadek's former appearance, but that was the one thing she didn't want to raise yet. And she couldn't think of anything else to ask him about.

Fortunately, Jude arrived at that moment with their interviewee's large vodka. As ever, her presence relaxed the atmosphere, though Ryan remained taut and watchful.

'Have the police been back to the shop since the weekend?' He shook his head and took a swig of vodka so urgent that it might have been some life-saving medicine. 'So you don't know what their current thinking on the murder is . . .?'

He shrugged. 'That the bloke was stabbed somewhere else and just came into the shop to sit down.'

'But he didn't sit down.'

'No. Thank goodness for that. If he'd actually died on the premises, I'd have had even more hassle.'

'You didn't see which direction he came from, did you?' asked Carole.

'No. The way that hailstorm was coming down, you couldn't see anything outside. I was only aware of him when he was actually inside the door.'

'And did you think anything particular when you saw him? Was there anything odd about him?'

'Well, he was swaying about a bit. I thought he might be trouble because he'd been on the booze.'

'Do people on the booze often cause trouble in betting shops?'

Ryan looked up sharply at Jude's question, then mumbled, 'Can happen.'

'And watching out for that kind of thing is part of your job?'

'Yes, we're trained to stop trouble before it starts.'

'Hm.' Jude twisted a tendril of hair around one of her fingers. 'And do you think the same as the police do, Ryan – that the young man came into the betting shop by chance?'

'What else is there to think?'

'Well, if you listen to Fethering gossip . . .'

'If you listen to Fethering gossip, you waste a lot of time.'

'But you must hear a lot, being in the shop all day.'

'I manage to tune most of it out.'

'Do you like your job?' asked Jude suddenly.

'What's that to you?' he responded aggressively.

'Just a detail that might shed light on other details.'

Jude wasn't sure whether her answer actually meant anything, but it seemed to contain some threat to Ryan, because with commendable honesty he said, 'No, I don't like my job.'

'Why not?'

'Well, it's dull and repetitive, for a start. The hours are long, particularly in the summer. And you have to spend your day smiling at people you wouldn't normally give the time of day to. You don't exactly choose your own company. Some of the punters are pretty rude. Then you get the down-and-outs and the Care in the Community lot. Some of them smell, too.'

'Then why do you stick at it?'

'It's secure. I'm paid just about enough to make me think that the idea of giving it up and retraining for something else is a bad one.' For a moment he looked haunted by self-doubt. 'Don't know whether I've got it in me to train for anything else now – don't know if I could hack it. Anyway, I've got a wife and two kids – not the time to cut loose. I can't afford to take risks.'

'Risks that might mean you'd get fired?'

Ryan evaded a direct answer to Jude's question. He just shrugged and said, 'It's a job. Probably no better and no worse than any other job. How many people do you know who enjoy what they do?'

Jude did actually know quite a lot, but it wasn't the moment to say so. 'Why did you agree to meet me?'

Her question seemed to make him even more nervous. He swallowed and his voice was strained as he replied, 'You wanted to talk. I can't really do that while I'm in the shop.'

'I said I wanted to talk about Tadeusz Jankowski.'

'Yes.'

'Which is why you agreed so readily to meet me.'

'OK, yes. Him coming into the shop and then dying wasn't exactly good for business. Head Office are keen that the publicity is kept to the minimum. They would approve of my meeting you if it means there's less chat around the shop about what happened.'

It was a relatively convincing answer, but Jude reckoned he was still holding something back. And a straight question seemed as good a way as any other of finding out what that was. 'Is there anything you know about the case that you've been keeping to yourself?'

'No,' he replied. 'I've given the police my full co-operation.'

There was a silence. Ryan took another desperate swallow of his vodka. Jude exchanged a look with Carole which confirmed that neither of them expected to get much more out of the interview. Time to put the big question.

Carole did the honours. 'I believe you told the police that you'd only seen Tadeusz Jankowski on one occasion.'

'I did, yes. The afternoon he died.'

'Well, we've heard from other regulars in the betting shop that he actually went in on a previous occasion.'

'Last October,' Jude supplied.

'Yes,' said Ryan. 'I heard that as well.'

'Then why didn't you tell the police you'd seen him before?'

'Because I hadn't. I was on holiday last October.'

He answered so readily that they could not doubt the honesty of his reply. As simple as that. Ryan

Masterson had not seen Tadeusz Jankowski the previous October because he had been on holiday with his family. Annual leave. It could be checked, presumably, with his employers, but neither Jude nor Carole thought the effort would be worth it. He was telling the truth.

And dealing with the question seemed to relax him. If that was all they were interested in, his manner seemed to say, then no problem. He downed the remainder of his drink – just melting ice, he'd long since finished the vodka – and said he should be on his way.

'Couple of other things we'd like to ask you . . .' said Jude.

The panic returned instantly to his dark eyes. He thought he had been off the hook; now it seemed he wasn't.

'Nikki . . .?'

'Yes.'

'She says she never notices anything that goes on in the shop.'

'Don't I bloody know it? Doesn't notice anything that goes on anywhere. Walks around in a dream, planning how she's going to decorate her sitting room when she gets married. Only thing she thinks about is her bloody wedding, and it's still over a year away.'

'That might be a front,' Carole suggested. 'And all the time she's really keeping her eye on everything that goes on?'

Ryan looked at her pityingly. 'Tell you, with Nikki, what you see is what you get. She is seriously thick.'

'Oh.' This didn't seem very gallant, but presumably he knew the woman he worked with.

'If that's it, I'd better . . .'

'One more thing . . .' Jude raised a hand to detain him. 'I asked you about this before. There's a woman who's a regular at the betting shop . . .'

'There are a few.'

'Well, I say she is a regular. I should have said *was* a regular. Stopped coming in around October last year.'

'People come and go, that's up to them.'

'This one was well dressed, sort of middle class.'

Ryan narrowed his eyes with the effort of recollection. 'I think I know the one you mean.'

'You wouldn't know her name, would you?'

He shook his head. 'Some people tell us their names, some don't. If they don't, we've no means of knowing.'

'No. And I suppose if you don't know her name, the chances of you knowing where she lives . . .'

'Are about as slender as those of one of Harold Peskett's bloody accumulators coming up.' This moment of levity showed how relaxed he now was. 'Why do you want to know about her?'

'Apparently Tadeusz Jankowski spoke to her when he went into the betting shop last October.'

'Ah, well, I wouldn't know about that,' said the manager with something approaching smugness. 'I was on holiday.'

Shortly after he reiterated that he must be on his way and left.

'There goes a relieved man,' said Jude.

'How do you mean?'

'He was very relieved when he found out what we were interested in – just whether he'd seen Tadeusz Jankowski before. He had no worries about answering that enquiry. Which means . . .' Jude grimaced '. . . that there was something else he was afraid we wanted to talk to him about.'

'Any idea what?'

'Well, only conjecture . . . but I'm pretty sure I'm right. Seeing the way he put away that vodka . . . and given the fact that he's always sucking peppermints, I would think it's a pretty fair bet that young Ryan has a drink problem.'

'And he thought we wanted to talk to him about that?'

'That's my theory. When I saw him in the back yard this morning, he was out there having a swig from his secret supply. He thought I'd actually seen him drinking. That's the only reason he agreed to meet us. He was afraid we might shop him to Head Office.'

'But why on earth would he think that?'

'Alcoholics are paranoid. Like all addicts. Including gamblers.'

'Well,' said Carole sniffily, 'you'd know about that.'

119

Chapter Thirteen

The decision to stay in the Crown and Anchor for another glass of the Chilean Chardonnay was quickly made. And they were soon joined by other after-work regulars. Shortly after six Ewan Urquhart and his younger clone Hamish appeared. Maybe they did this every evening after a hard day's estate agenting (though Jude sometimes wondered whether 'a hard day's estate agenting' wasn't the perfect definition of an oxymoron). Certainly the speed with which Ted Crisp set up a pair of unordered pints for them suggested a daily ritual.

Father and son took the first sip together and both smacked their lips in appreciation, another part of the ritual that needed to be observed. Then Ewan Urquhart took in the occupants of the pub and nodded recognition to Jude. She smiled back.

'Cold enough for you?' he asked, falling back, as most Englishmen do in casual conversation, on the weather.

'Pretty nippy,' Jude agreed, following the convention. She decided it wasn't the moment to engage in further talk. On their previous encounter Ewan

Urquhart had not endeared himself to her. But the introduction had been made and who could say when a tame estate agent might suddenly become a useful source of information? She continued to talk to Carole about Friday's impending visit of Gaby and Lily. But through their desultory conversation they managed to hear what the Urquharts were saying at the bar. Doing so was in fact unavoidable. Ewan Urquhart was one of those men who thought it was his God-given right to talk loudly.

'Do you know, Ted, what an absolute chump my son has been today . . .?'

'Tell me about it,' said the landlord.

'He only managed to turn up for a viewing of a property having left the keys in the office. Client wasn't best pleased about that, let me tell you.' While the litany of his incompetence was spelt out, Hamish's reaction was interesting. He looked apologetic, but at the same time almost grateful for the attention, as though undergoing such criticism was an essential part of the bond with his father. Hamish had apparently been cast early as the family buffoon, and it was a role that he played up to.

'Client was one of these city slickers,' Ewan Urquhart went on, 'investing his obscene bonus in a country cottage. Kind of guy for whom time is money. Wasn't best pleased to turn up to the property and find he couldn't get in. Gave you a bit of an ear-bashing, didn't he, Hamish?'

'Yes, Dad,' came the sheepish reply.

'So, needless to say, a call comes through to the

office and I have to leap into the Lexus, take the keys and smooth the city slicker's ruffled feathers. Turns out all right, actually, because when I get chatting to the chap, turns out he's an Old Carthusian just like me.'

'What's that when it's at home?' asked Ted Crisp.

'Old Carthusian? Means I went to a little educational establishment that goes by the name of Charterhouse. Rather decent public school, as it happens. So of course when the city slicker finds out we went to the same school we're all chums . . . and of course Hamish wouldn't have had the same connection, because you were too thick to pass the Common Entrance, weren't you?'

'Yes, Dad,' Hamish agreed, once again apparently proud of his inadequacy.

'Anyway, so once again I got the boy out of a mess. Which means that you're bloody well paying for the drinks tonight.'

'Of course, Dad.' The young man's wallet was out immediately; as yet no money had changed hands.

'And you can buy a drink for your sister when she arrives too.'

'Will do.' Hamish Urquhart looked at his watch. 'She said she'd be along about six-fifteen. Got some class or other up at Clincham College.' Carole and Jude pricked up their ears at that. 'Guarantee she'll be on the G and Ts. Ted, could you take for the pints and do me a large G and T too?' The young man's bluff bonhomie sounded like a parody of his father's. 'And won't you have one yourself?'

'No, thanks,' the landlord replied. 'I don't have anything till the end of the evening. Otherwise I'd drink myself into an early grave.'

'And we don't want that happening, do we?' said Ewan Urquhart heartily. 'I'm sure you're just like me, Ted, want to keep going as long as possible, becoming more and more curmudgeonly with every passing year, eh?'

'I reckon I'm pretty curmudgeonly already,' said the landlord as he poured tonic into a double gin with ice and lemon.

'Nonsense, nonsense. You're a fine upstanding English gentleman. Which is more than can be said for that fellow we had in the office this afternoon, eh, Hamish?'

'I'll say. He was very much an "oriental visitor".' The young man put on a very bad cod-Indian accent for the words.

'Not that we weren't punctiliously polite to him, of course. And, actually, nowadays it's all right. I mean, even ten years back I'd have had to be very discreet with someone like that . . . you know, suggesting that the Shorelands Estate in Fethering was maybe not quite where they should be looking . . . maybe they could find something more suitable in Brighton. But now half of the people on the Shorelands Estate are of dusky hue.' Ewan Urquhart let out a bark of laughter. 'Soon I would imagine the Residents' Committee there will be worrying about white people moving in next door to them!'

Ted Crisp guffawed too readily at this for Jude's liking. But she and Carole were distracted by the appearance through the door of a girl who was undoubtedly Hamish's anticipated sister. In her the ginger tendency of her father and brother was transformed into a mane of pale golden hair and their thickset bodies had been fined down into a slender voluptuousness. Her pale skin was flushed red, presumably by the February cold. She wore a Barbour over jeans and big fleece-topped boots. There was no doubt from the expression that took over Ewan Urquhart's face that she was the apple of her father's eye.

'So what's kept you, Soph?' he asked, as he enveloped her in a large hug. 'I didn't think you had classes as late as this.'

'No,' she said lightly. 'Had to do some work in the library.' Her voice had been trained at the female equivalent of Charterhouse.

'Well, I'm not sure I approve of all this book-learning for women. Women are only really good for three things. Cooking and cleaning are two of them . . . and . . .' Hamish and Ted Crisp joined him in a chortle of male complicity. He had spoken in an over-inflated tone of self-parody, but deep down he clearly believed in what he was saying.

'Anyway, your timing's good in one respect. Your brother's just bought you a drink.'

'Oh, thank you, Hamish.' She took a grateful swig of the gin and tonic.

'No prob, Soph.'

'And shall I tell you why the drinks are on him tonight?' Without waiting for a prompt, Ewan Urquhart once again recounted the tale of his son's ineptitude. At the end the girl gave her brother a little hug and said, 'You are an idiot.' Her tone was the affectionate one that might be used to an over-eager puppy.

'So what have they taught you today?' asked Ewan, sharing his next observation with Ted Crisp. 'Have to be doing a constant cost analysis on this higher education lark, you know. The amount they get charged for tuition fees these days, you want to know where the money's going.'

'Yes,' the landlord commiserated, 'I've heard about it. The debts these kids come away from university with, all those student loans, they're never going to get out of the red, are they?'

'Well, at least young Sophia doesn't have that problem.' He pronounced the second two syllables of her name like 'fire'. Then, with a tap to his back pocket in the vague proximity of his wallet, he explained, 'Muggins here's footing the bills for everything. So come on, what did they teach you today?'

'We had a class on Eisenstein, and then some workshopping in the Drama Studio. It's for this show we're doing.'

'Huh, play-acting,' her father snorted. 'Not my idea of hard work. You know what my daughter's studying, Ted? Drama and Film Studies. They seem to be able to do degree courses in anything these days. Media Studies, Dance, Pop Music, Fashion, you name it. Probably be doing degrees in bloody Shopping before too long. Wasn't like that in my day . . .'

'Why, what did you study at university then, Ewan?'

For the first time the estate agent looked discomfited

by Ted's question. 'Oh,' he replied, quickly recovering, 'didn't go down the university route myself. Got out into the real world, got down to some real work. I'm sure you'd agree that's the best way to go about things, wouldn't you?'

'Dunno,' the landlord replied. 'It's not what I did. I went to university.'

'Really?' The surprise of the eavesdropping Carole and Jude was as great as that of Ewan Urquhart.

'Well, of course,' Ewan continued defensively, 'I studied later. You know, got my ARICS qualifications . . . eventually.' The recollection was clearly not a happy one, so he moved swiftly on. 'What did you study then?'

'Nuclear Physics.'

'Good Lord. So you have a degree in Nuclear Physics, do you, Ted?'

'Well, no, I don't actually. I left halfway through my second year. I was starting to spend more of my time doing stand-up than on my studies, so I thought I'd give it a go professionally.'

'And did it work out?'

'Ewan, do you have to ask?' Ted Crisp's large gesture, encompassing the whole of the Crown and Anchor, was sufficient reply.

'Anyway, Soph, I wonder if what you learnt today is ever going to prove of any use to you . . .'

The girl shrugged easily. 'Who knows, Daddy? Some people say that education shouldn't be about direct application of skills to commercial challenges, that it should be about training and broadening the mind.'

'What a load of poppycock. It's not a broad mind that's going to help you succeed in the marketplace, it's applied skills. Isn't that true, Hamish?'

'Certainly is, Dad.'

The set-up was perfect. With a guffaw, his father responded, 'And maybe, when you get some applied skills, you'll have a chance of succeeding in the market-place too!'

Shamefacedly, Hamish Urquhart rode the laughter. Carole and Jude exchanged looks and decided it was time to be getting back home.

Chapter Fourteen

The next morning, the Thursday, Carole drove Jude in her neat Renault up to Clincham College. They had tried ringing, but the woman who answered the phone said she wasn't allowed to give out any details about the students. Maybe an in-person approach would prove more productive.

The entrance to the campus was flanked by boards thanking local companies and other institutions for their sponsorship, giving the impression of a business park rather than a seat of learning. As the Renault nosed its way up the drive towards the visitors' car park, they passed a few students, looking impossibly young and clutching armfuls of books and folders. In warmer weather they might have been drifting more lethargically, but the brisk February air kept them on the move.

The main building of Clincham College had always been an educational institution, though it had undergone various metamorphoses before its recent attainment of university status. Originally built by a late Victorian philanthropist as 'an academy for the furtherance of Christian knowledge', the humourless tall grey edifice had at various times been a boys' prep school, a girls' public school and an outpost of a minor American university, peddling expensive degrees to students mostly from the Middle and Far East. Before its recent elevation it had for some years been a technical college. Now, as the biggest board at the entrance proudly proclaimed, it was 'The University of Clincham'.

The portico through which Carole and Jude made their way to the Reception area was elaborate and imposing, though it presented that quality of tired shabbiness which infects all educational establishments. The modern lettering of the various signs attached to the tall pillars was at odds with the period of their design.

Inside, more students were draped around the central hall, talking in groups or on their mobile phones. Their manner was loud and over-dramatic, trying to assert their personalities in their new supposed maturity.

Carole and Jude followed the signs to Reception, a glassed-off area with a counter, at which sat a daunting woman in a black business suit. Behind her in the office area stood a tall man reading through a stapled set of spreadsheets.

'Good morning,' said the woman, following some script that had been imposed on her. 'Welcome to Clincham College.'

'Hello, my name's Carole Seddon, and I wonder whether you could help me?'

'That's what I'm here to do,' said the woman, though her manner belied the welcome in her words.

'We're trying to make contact with someone who we believe may have been a student here.'

The woman's face shut down immediately. 'I'm afraid I'm not allowed to give out information about the students at the university.'

Jude thought she'd see whether charm might succeed where Carole's confrontational approach had failed. 'No, I'm sure that's the rule, but all we wanted to know—'

'I'm sorry,' the woman interrupted. 'I cannot let you have any information about the students.'

'Is there someone else we could speak to?' asked Carole frostily.

'You could write to the Principal with your enquiry, and it's possible that he might reply to you.' The woman didn't make that sound a very likely scenario.

'Look,' Jude persisted, 'all we want to know is the answer to one very simple question.' There was no point in pretence. Everyone in the locality knew the name of the recent murder victim. 'We want to know whether Tadeusz Jankowski, the man who was stabbed in Fethering last week, was ever actually enrolled in the college here.'

The woman went into automaton mode. 'I am not allowed to give out any information about any of the students in—'

'Ah, so you're admitting he was a student here?'

'I am not doing—'

She was interrupted by a voice from behind her.

Tadek's name had distracted the man from his spread-sheets. 'It's all right, Isobel, I'll deal with this.'

Leaving his papers, he emerged through the door from Reception and approached the two women. 'My name's Andy Constant. Lecturer in Drama Studies. Also Admissions Tutor.' Carole and Jude gave their names. 'Would you like to come and have a cup of coffee?'

They agreed that they would and, without further words, he led them to an adjacent snack bar. 'Don't worry, the coffee's all right.' He gestured to a well-known logo over the door. 'Outside franchise. Like everything else in this place. The academic life has ceased to be about learning. It's now all about raising funds and doing deals. I'll get the coffees. What would you like?'

As he went to the counter, Carole and Jude found a table and studied him. Long and gangly, Andy Constant moved with a laid-back swagger. His face receded from a beak of a nose and surprisingly full lips. His grey hair was worn long, rather in the style of Charles I. He had on black jeans, Timberland boots and a grey denim blouson over a white T-shirt. His voice was as languid as his manner.

He brought over the coffees, a cappuccino for Jude, the 'ordinary black' Carole had ordered, a tiny cup of espresso for himself, and sat down opposite them.

'Bit of excitement in a little place like Fethering, a murder, isn't it?' His tone was joshing, sending up the intensity of their interest. But he was at the same time alert, apparently trying to deduce the agenda that had brought them to the college.

'Bound to be,' said Jude easily.

For the first time he seemed to take her in, and he liked what he saw. 'Yes. And everyone's got their own theory about what happened.'

'The students too?'

'And how. Big excitement for them. Also rather frightening. A young man killed, possibly murdered, only a few miles away in Fethering. Comes a bit near home for them. Current crop of students have been brought up to be afraid of everything. The Health and Safety Generation, I call the poor saps. All afraid of being attacked, the girls afraid of being raped . . . Whatever happened to the innocence of youth?'

'Did it ever exist?' asked Carole.

'Maybe not, but I think when I was their age I did at least have the *illusion* of innocence. I kind of trusted the world, was prepared to give it a chance. I wasn't afraid of everything.'

'You say they're afraid of everything,' said Jude, 'but you're talking about a generation who think nothing of shooting off round the world on their gap years.'

'True. Except that's just become another form of package tourism these days. For me it takes the excitement out of far-flung places, knowing there'll be a nice familiar Macdonald's waiting when you get there.'

'Maybe.' He had taken over the conversation so effortlessly that Jude wanted to find out more about Andy Constant. 'You said you lecture in Drama. Does that mean you used to be an actor?' A theatricality about him made this quite a possibility.

'Very early in my career. Moved into directing for a while. Since then, teaching. Mind you, that involves a certain amount of directing too. And acting, come to think of it.'

He had considerable charm, and a strong sexual magnetism. The latter got through to Jude at an instinctive, visceral level, and she wondered whether Carole was aware of it too.

'Anyway,' Andy went on, 'I couldn't help overhearing what you said to Isobel at Reception. Sorry, I'm afraid she's not the most imaginative of women. Whatever the question, she always comes up with the party line. But I heard you mentioning the name of Tadeusz Jankowski. I wondered why you were interested. Are you just another pair of Fethering residents fascinated by their proximity to a murder?'

Carole and Jude exchanged a look. The true answer was probably a yes, but they needed to come up with something a bit better than that. Jude thought of a solution which certainly had elements of truth in it. 'The sister of the dead man came to see me. Naturally enough, she's trying to find out everything she can about her brother. I just thought Carole and I could possibly help her.'

He nodded, as if he accepted this justification for their presence. 'But why have you come here? What reason do you have for connecting the young man with Clincham College?'

Quickly Jude recounted what she had heard from

Harold Peskett, about the young Pole's earlier visit to the betting shop.

'Ah. That would explain something else.'

'What?'

'The police have been here too.'

'Asking about Tadeusz Jankowski?'

'Yes, Carole. Maybe they got the lead from the same source as you did.'

'When were they here?' asked Jude.

'Monday.'

'Then it wasn't the same source as mine. I only suggested they should contact Harold yesterday – and up to then he said they hadn't had any contact with him. So they must have heard about the Clincham College connection from someone else.'

'Not necessarily,' said Andy Constant. 'Apparently they didn't seem very focused when they came here, more like it was just a routine enquiry.' Yes, thought Jude, 'unfocused' is a pretty good description of the approach Baines and Yelland had used when they interviewed her.

'I mean, I suppose it makes sense,' Andy went on. 'Young people tend to congregate together. The dead man was young and had been living round here, so there's quite a reasonable chance that he would have hooked up with some of the students from the college.' Carole noticed he didn't use the word 'university' and wondered whether this was because he hadn't yet got used to the idea or whether he was as cynical about the place's status as she was.

The lecturer took a sip of his espresso and then continued in a different tone. 'Anyway, one thing the police did say was that we on the staff here should keep our eyes and ears open for anyone who came here expressing interest in the murder victim . . .'

'Oh.'

'I thought I should warn you.'

'Why warn us?'

'Well, I'm sure you don't want to be questioned by the police, do you? It's very time-consuming and can, I believe, be quite unpleasant. I mean, you're fine now. Isobel at Reception won't say anything – that would involve her using her initiative and she doesn't do that. And you can rely on me to keep quiet, but I can't guarantee that the rest of the staff here would be so accommodating.'

'So what are you actually saying?' asked Carole.

'I'm saying that we've been told to let the police know if anyone comes here enquiring about Tadeusz Jankowski, and so I think there might be an argument for you not taking your investigations at Clincham College much further.'

'You're warning us off,' said Jude.

He gave a relaxed laugh. 'That sounds a little over-dramatic. Let's just say I'm trying to avoid your being inconvenienced.'

'That's very thoughtful of you. But the police have already questioned me, and I didn't find it a particularly inconvenient experience.'

'Fine.' He shrugged. 'Only trying to save you hassle.' Jude felt his grey eyes seeking out her brown ones and saw the half-insolent smile on his face. Andy Constant

135

knew he was attractive and he knew that she was responding to him. He couldn't know that part of the attraction came from his similarity to Laurence Hawker, another tall academic with whom she had spent time until his premature death a few years before. While she couldn't deny the pull that Andy Constant exerted, Jude resented feeling it. In spite of the superficial likeness to Laurence, there was something about him that struck warning chords within her, something dangerous. Which of course only served to add to his appeal.

Carole, who seemed unaware of the subtext between them, took up the conversation. 'You said you were Admissions Tutor.'

'I did, yes.'

'Then maybe you can at least answer the question we came here to ask.'

'Try me.'

'Was Tadeusz Jankowski ever enrolled here as a student?'

Andy Constant was silent for a moment, as if deliberating over his reply. He took another sip of his espresso, then put the tiny cup down on its tiny saucer. 'I can't actually see what harm my giving you that information can cause. Well, the answer's no. Tadeusz Jankowski was never enrolled in any course at this university.' It was the first time he had used the word.

'And had he ever made enquiries about the courses he might have enrolled in?' asked Carole, pushing her luck.

'Not so far as I know. I suppose he might have made

an approach by letter or email, but none of my colleagues has mentioned anything about his doing so. And, needless to say, given the amount of media coverage, people have been talking a lot about him. I think if anyone had had an approach from someone called Tadeusz Jankowski, they'd have said so. It's not the kind of name you'd forget, is it?'

Jude joined in. 'So you can't think of any connection he might have had with Clincham College?'

'No.'

'Do you know if he'd ever even been on the premises?'

'Not to my knowledge,' replied Andy Constant, and then he gave Jude another of his lazy, but undeniably sexy smiles. 'Still, if I hear from anyone that he has been seen here, I'll let you know.' He smiled again. 'Maybe you'd like to give me your number, Jude . . .?'

As she was scribbling it out on a scrap of paper, a girl came into the canteen. She was dark and pretty in a Hispanic way, dressed in the typical student uniform of jeans and layers of sweatshirts. Long black hair curtained her face. 'Andy,' she said as she approached their table. Her voice sounded slightly Spanish.

He looked up and seemed pleased with what he saw. 'Yes?'

'Andy, I thought you said we'd meet up in the Drama Studio at eleven.'

He looked at his watch. 'Oh, sorry. Hadn't noticed the time.' He turned the full power of his smile on to Carole and Jude. 'Ladies, you will excuse me?'

And, pausing only to snatch up the piece of paper

with Jude's number on it, he walked with long strides out of the café. The dark-haired girl followed, her eyes glowing with puppy love.

Jude was too old for puppy love, but she couldn't deny that Andy Constant was a very attractive man.

Chapter Fifteen

Jude heard the sound of crying as soon as she came through the door of Woodside Cottage. Zofia was hunched up on one of the sitting room's heavily draped sofas, her shoulders shaken by the sobs that ran through her body. On the floor beside her were a battered suitcase and a scruffy backpack. Immediately Jude's arms were round the girl and her lips were murmuring soothing words.

'I am sorry,' was the first thing that Zofia managed to say. 'I hear from the police this morning that I can come and collect Tadek's things, his possessions, and seeing them . . .' She indicated the bags '. . . it makes me realize that he is really gone from me.'

'Do you want me to put them away somewhere, until you are ready to deal with them?'

'No, Jude, thank you.' Zofia wiped the back of her hand against her face to dismiss the tears. 'No, I am ready to deal with them now. Maybe there is something in here that tells me what has happened to Tadek. I must not be emotional. I must try to piece together from his possessions what he was doing here in

England, and perhaps the reason why someone want to kill him.'

'All right,' said Jude. 'I'll help you. But first let's have a drink of something. What would you like, Zosia?'

'Coffee, please. Black, that would be good.'

'Don't start opening the bags until I'm there.' Jude didn't fool herself that her words were spoken from pure altruism. She was being offered a unique chance to further her investigation into Tadek's death.

'Did the police say anything,' she called through from the kitchen, 'about why they were letting you have his belongings so soon?'

'They just said they'd finished what they needed to do with them, and the landlord wants to rent out the room again as soon as possible so the stuff can't go back to Littlehampton. Would I like to take it, please?'

'Did you go back to the house?'

'No, I collect from police station.'

'I wonder if their letting you take the stuff suggests the police are winding up their investigation?'

'I do not know.'

'Well, if they've made an arrest, we'll hear pretty soon on the news.'

'Yes.'

When Jude came through with the coffee, Zofia had curbed her tears but she still looked lost and waiflike on the sofa. Her pigtails emphasized her vulnerability. 'Come on,' said Jude, once the drinks were poured, 'let's be very unemotional about this. Try to distance yourself from what you're looking at, Zosia.'

'I will try, but it is not easy.'

'I'm sure it isn't. But just try to forget it is your brother whose things we are looking at. Imagine it is an assignment you are doing as a journalist. You have to write a story based on the information you can glean from what you find here.'

'Yes, this is a good way. I will try this.' She produced her blue notebook and opened it at a clean page. 'I am writing a story about a murder investigation. And I will write my notes in English.'

'Right. Open the suitcase first.'

Zofia did as she was told. The contents of the case were pitifully few, mostly clothes, and fairly worn and threadbare clothes at that. Though they must all have been redolent of memories, the girl was commendably restrained as she neatly piled them up. She made a kind of inventory in her notebook.

'Nothing here that he didn't have at the time he left Warsaw,' she announced when the suitcase was nearly empty. She picked up the last item, a sponge bag, and unzipped it.

The contents once again were unsurprising. Shaving kit, deodorant, shampoo, toothpaste, toothbrush, paracetamol. And in one compartment a pack of condoms.

'So it looks like something was happening in his life . . .' suggested Jude.

'Or just that Tadek was, as he always was, optimistic.' Zofia was making a joke at the expense of her brother's romantic aspirations, but she could not say it without a tear glinting in her eye.

She moved on to the backpack. This had seen a lot

of service. Its fabric was slack and discoloured, covered with a rough patchwork of stickers, old and illegible ones covered over by newer designs whose colours showed up against them.

'Are these all from your brother's travels?'

'No. He was given the backpack by a friend, who I think himself had bought it second-hand. The only ones Tadek would have put on are those from music festivals he goes to.' She pointed to a bright printed circle. 'This one in Leipzig . . . I remember he goes there after he finish university last summer. A celebration . . . to play some of his own music, he said, and to listen to people who play music better than he does.'

She pulled the backpack towards her and tackled the buckles. 'Maybe here we will find more secrets about what he do in England.'

There was some evidence of Tadek's activities, but nothing very interesting. Zofia itemized everything in her blue notebook. Programmes and tickets suggested he'd been to a few music gigs, but none further afield than Brighton. Some torn-out newspaper advertisements indicated that his career ambitions might have extended beyond bar work. A well-thumbed dictionary and an old language course on cassette bore witness to a determination to improve his English.

And there was also an English rhyming dictionary. Zofia looked at this with some confusion, before opening it to check the contents. Then she nodded slowly.

'Does that tell you something?' asked Jude.

'I think, yes. It is something Tadek speak of occasionally. He say writing good songs in Polish is good for

Poland, but not for the world. To write songs that are very successful, you must write in English – or American.'

'So you think he was writing songs in English?'

'I think he tries, yes.'

'He wanted to be very successful?'

Zofia Jankowska grimaced. 'Not exactly that. Tadek did not want a lot of money. Well, we would not have minded, but for him money was a . . . was what he could do with it . . . I think there is an expression in English . . .?'

'"A means to an end".'

'Yes, this is good. This is how Tadek see money. It helps him to do things he want to do. For him money is "a means to an end".'

'So writing songs in English would have made him more money? That would be his reason for doing it?'

'Perhaps. More with Tadek, though . . .' The girl smiled wistfully '. . . he might want to write songs for English women.'

'What do you mean?'

'I tell you he is romantic. He fall for women who are not right for him . . .'

'Yes, you said. And often older women.'

'That is what Tadek does, very often. And because he is romantic, and because he does not have much money to buy presents for the women he loves . . .'

'He used to write songs for them?'

Zofia nodded. 'That is what he always does.' She picked up the rhyming dictionary again. 'So perhaps this means he had fallen in love with an Englishwoman.'

She pulled a small pile of songbooks out of the backpack. They were mostly much-used copies of folk and protest songs from the nineteen-sixties, songs made popular by artistes like Bob Dylan, Joan Baez, Donovan and the Byrds.

'Your brother had rather old-fashioned tastes.'

'Yes, this is the music he likes. He plays a lot of these. Not electric guitar. The songs he write are in this style too. Perhaps that is why he does not make money from his songs, in any language. As you say, they are old-fashioned.' Emotion threatened for a moment, as she realized that she had heard the last of her brother's songs, but she controlled it. 'Right, that is nearly everything. Just a few more bits.'

She took out the remaining contents of the backpack, again arranging them neatly in piles on the floor. She made more notes in the little blue book. A couple of novels in Polish, a crucifix, other small ornaments. There was nothing that seemed out of place to Jude, but Zofia sat there for a long time saying, 'It is strange, it is very strange.'

'What's strange? Is there something there that shouldn't be?'

'No,' the girl replied. 'It is the other way round. There is things not here that should be here.'

'What?'

The pained hazel eyes fixed on Jude's. 'Tadek lived for his music. There is nothing of that here, except for the sheet music. No notebooks with songs written out, no lyrics, no cassettes, no CDs. Most of all, there is not his guitar.'

'What was the guitar like?'

'It was not electrical. It was . . . I don't know the word.'

'Acoustic.'

'Yes, it was acoustic. An acoustic guitar.' Zofia seemed to savour the adjective on her lips. 'Tadek would never give his guitar away. Where is it? It is such a special guitar.'

'Special meaning valuable?'

'No, no, probably after what Tadek has done to it, it is less valuable. He painted it red and he paint two eyes on the front, you know, like the hole behind the strings is the mouth, so the guitar has a face. In the band he play with with his friends, they all paint faces on their instruments. It is something they do, so that always people recognize them. And they call the band "Twarz". That means "face" in Polish.'

'Did you ask the police about the guitar when you picked up this lot?'

'I wasn't thinking. But they tell me here is everything they find in his room.'

'It might be worth checking. They could still be doing forensic tests on the guitar. Have you got a number for them?'

Zofia Jankowska had. She rang through and spoke to the officer from whom she had picked up the bags that morning. He told her everything was there except for the clothes her brother had been wearing at the time of his death. There had been no sign of a guitar amongst his belongings.

Being told this prompted another question from Jude. 'That overcoat he was wearing, was that his?'

Zofia nodded. 'I was with him when he bought it. In a street market in Warsaw for old clothes. It was from Russian navy. A lot of clothes like that are for sale in Poland.' Jude remembered thinking at the time that the coat had looked naval.

'You don't think he might have sold the guitar? If he needed the money?'

'Tadek would never do that. He might sell anything else, he might go without food, he would never sell his guitar. That was like part of him. Besides . . .' She picked up something that looked like a polished wooden cigar-box, turned it over and clicked a secret catch that revealed a false bottom. Inside was probably two hundred pounds in English notes. 'You see, Tadek had money.'

Zofia squatted back on her haunches in something like despair. 'So where do we find his guitar?'

'And where,' asked Jude thoughtfully, 'do we find the English woman to whom he was writing love songs?'

On her walk with Gulliver late that afternoon, Carole found herself passing Fethering's parade of shops and felt a very uncharacteristic urge to go into the bookie's. She managed to curb it and keep walking, but the strength of the impulse surprised her.

She knew it was partly to do with Gerald Hume. She didn't know whether she was attracted to him – she'd hardly been in the man's company long enough to form an opinion – but she was still warmed by the impression that she'd received of his being very definitely attracted to her. She wasn't convinced that the attraction was sexual, but they had definitely clicked at some level. The knowledge gave her a slightly heady feeling of power.

But Gerald Hume wasn't the only cause of her urge to go in. The betting shop remained the focus of the enquiry into Tadek's death. Perhaps it was no longer the focus for the official investigation – the police no doubt had new avenues to explore – but for Carole and Jude everything still came back to the betting shop.

Not for the first time Carole tried to guess at the young man's movements in the moments before he entered the place the previous week. That was the big question: where had he actually been when he was attacked? His thick coat could only have served as a temporary barrier to the flow of blood, so the scene of the stabbing could not have been very far away. Had the confrontation taken place on the beach or in one of the nearby houses or shops? Surely if it had happened in public there would have been some witnesses? And yet the powerful news-gathering agency of Fethering gossip had produced not a single clue even as to the direction from which the dying man had entered the betting shop.

Then Carole remembered the hailstorm. Under her duvet, drowned in flu, she had only been aware of the rattling of the icy downpour against her windows, but from Jude's description it had been really ferocious, obliterating all of the town's familiar landmarks. That was why no one had witnessed Tadek's approach to the betting shop.

Carole looked again along the parade. Allinstore, Marnie's Hairdressing, Polly's Cake Shop, the estate agents, the charity shops. It seemed unlikely that the young Pole had come out of one of them and yet what other explanation was there for his sudden appearance?

At that moment a car drawing up alongside her reminded Carole of another possibility. The young Pole could have arrived at the parade by car. But if he did, where had he come from? And who with?

Chapter Sixteen

Any social encounter that involved Lily had to be arranged around her schedule. Like most babies – particularly first babies – her arrival had immediately changed the pecking order in her parents' household. Gaby and Stephen were her slaves, and their lives now revolved around the vagaries of their daughter's feeding and sleeping patterns.

As a result the visit to Carole on the Friday was rigidly circumscribed by time. If Gaby left Fulham on the dot of ten, Lily would sleep all of the hour and three-quarters' drive to Fethering. Then they'd have to leave on the dot of two to ensure an equally peaceful return journey.

This suited Carole well. She liked arrangements to be fixed and defined. Nothing caused her greater anxiety than the concept of 'an open-ended visit'.

And she was hungry for the sight of Lily. Even in the few weeks since their last meeting, the baby had developed exponentially. Her smile was no longer something that could have been mistaken for wind. It was now a definite expression of pleasure, and one that could be bestowed on those around her like a rich gift.

Her mother still got most of the smiles. She and Lily had bonded instantly, and the baby's arrival had changed Gaby's personality. Though she hadn't lost her sparkle, she was calmer. And her conversation no longer revolved about show business. She seemed to have no wistful nostalgia for her work as a theatrical agent, she was totally absorbed in the new life which had come into hers. Carole thought it might be some time before her employers would see Gaby back in the office.

Serenely even-handed, that day Lily granted smiles to her grandmother as well as her mother. There had been some discussion with Stephen and Gaby as to what Carole should be called in her new role. All the possibles – Gran, Granny, Grandma, Nan – sounded dispiritingly old, but there was no avoiding making a choice. She had settled for 'Granny' as the least offensive, and indeed the name her own almost-forgotten grandmother had been known by.

With Lily there as a catalyst, Carole was surprised how much more relaxed she felt with her daughter-in-law. She had always liked Gaby, but felt an edge of unease when Stephen was not there and there were just the two of them. She had a bit of that feeling when she was alone with anyone. Her insecurities rose to the surface, she was always afraid that the other person was making judgements and finding her wanting.

But now with Gaby and the baby, Carole experienced something she had never relaxed into before, a kind of gender solidarity. Though she didn't rate her own maternal skills very highly, the shared experience of motherhood had brought the two women closer. Carole was amazed how unperturbed she could be by Gaby openly feeding Lily. She felt a kind of regret for her own time with Stephen as a small baby, when social convention and her own modesty had made breast-feeding a rather furtive exercise.

But perhaps what she appreciated most was the ease that her daughter-in-law showed in her presence. Gaby did not question Carole's right to be included in the care of her baby. She even asked for advice and reassurance over Lily's little quirks of development.

So at two o'clock sharp Carole was sorry to see them go, but warmed by the encounter. She felt bonded with the next two generations of women, and she looked forward to watching the development of the new person in her life.

She also knew that the visit would not have been nearly so satisfactory had her ex-husband been present.

So she was already in a good mood when the phone rang at about half-past two, and the ensuing conversation cheered her even more.

'Is that Carole Seddon?' The voice was cultivated, precise and vaguely familiar.

'Yes.'

'I found your number in the local directory.'

'Well, you would. It's in there,' said Carole rather fatuously. She still couldn't identify the voice, but was not left in ignorance for long.

'It's Gerald Hume speaking. Remember, we met in the betting shop yesterday.'

'Yes, I remember. I'm surprised you're not there now.'

'Oh, I am. As you may recall my saying, I am an habitué.' His use of the word echoed their conversation of the previous day. 'Well, to be strictly accurate, I am not inside the betting shop. I'm standing outside the premises. The mobile phone signal is better here, and also I don't like having my telephone conversations listened to by all and sundry.'

'Nor do I. That's one of the reasons I don't want a mobile phone.'

'I understand.' There was a brief silence. 'I thought you might have come in today.'

'Good heavens, no. As I believe I told you, yesterday was the first time I've crossed the threshold of a betting shop.'

'I thought you might have got the taste for it.'

'Certainly not,' came the instinctive, Calvinist response.

'Well, Carole,' said Gerald Hume with a sudden change of tone, 'I wondered if we could meet for a drink.'

'Meet for a drink?' she echoed stupidly. 'You and me?'

'Yes. I enjoyed meeting you yesterday. I thought it would be nice to talk at further length.'

'Well . . .'

'I'm sorry. I hope you don't think me forward.' Which was a comfortingly old-fashioned word for him to use. 'If you don't relish the idea, you have only to say no.'

Carole found herself saying 'Well . . .' again. The proposition was so unexpected that she couldn't immediately adjust to the idea.

'If you'd rather not, you needn't be embarrassed by refusing.'

'No, I'm not embarrassed.' To her surprise, Carole realized this was true. And suddenly she could see no reason to refuse his suggestion. 'Yes,' she said. 'Yes. Let's meet for a drink. When were you thinking of?'

'Would this evening be convenient?'

'This evening would be most convenient.'

Jude also had an invitation that afternoon. She had been half-expecting the call, with foreboding but an undercurrent of excitement. From the moment she'd met Andy Constant, she knew that something had connected between them.

On the phone he sounded even more languid and laid-back. The offer was made very casually, as if the manner of asking somehow took the curse off it. If she refused, his manner implied, it had never been any big deal anyway.

'Thought it'd be nice to meet again,' he said.

He was taking a risk. He knew nothing about her. She might be in a long-term relationship. But still he asked. Jude had already got the impression that Andy Constant was used to getting his own way with women.

'Well, yes, it might be,' she responded. She was taking a risk too. But she reassured herself that it wasn't only because she was attracted to him. He still might

153

have some information that was of relevance to the murder of Tadek. To keep in touch with him would be in the cause of pursuing their investigation, she told herself with knowing casuistry.

'Thing is, I'm doing a show at the college with some of the Drama students. Wondered if you'd like to come and see it. Then we could have a drink afterwards.'

Again, he made it sound very casual. Quite clever too, Jude thought. Not a direct request for a date. He made it sound as if the main purpose of the invitation was for her to see the show. And hopefully be impressed by it, perhaps warm to him because of his skills as a director. Then have a few drinks and maybe fix to meet again. There was something disquietingly practised about his approach.

'What is the show?' she asked.

'It's called *Rumours of Wars*. Something the students have built up through improvisation and I've kind of tailored into a script. I promise you it's less dreary than it sounds. They're a bright lot of kids, some real talent in there.'

'When are you talking about?'

'Short notice, I'm afraid. Show only runs for three performances. Saturday I have to entertain a lot of college bigwigs. So I'm talking about this evening.' Jude hadn't complained about the short notice, but he still seemed to feel the need to apologize. 'Ideally, I'd have asked you further in advance, but I hadn't met you then, had I? And I do think the show's something you might enjoy.'

Which Jude considered was a rather bold claim, since he'd had no time to assess her theatrical interests.

'It's in the college's new theatre. Building's worth seeing, apart from anything else. So tell me, do you fancy it?'

Again, he fostered the illusion of distancing himself. It was the show she'd be coming to see, not him. Jude had to acknowledge that his technique, though obviously well practised, was rather good.

'All right,' she said. 'I'd like to come.'

Chapter Seventeen

On a day when she had been feeling less good about herself Carole Seddon might have balked at Gerald Hume's suggestion that their meeting that evening should take place in the Crown and Anchor. The proposed encounter did have elements of a 'date' about it, and the pub's landlord was one of the very few men in Fethering who had ever shown an emotional interest in her. In less certain moods she might have agonized about some awkward scene arising between the two men. But that Friday evening Carole had no qualms about the venue. For a start, her affair with Ted Crisp was long over and their relationship had settled down into an easy friendship. Besides, the Crown and Anchor did have certain advantages. Apart from anything else, she would be on home territory and not far from High Tor, should the meeting prove to be uncomfortable. After all, she knew nothing about Gerald Hume.

He was sitting in one of the alcoves nursing a half-pint of lager when she arrived. Dressed, as ever, in pin-striped suit and tie, his briefcase on the banquette beside him. Carole greeted Ted Crisp immediately, to establish her familiarity with the pub. Now the moment had arisen, it gave her a slight *frisson* actually to be in a pub talking to an ex-lover when she was about to meet another man.

She sat down while Gerald Hume went to the bar to buy her requested Chilean Chardonnay, and wondered what kind of man he would prove to be. She wasn't worried about finding out, though, just intrigued.

'Perhaps,' he announced when he had supplied her drink, 'I should explain why I wanted to meet up with you.'

To her surprise, Carole found herself saying, 'I don't think you need to especially. As you said on the phone, it's nice for us to have a chance to talk.'

'Yes.'

He hesitated, still seeming to feel he should provide some explanation, so she moved on, 'Did you have a good day on the horses?'

'A profit of three pounds fifty pence.' He spoke in a considered manner, as if carefully selecting each word with a pair of tweezers.

'And is that a good day?'

'Would you regard three pounds fifty pence as adequate recompense for five hours' work?'

'No, I suppose not. So you do think of what you do in the betting shop as work, do you?'

'Well, it's the only work I have now.'

'I heard a rumour that you used to be an accountant.'

'That's a very unusual rumour to hear.'

'In what way unusual?'

'Because it's accurate. Very few rumours in

Fethering share that quality.' Carole smiled. He clearly knew the area well. 'Yes,' he went on, 'I was an account-ant with the same company for thirty-six years. They then deemed that I was no longer fit to be an account-ant.'

Carole didn't quite like to ask for amplification, but seeing her reaction he provided it. 'No, no skulduggery on my part, no embezzlement of funds. Merely a company policy of retirement at sixty. Drinks with colleagues, a hastily mugged-up speech from my new much younger boss, the presentation of an unwanted carriage clock and "Goodbye, Mr Hume." So, given the fact that I used to spend eight hours of every weekday in the office, that did leave rather a large gap in my life.'

'Surely there were other things you could have done?'

'I suppose so. I could have set up in private prac-tice. I could have offered my services as treasurer for various local societies. But such options did not appeal to me. My pension was adequate and I had made some prudent though not very adventurous investments over the years. So I didn't need to do anything else to make money.'

'Isn't retirement when people are supposed to devote themselves to their hobbies in a way that they previously never had time for?' asked Carole, reflecting that in her own case this hadn't worked out. The only hobby she had was being an amateur detective and that was one she had developed after she retired.

'Perhaps. And I am quite a keen photographer. But I can't do that every day. I get bored, so it remains just a hobby. Spending time in the betting shop, however, does impose some kind of structure on my life. It also enables me to study the vagaries of horse racing over a sustained period.'

'You mean you . . . "study the form"? Is that the right expression? And, incidentally, Gerald, I should tell you here and now that, whatever impression I may have given to the contrary yesterday, I know absolutely nothing about horses.'

'That, Carole, was abundantly clear.'

'Oh.' She couldn't help being disappointed. She thought the way she'd behaved the previous day had been pretty damned convincing.

'Anyway, you asked if I study the form, and yes, I do do a certain amount of that, but I am more interested in the mathematical probabilities involved in the business.'

'Do you mean you are trying to work out a foolproof system to win on the horses?'

Gerald Hume chuckled. 'If I were doing that, today's profit of three pounds fifty pence might suggest that my system is as yet far from foolproof. But you're right in a way. I am trying to draw some conclusions from the many races that I watch every day. I analyse the results and, yes, there is the hope that such analysis might lead to a more informed pattern of investment.'

'And do you ever have big wins?'

'A few hundred pounds now and then. But such days are rare.'

'I still can't quite understand why you do it.'

'No, it may seem inexplicable. There is a commonly held view that racing is a mug's game, that there are too many variables for any kind of logical pattern to be discernible. But the attempt to impose order on such chaos does sometimes bring me the same kind of satisfaction that I used to derive during my working life from balancing columns of figures. Perhaps because my life has followed a relatively predictable course, I am fascinated by the random. Maybe, in my own perhaps pernickety way, I am trying to impose logic on the random.'

'I see.' And now she almost did.

'And it keeps me off the streets.' He smiled rather wanly. 'I'm not sure how I would fill my time without my regular attendance at the betting shop.'

There was a moment of silence before Gerald Hume, realizing the danger of sounding pitiable, abruptly changed the direction of the conversation. 'Still, enough about me. I don't have nearly that amount of information about you yet, Carole.'

'No.'

Her retirement from the Home Office and divorce were established with the minimum of comment.

'I see,' said Gerald. 'I never married.'

'Is that a cause for regret?'

'Rarely. I think I am probably not designed for connubial bliss. I tend to be rather analytical in all my dealings, which may lead to a level of detachment in my behaviour. And I have been given to understand that marriage requires engagement with the partner rather than detachment from them.'

'I think that is usually thought desirable, yes.'

Carole was touched by his quaintness, and found her own speech beginning to echo the formality of his. She had also by now realized that Gerald Hume wasn't and never would be a 'date'. The attraction between them was not physical, it was purely intellectual. This revelation did not bring her even the mildest flicker of disappointment. In fact it reassured her, clarified her feelings.

'May I go off on a complete tangent, Gerald . . .?'

'By all means.'

'. . . and ask whether you do crosswords?'

As Carole knew he would, he confirmed that he did. 'I do the *Times* and the *Telegraph* every morning before I go to the betting shop. One might imagine, given my interest in numbers, it would be the Su Doku that monopolized my attention, but no, it's words. Maybe because words are more resonant than numbers, because they carry with them a greater burden of semi-otic information. And do I gather you are also an aficionado of the crossword . . .?'

'I usually do the *Times*,' said Carole.

'I knew you would.' This confirmation of his conjecture seemed to make him particularly happy. 'I am very glad that we have met, Carole. I think there are a lot of similarities in our personalities.'

Deciding that this was not a completely undiluted compliment, she moved on to another possible area of mutual interest. 'Gerald, have you ever applied your analytical mind to the subject of crime?'

He smiled with relish. 'I most certainly have. I

enjoy the process of deduction, very similar in fact to that required in the solution of a crossword. But I'm afraid the crime writing I favour is of an older genera- tion. The so-called Golden Age, when authors played fair with their readers in regard to plotting. Though contemporary crime fiction may have gained in psy- chological reality, that has always been at the expense of the puzzle element. And for me it is in the puzzle that the appeal of the genre lies.'

'But have you ever applied your deductive powers to a real crime?' asked Carole.

'Might you be thinking of the recent regrettable incident, which occurred at the place where I spend a large portion of my days?'

'I was thinking of that, yes, Gerald.'

'Hm. The first time I have been so close to a mur- der, outside of fiction. I'm afraid, in my professional life – though accountants may frequently be thought to get away with murder . . .' He let out a small dry laugh at this small dry joke '. . . they are – perhaps fortunately – rarely involved in the real thing.'

'So have you joined in the increasingly popular Fethering pastime of trying to work out whodunit?'

'I have.' He sighed. 'But without much progress. I regret in this instance the Almighty Author has pro- vided us with an inadequacy of information. Dame Agatha would never have been so parsimonious with the clues. Though we habitués of the betting shop were witnesses to one part of the tragedy – and your friend Jude witness to a further part – we have very few facts that link the poor young man to his penultimate destination.'

'Were you particularly aware of him when he came in that afternoon?'

'I can't say that I was, Carole. Yes, I noticed a young man I had not seen before come into the shop. The noise of the hailstorm was very loud when the door was opened, so I looked in his direction. But I very quickly returned to my investments. I can't honestly say that the young man made any impression on me at all.'

'Gerald, you said then that you had not seen the victim before . . .'

'That is correct, yes.'

'But last week's visit was the second time he had been in the betting shop.'

'Was it?' The ex-accountant looked genuinely amazed by this news. 'I had certainly never seen him before.'

'And you are there most days during opening hours?'

'Well, not opening hours – betting shops tend to be open for an increasingly long time these days – but I'm there during afternoon racing hours. I tend to arrive about half an hour before the first race and stay there until after the last.'

'And would you say you tend to notice everyone who comes in and out?'

'I do. I make a point of that. My researches into the randomness of gambling are obviously related to the demographic profile of the people who participate.'

'So you're sure you'd never seen Tadek before last week?'

'Tadek?'

'I'm sorry. Tadeusz Jankowski was always called Tadek.'

'I understand. No, I had definitely never encountered him before last week. When was he seen?'

'Round the beginning of last October.'

Gerald Hume's brow clouded as he tried to explain the anomaly, but then it cleared. 'Last October, yes. I remember now. I was unwell. I had a serious throat infection which kept me to my bed for a few days. I think it must have been during that period. Did Ryan the Manager see him?'

'It was while Ryan was on holiday.'

'So how do you know the young man was in there?'

Carole explained about Jude's conversation with Pauline.

'Ah yes. That would make sense. Pauline never does much in the way of gambling, but she always keeps her eyes on everything that's going on. A habit that she learnt from her late husband.'

'Oh?'

'He was a fairly considerable crook. Or so Fethering gossip has it . . . and this is another instance when I would be inclined to believe Fethering gossip.'

'Jude said that Pauline was one of very few women who go into the betting shop.'

'That is true. It is more of a male enclave . . . though a lot of the ladies put in an appearance round the

164

Derby or Grand National. Or down here when Glorious Goodwood is on, of course.'

A new thought came suddenly to Carole. 'Ooh, that reminds me. Other women in the betting shop!'

'I'm sorry?'

'Apparently when Tadeusz Jankowski went into the betting shop last year, he spoke to a woman who was often in there. Another regular. Very well-dressed, middle-class woman . . . does that ring any bells, Gerald?'

'Well, there are one or two fitting that description who come in from time to time . . .'

'This one used to be very regular, but then stopped coming . . . round about last October. Any idea who it might be?'

Gerald Hume beamed as the recollection came to him. 'Oh yes. I know exactly who you mean. I'm sorry, with her not having been in for a few months, I'd completely forgotten about her. But yes, she fits your description exactly.'

'Did you ever talk to her?'

'No. She kept herself to herself.'

More or less exactly what Pauline and Ryan had said. Carole asked, without much hope, 'So you wouldn't know her name, would you?'

This question produced another beam. 'As a matter of fact I do. Melanie Newton.'

'But if you didn't speak to her, how do you know that?'

Gerald Hume's expression combined shame with pride as he replied, 'One day when she was in the betting shop, she had made a note of her fancies on an envelope. When she went, she screwed it up and left it on a shelf. I'm afraid, out of pure curiosity – and because she seemed rather different from the average run of betting shop habitué – I uncrumpled the envelope and looked at it.'

'So do you have an address for her too?' asked Carole excitedly.

Gerald shook his head apologetically. 'I'm afraid I don't have a photographic memory for such things. Though I do have a vague recollection that she lived in Fedborough.'

Carole still felt good about herself when she got back to High Tor at about eight o'clock. She had a new lead. Melanie Newton. She was going to share the good news with Jude, when she remembered that her friend was out seeing some theatre show at Clincham College.

But as well as a new lead, she thought she might have something else. Though Gerald Hume would never be a lover (which was, if she was honest with herself, quite a relief), it was not impossible that over time he could turn into a very good friend.

Chapter Eighteen

Jude picked up the ticket that Andy Constant had promised would be left at the box office and went through into the theatre. The building was named after the company which had stumped up the money for its construction, with a view to raising their local charitable profile. (They had made a very favourable deal with the university, which would allow them free use of the halls of residence for conferences during the vacations.) As Andy had said, the theatre was new, new even to the extent of still smelling of paint and freshly varnished wood. And it was a rather splendid structure.

The auditorium was buzzing with the sounds of young people, fellow students there to support their mates, but there were also quite a few parents, coming to see what all those tuition fees were being spent on.

Jude had been presented with a programme, just an A5 sheet printed in black with a list of actors and production credits. The title of the evening's entertainment was *Rumours of Wars: The Interface Between Society and Violence*. She noted that the show had been 'Conceived and Directed by Andy Constant'.

She saw him briefly before the show. He gave her a

wave of acknowledgement as he bustled busily up the aisle from the pass-door by the stage. He was dressed exactly as when she'd last seen him, but there was now a greater aura of importance about him. In his wake scuttled the pretty dark-haired girl who had summoned him from the university coffee shop on their last encounter. As he passed Jude, Andy Constant said, 'If I don't see you in all the confusion after the show, let's meet up in the Bull. Just opposite the gates of the campus – do you know it?'

'I'll find it.'

'Won't be such a scrum there as there will in the student bar.'

'Can I set one up for you?'

'Pint of Stella would be wonderful.'

And he whisked his important way to the back of the auditorium, where the dark-haired girl was now waiting for him.

Just as the lights were dimming, Jude caught sight of Ewan and Hamish Urquhart a few rows in front, presumably there to cheer on Sophia.

The show was not bad, but it did feel slightly over-inflated for its own good. The subject of war is a big one and *Rumours of Wars* tried to take on all of it. There were the obligatory scenes of carnage from 1914–18, juxtaposed with the clinical battles of new technologies. There were scenes of everyman squaddies punctiliously obeying orders given to them by idiots, of bereaved mothers weeping over the deaths of children in air raids, of blimpish generals planning mass slaughter over post-prandial port.

All of this was realized in a form that involved much shouting, a certain amount of dance, some a cappella singing and a lot of mime (which was about as interesting as mime usually is). The show was built about a lot of tableaux of human bodies, dramatic images precisely engineered. It was all impressive and just a tad worthy.

Also old-fashioned. Andy Constant must have been very young during the sixties, but that was definitely the period when his ideas of theatre had been formed. Jude got the feeling that he'd definitely seen *Oh! What A Lovely War* at an impressionable age. There was a simplicity in his anti-war message which accorded better with the protest years of Vietnam, when there were still perhaps some illusions remaining to be shattered, than the cynical wartime of Iraq. The show seemed to be taking a battering ram to a door that was already wide open.

And the acting wasn't terribly good. The kind of slick ensemble playing required by that kind of theatre was beyond the capacity of the University of Clincham's Drama students. Though individual talents shone through in various areas, none had the all-round versatility that the piece demanded. And of all the cast Sophia Urquhart was probably the weakest. She looked pretty enough and went through the motions of what she had rehearsed, but didn't convince. However much she threw herself around the stage, she remained quintessentially a young lady of the Home Counties who had been to all the right schools. Wherever the girl's future lay, it wasn't in acting.

Her singing voice, though, was something else. In the one solo number she had, she was transformed. This, again harking back to the sixties, was Pete Seeger's 'Where Have All the Flowers Gone?' As the girl's pure unaccompanied soprano spelt out the message of pacifism, she seemed not only to evoke an earlier era, but also to swell with confidence and to take effortless control of the whole auditorium. As a singer, Sophia Urquhart might make it.

The best thing about *Rumours of Wars*, in Jude's view, was its length. An hour and twenty minutes with no interval. Quite long enough to preach to the converted that *war is a bad thing*.

Jude's overall impression of the evening was the dominance of Andy Constant. The show was supposedly built up from improvisation, but had all the hallmarks of contrivance. Yes, the students may have come up with individual ideas, but they had been welded into a preconceived form by the director. The iron will of Andy Constant lay behind every line and every gesture. In a way, the weakness of the material served only to highlight the skill with which it had been pressed into theatrical shape.

In her brief experience as an actress Jude had come across directors like that. For them the written text was an irrelevance, an obstacle to be overcome by their stagecraft. And working from improvisation gave them the perfect opportunity to impose their wills on actors. The aim of the production was only to show how clever they, the directors, were. The whole exercise was an ego-trip.

Jude knew that that was exactly how Andy Constant would have treated his students during the rehearsal period. What he was after was control, pure and simple.

And even as she identified the kind of man he was, she was aware of the way she was drawn towards him. She could regret, but she couldn't deny it.

Andy had said that the Bull pub would be less of a scrum than the student bar, but it was still pretty crowded, the regular clientele augmented by parents who had just experienced *Rumours of Wars*. From the conversations Jude overheard as she struggled towards the bar, they had thought rather more of the show than she had. Or maybe it was just because their offspring had been participating.

There were also quite a few of the students who'd been in the show, and a lot of their friends who hadn't. Jude saw the girl with long dark hair at the centre of a giggling bunch of youngsters.

Given the crowd, she was glad she'd suggested setting up a drink for Andy Constant. One trip to the bar took long enough. As she eased her way through the crowd with a Chardonnay and a pint of Stella, she found herself face to face with Ewan and Hamish Urquhart, both dressed in Drizabone coats over their corduroy.

'Ah, Jude, isn't it? I thought I saw you in there. So, what did you think of my little Sophia, eh?'

'I thought there was a lot of talent there,' she said tactfully.

'Yes. Bloody stupid thing for a girl to do, though,

isn't it? No security in acting. Hope she'll see the light soon and start doing something sensible. Mind you,' he couldn't help saying, with a father's pride, 'she is rather gifted, and she's pretty enough to make a go of it.'

'Let's hope so. Her singing is really excellent.' No need to say anything about the acting.

'Yes. Hamish, you get them in, will you?' Ewan Urquhart's son obediently scuttled into the melee around the bar. 'No, she's a good little singer, my Soph. You can catch her singing in here most Friday nights.'

'Really?'

He pointed to a poster pinned on to a board nearby. It had been printed up on a home computer by some-one who had only just discovered how many fonts and colours it was possible to use, and advertised 'MAGIC DRAGON, Clincham Uni's Number One Folk/Rock Band'. A rather smudged photograph showed a long-haired figure who was recognizably Sophia Urquhart fronting two guitarists and a fiddler.

'Obviously they're not doing it tonight because of the show. But most other Fridays during term-time you'll find her in here singing her little heart out.'

'I must try and catch them one day. As I say, she has got an exceptional voice.'

'Yes.' Ewan Urquhart agreed in a voice that mixed pride with scepticism. 'Trouble is, if she goes into that kind of business – singing, acting – God knows what kind of riff-raff she's going to mix with. Funny lot, actors, aren't they?'

'Some of them. So there isn't any showbiz in your family?'

'Good God, no. I went to Charterhouse, spent all my time doing sport. No time for bloody acting.' Ewan Urquhart seemed to need to shoehorn his status as an Old Carthusian into every conversation.

'I thought maybe Sophia's mother . . .'

'Sophia's mother and I parted company some years ago,' he responded with some asperity. 'And if you're wondering whether Sophia got her acting or singing talent from that source, let me tell you my ex-wife had no talent of any description.'

Jude deduced from the vehemence of this response that it was Mrs Urquhart who had left her husband, rather than vice versa. And she didn't blame her.

She noticed that Andy Constant had just entered the pub and so, with an 'Excuse me', edged her way towards a table for two she'd just seen vacated.

He flopped down in front of his pint, long limbs drooping in a parody of exhaustion. 'God, I'm wiped out. I find directing takes more out of me than acting ever did. Particularly with these kids . . . you never quite know what they're going to do from minute to minute.'

'They seemed very disciplined to me, from what I saw on stage.'

'Yes, but it takes a while to get into their heads what acting's about. Very few of them understand the concept of an ensemble. They don't know that acting's not about the individual, it's about everyone working together.' Which Jude understood as 'everyone doing what I tell them'.

'Still, the show played pretty well tonight,' Andy

Constant went on complacently. 'I like it when the audience gasps.' The audience had indeed gasped, but only at the crowbarring-in of a few four-letter words, which Jude hadn't reckoned added anything.

'I'm intrigued that the show was worked out through improvisation,' said Jude. 'It all felt very structured.'

He grinned, as if she had given him a compliment. 'Yes, well, the ideas the kids come up with are not always very practical. You have to have someone there who's shaping the thing.'

'And in this case that person was you?'

He acknowledged the fact with a nod, took a long sip of his lager and then looked at Jude through narrowed eyes. She guessed that at some stage he had been told he looked sexy doing that, and was annoyed with herself for actually finding it sexy.

'So . . . Jude . . . I don't know much about you.'

'No.' That was, generally speaking, the way she liked things to stay. 'Well, I live in Fethering. Is that enough information?'

'I'd like to know whether you're married?'

'No.'

'In a long-term relationship?'

'No.'

'I'm surprised. You're an attractive woman.'

'Thank you.' Jude had never been coy about accepting compliments. 'And what about you . . . in the marital stakes?'

He ran his fingers through his long grey hair, flattening it either side of the central parting. 'I am technically married, in that my wife and I haven't bothered to divorce, but we haven't really been married for sixteen years . . . no, I tell a lie, it's seventeen now.'

'Children?'

'A couple.'

'How old?'

'Oh, finished with education. Off our hands.' The answer was airy and, to Jude's mind, calculatedly vague. He didn't want her to know exactly how old he was, which probably meant he was older than he looked.

This impression was confirmed by the way he immediately moved the conversation on. 'You haven't got any further in your search for the killer of Tadeusz Jankowski?'

'No further progress. Nor in finding a connection between him and Clincham College.'

That caught him on the hop. A momentary expression of anxiety was quickly quelled as he said, 'Well, I think you're very unlikely to find one.'

'Carole and I can keep looking.'

'Of course you can. It's a free country. Though, with the current government, I'm beginning to wonder . . .' It was a line he had to say, to maintain his pose as the free-thinking outsider.

Their exchange of information was still incomplete, so Jude asked, 'And are you in a relationship at the moment?'

He did the narrowed eyes routine again. 'Nothing I couldn't get out of if something better came along,' he murmured. God, the arrogance of the man.

'I think we should meet again,' he announced suddenly. 'When we have more time to . . . appreciate each other.'

'It's a thought,' said Jude, against her better judgement.

'A good thought.' He smiled lazily. 'I'd suggest extending this evening's encounter, but . . .' He shrugged '. . . I'm afraid there's some stuff I've still got to sort out back at the college.'

Jude didn't say anything. The bar was quieter now. The first rush of students had gone back to the campus. Her hand was lying on the table. Andy Constant moved his forward as if to touch it, then abruptly changed his mind as he caught sight of the approaching Sophia Urquhart.

'Andy, bit of a problem.'

He looked shaken and turned to face the girl. 'Something to do with the show?'

'No. A message from Joan.' She looked piercingly at Jude, not recognizing her but perhaps with a degree of suspicion. 'If I could just have a quick word, Andy . . .'

'Excuse me.' He shrugged, as if to apologize for the bad timing of all young people, and uncoiled his lanky body from the chair.

There was a short exchange between him and Sophia, then he ambled back to the table with a magnanimous smile. 'Sorry, she was just picking up on a note I gave her about tonight's performance.'

Which was a perfectly reasonable explanation for what had happened. But for the fact that Jude had exceptionally good hearing and had caught the words the two of them had whispered to each other.

Sophia had said, 'Joan thought her father would have gone straight after the show, but he's just offered her a lift home. So she can't come back with you tonight. She says she probably could tomorrow.'

'Tell her she'd better be able to,' Andy Constant had hissed. 'I want her.'

'I'll pass on the message.'

'Make sure you do,' he said intensely. 'Make sure she knows what I feel.'

Jude found the exchange, to say the least, intriguing.

Chapter Nineteen

Andy Constant looked at his watch, before turning his narrowed eyes back on to Jude. 'Actually, I could show you the college's Drama facilities now if you like . . .'

'I've seen the theatre.'

'But not the Drama Studio. I keep a secret supply of hooch in the Drama Studio. We could have our second drink there.'

'No, thank you,' said Jude firmly.

Andy Constant's reaction was like that of a spoiled child. He swallowed down the rest of his lager and, with a brusque 'Thank you for the drink – I'd better go and sort things out back at the college', left the pub.

Jude was appalled by his behaviour. If she read what had happened right, Andy Constant had had some kind of assignation set up with the Joan that Sophia Urquhart had mentioned . . . quite possibly back in the Drama Studio. Within seconds of hearing that Joan couldn't make it, he had, presumably on the 'bird in the hand' principle, asked Jude to share the delights of the Drama Studio with him. And when she, who hardly knew him, had refused, he had immediately thrown his toys out of the pram.

But Jude had a feeling that wouldn't be the last she heard from Andy Constant. She recognized the kind of man who wouldn't acknowledge failure when it came to women. He'd be on the phone again before too long, suggesting another meeting. And Jude hated herself for knowing that she'd probably respond to his invitation.

Oh dear, how weak she could sometimes be. Time to get back to Woodside Cottage. She reached into her handbag for her mobile to call a cab, and then realized she'd left it on charge in her bedroom. Never mind, there was bound to be a public phone in the pub. In fact there was a sign to it over the far side of the room.

As she approached the bar, she found herself passing the three Urquharts. 'Jude,' said Ewan bonhomously, 'are you after another drink? Please, allow me to do the honours.'

'That's very kind, but actually I was just on my way. Going to phone for a cab.'

'Oh, you don't need to do that. You're in Fethering, aren't you? So are we. I'll give you a lift.'

'Well, thank you.'

'And since the massed Urquhart clan are not leaving till we've had another dram, what can I get for you?'

Ewan Urquhart, as he never missed telling everyone, drove a large sleek black Lexus. It must have been recently cleaned. In the damp February weather cars in West Sussex were very quickly spattered with mud from the roads, and his shone as though it had just come out of the showroom.

The interior was also immaculate. Hamish had offered her the passenger seat, but Jude had said she was sure he needed the leg-room, so sat in the back with Sophia. She was aware of the girl's distinctive and very expensive perfume. She was also aware that Sophia seemed subdued and out of sorts. Perhaps it was just the come-down after giving of herself in *Rumours of Wars*.

The relative silence of his children didn't appear to worry Ewan Urquhart, as he continued the monologue which, from what Jude had seen, filled his every waking hour. 'I thought the show was pretty well done, but I'm not sure what the point of it was. I mean, good as a showcase for student talent perhaps, but not what you'd call entertainment. I can't imagine anyone who hadn't a vested interest . . . you know, some connection with the cast . . . voluntarily going to a show like that.'

'You don't know anything about theatre, Daddy,' said his daughter truculently.

'I may not know about theatre, but I know what I like,' he riposted with a self-satisfied guffaw. 'And what I like is something with a structure. A "well-made play" I think it's called.'

'An "old-fashioned play" is what I think you mean.'

'Nonsense, Soph. Certain standards are always viable. In my young day plays were crafted, not thrown together from the ideas of a bunch of self-dramatizing students. And craft is what plays should be about.'

'I didn't know you were a lover of the theatre, Ewan,' said Jude.

'Oh yes, there's some stuff I enjoy.'

'Really?' asked his daughter. 'But you never go to the theatre, Daddy.'

'I do.'

'Come on, before tonight, when was the last time you went to the theatre?'

'Well . . . Well, I . .'

'See, you can't remember. Honestly, Daddy, sometimes you're so full of shit.'

He wouldn't have taken a line like that from anyone else, but when his beloved daughter said it, Ewan Urquhart just chuckled. 'You may be right, but I know what I like.'

'Do you get to see a lot of theatre, Sophia?' asked Jude.

'Oh yes, I go whenever I can. It's important, you know, because of the course I'm on. Andy sometimes organizes trips to the West End for us, and we get to see most of what's on in Brighton and Chichester.'

'Now Chichester used to do some good plays,' said her father.

'Yes, but you never went to see any of those either.'

'I remember you and Mum taking us to see some pantomimes there when we were little,' said Hamish, rather pathetically.

But his contribution to the dialogue was, as ever, ignored, as his father chuntered on. 'It's a very insecure business, though, the theatre. I'm just waiting, Jude, till young Sophia sees the error of her ways and starts doing something sensible.'

'It's my life,' said his daughter passionately, 'and I'll do what I want with it!'

Her father was instantly contrite. Clearly he didn't like to upset his precious Sophia. 'Yes, of course you will,' he said soothingly. 'I was only joking.'

'Dad's always joking,' said Hamish, contributing his bit to the reassurance. 'He's really not getting at you.'

'Huh,' was all the response they got from the girl.

There was then a moment of silence, which Jude broke by asking, 'Have you had singing lessons, Sophia? You've got a really good voice.'

'Not much. We cover it a bit in general voice work on the course. But I have sung a bit with bands round here, and I did some singing with people when I was on my gap year.'

'Gap year,' her father snorted. 'Weren't any gap years when I was growing up. You finished your education and you got down to work. Mind you, we didn't have a government then that wanted to keep as many kids as possible as students to massage the unemployment figures.'

Carole would agree with you on that, thought Jude.

'I think,' he went on, 'that university is just an excuse for not facing up to real life. I didn't go to university and it hasn't done me any harm.'

'Nor me,' Hamish agreed.

But of course he was just setting himself up for another parental put-down. 'Yes, but the cases were slightly different. I didn't go to university as a career decision. I reckoned the education I'd had at Charterhouse would be quite sufficient to see me through life. Which indeed has proved to be the case.

Whereas you, Hamish, didn't go to university because you were too thick to get in!'

As before, all the Urquharts, including Hamish, enjoyed this joke at his expense.

'So, Sophia, where did you go on your gap year?' asked Jude.

'Oh, just round Europe. InterRailing, you know. France, Germany, Denmark.'

'Did you get into any of the old Eastern Bloc countries?'

'No.'

'Thought you said you went to East Germany,' her father pointed out, nitpicking as ever.

'Oh yes, I did. Sorry, I wasn't counting that, because it's part of Germany now.'

'Geography never was your strong point, was it, Soph?' Another guffaw. 'Though I think that's actually just a women's thing. No good at navigating, women – have to keep stopping to ask for directions.'

'Whereas men get lost,' said Jude, 'because they never will stop to ask for directions.'

'Oh, touché,' came the response, but nothing was actually going to change Ewan Urquhart's view of the opposite sex. 'Now tell me, Jude, where is it you live?'

'On the High Street. Just drop me anywhere now, it's no distance.'

'Nonsense. I will escort you to your front door. One hears of such terrible things happening to unaccompanied women these days.'

'Well, thank you, I'm sure I'll be fine.'

But the Lexus had already turned into the High Street. 'So tell me, which house is it?'

'Just along there on the right. Beyond the lamp-post.'

'Oh, I've sold a good few properties along here, let me tell you. Prices skyrocketing. If you're ever thinking of selling, Jude . . .'

'Well, I had thought of having the place valued. You know, to sort of see where I stand.'

'We'd be happy to do it. All part of the service at Urquhart & Pease. Isn't that right, Hamish?'

'Yes, Dad.'

'By the way, I'm intrigued to know . . .' Jude asked. 'Who's Pease?'

'My partner?'

'Yes, the other part of Urquhart & Pease.'

'Ah.' Ewan Urquhart chuckled, before producing another well-rehearsed line. 'He doesn't exist. When I set up the business, I reckoned two names sounded more authoritative than one. So that's how Mr Pease got invented.'

'Thank you for explaining that. It'd been intriguing me. Anyway, I might take you up on your offer of a valuation.'

'Do, by all means.'

Then, as the big car slowed down, Jude asked Sophia, 'Tell me, while you were in East Germany, did you go to Leipzig?'

The girl looked at her with some surprise. Then the line of her mouth hardened as she replied, 'No. I've never been there.'

Chapter Twenty

Both Carole and Jude had shopping to do on the Saturday morning, but they joined up for coffee in the kitchen of High Tor at about eleven. Jude had not suggested meeting at Woodside Cottage because Zofia Jankowska had come in very late the night before and the poor girl needed her sleep. She was exhausted by the emotional rollercoaster she had been riding since she heard of her brother's death.

Carole was very pleased with herself about the information she had received from Gerald Hume and presented it to Jude with considerable aplomb. 'So at last we have a name. Someone who did actually know Tadek – or at least spoke to him in the betting shop.'

'Pauline implied that he knew the woman. Melanie Newton, eh?'

'And Gerald seemed to think she lived in Fedborough.'

'Sounds like a job for the local phone book.'

Flicking through the directory, they were beginning to wish their quarry had a less common name. There were forty Newtons listed. But when they narrowed the search down to Fedborough addresses, it looked easier.

Only four. None of them had the initial 'M', but, as Carole and Jude agreed, the listing might well be under the name of Melanie Newton's husband or another relation.

'Well, let's see if we get any joy. Are you going to call them or shall I?'

'You do it, Jude.' Carole was suddenly embarrassed by the idea of phoning up complete strangers. 'You're better at lying than I am.'

'Why do I need to lie?'

'You can't just ring up someone out of the blue, can you?'

'A lot of people do. The number of calls I get about replacement windows and making wills and investing in land . . .'

'Yes, or trying to sell you a mobile phone . . .'

'Perhaps I should do that. Make up some story. Pretend I'm from a call centre.' Jude made up her mind. 'No, I think it'd be simpler – as usual – just to tell the truth.'

'"Hello, I want to talk to you about someone you spoke to five months ago"?' suggested Carole with dis-belief.

'Something along those lines, yes.' Jude phoned the first of the numbers. An answering machine message. She pressed the red button to end the call. 'Bob and Marie Newton are not available at the moment. No Melanie.'

She keyed in the next number. 'Oh, hello, could I speak to Melanie?'

She was informed, with some huffiness, that there was no one of that name living at the address.

'Two more to go,' she said as she tried the third. Again someone answered. A woman's voice.

'Oh, hello, could I speak to Melanie Newton, please?'

'I'm sorry. She no longer lives here.'

'You don't by any chance know where she lives now, do you?'

'I'm not sure. I got the impression the marriage was breaking up and I think she and her husband went their separate ways.'

'So don't you have any means of contacting her?'

'I've got a mobile number for her husband, Giles. I've never used it, so I don't know if it's still current.'

'Could you give it to me?'

For the first time the voice at the other end of the line sounded suspicious. 'Who am I talking to here?'

'My name's Jude.' Which was true. 'I'm an old friend of Melanie's.' Which was a lie. Carole raised her eyes to heaven.

'All right.' And the voice gave the mobile number.

'Thank you so much. And can you tell me how long ago the Newtons moved?'

'We moved in here on the third of November.'

As soon as she had finished the call, Jude keyed in the mobile number she'd been given.

'Hello?' said a wary answering voice.

'Is that Giles Newton?'

'Yes.' He still sounded guarded.

'You don't know me, but I'm trying to contact Melanie Newton and—'

Giles Newton ended the call.

When Jude returned to Woodside Cottage, Zofia Jankowska was up and dressed, making coffee in the kitchen. 'Aren't you going to have something to eat too?' asked Jude.

'No, I have too much food of yours already. You do not let me pay.'

'You don't need to pay.'

'It makes me feel not good. I do not like to be . . . what is the word I heard? A "sponger"? I read in newspaper that many Poles in England are spongers.'

'Then you should read different newspapers. You're not sponging off me. You're here as my guest.'

'I should be paying something. I do not know how long I will be here. If I could get a few hours' work, I could pay you.'

'Well, I'm sure you could get something if you really wanted to.' A thought came to Jude. 'Tell you what . . . the landlord of the Crown and Anchor was complaining how he couldn't get any decent bar staff.'

'That is the pub here in Fethering?'

'Yes.'

'Well, if I could work some hours for him, I could pay you some rent.'

'I've told you, you don't need to.'

'It would make me feel better. And I have worked in a bar a lot. I know what to do. In Warsaw I work in bars.

There of course I take money in zlotys, but I am quick learner. I soon catch on to money in pounds.'

'Well, I'll give him a call. His name's Ted Crisp.' Jude hesitated. 'I just wonder, though . . .'

'What?'

'Ted's . . . um, how shall I put this? Very English.'

'English in the way that he does not like foreigners?'

'Yes,' Jude admitted.

'This is perhaps because he has not met many foreigners?'

'Quite possibly, yes.'

'Then I think he should meet one. Me. Zofia Jankowska. I will show him how a good worker works.'

Jude chuckled and looked at her watch. 'I'll give him a call later. After the Saturday lunchtime rush. Ooh, by the way, there is something more we've found out about that woman your brother spoke to in October.' And she told Zofia the information she'd had from Carole. 'As I say, the husband hung up on me, but at least we've got a name, which is more than we had this time yesterday.'

'Maybe you will be able to find her.'

'I hope so.'

'I also thought of two people I could try to talk to.'

'Oh?'

'One is back in Warsaw. A friend of Tadek, called Pavel. He was in the band. I try to call him this morning, but his mother say he off playing music in Krakow. She will pass on message when he call her. But I think that will not be soon.'

'Why not?'

Zofia shrugged ruefully. 'Pavel like Tadek. Not good keeping in touch.'

'But your message will get through eventually?'

'Eventually, yes. But his mother say he not even picking up emails in Krakow.' She looked glum for a moment, but then a spark returned to her eyes. 'A second person I think of, though. I had forgotten about him until this morning, but there was another friend of Tadek who used to play in the band with him. In Twarz. Not for a long time. He was the drummer, but not a very good drummer. He left the band a year before Tadek finished at the university. He was called Marek Wisniewski and he used to get on well with my brother. But why I think of him is I remember he came to England. I think he get work as a waiter.'

'How long has he been here?'

'More than a year. A year and a half perhaps. But perhaps Tadek get in touch with Marek when he come to England.'

'Have you got a contact for him?'

'Not here in England, no. But I know his brother in Warsaw. I will ring him, see if he knows where Marek is working now.' The girl shrugged. 'It may be nothing, but everything is worth trying, isn't it?'

'Certainly,' said Jude.

They both made their phone calls that afternoon. Zofia got through to Warsaw and was given the address of a Brighton restaurant where Marek had been working when his brother had last heard from him. A bored man at the restaurant said he still worked there, but he was off on a few days' leave. He thought he would be back on the Tuesday. She asked the man to give Marek her mobile number, but she didn't feel very optimistic that the message would get through.

'Nothing else we can do at the moment,' Zofia said gloomily when she'd ended the call.

'No, but if you don't hear, we can go and see him. Brighton's not far away. Anyway, now I'll phone Ted.'

The timing couldn't have been better. The landlord of the Crown and Anchor had just been let down by one of the barmaids who was meant to be doing a shift that evening. If the girl Jude was talking about could come down straight away . . . 'That is, if she has had experience of bar work. I haven't got time to train anyone up.'

'Oh, she's had experience of bar work,' said Jude. She and Zofia had agreed that they would not mention her relationship to Tadek. That might make for an uncomfortable atmosphere in the bar of the Crown and Anchor. Nor on the phone did Jude mention the fact that Zofia was Polish.

Of course, it was something that Ted couldn't fail to notice when they were introduced. Behind the ragged beard his face took on a look of suspicion. 'From Poland, you say?'

Zofia Jankowska smiled brightly. 'Yes.'

'Well, you can help out tonight, because I've been let down,' he said grudgingly. 'But I don't know if I'll be able to offer you anything more.'

'Let's see how tonight goes, yes?' said Zofia, unfazed by his less than enthusiastic welcome.

'All right,' he conceded.

'Please, you show me where everything is, and where is written down the costs of the drinks.'

As Ted Crisp turned to get a price-list, he cast a reproachful eye on Jude. She'd put him in a situation where he couldn't really make a scene, and he felt she'd rather pulled a fast one on him. There were already far too many foreigners around the country; he didn't want any of them actually working for him.

Jude, however, went home happy. She felt confident that Zofia would do everything that was required of her. And also from behind the bar of the Crown and Anchor, the girl would be perfectly placed to hear any gossip relating to the death of her brother.

Chapter Twenty-one

Though Carole was not good at lying, that did not mean that she was incapable of deviousness. She woke in the small hours of the Sunday morning, frustrated by their inability to contact Melanie Newton. The only way to the woman was through her husband's mobile phone, and when Jude rang him Giles Newton clearly had not wanted to play ball. There had to be another approach. And by the time, an hour later, Carole drifted back into sleep, she felt confident she had found it.

She reckoned half-past ten was a reasonable hour to call someone on a Sunday, so after a brisk walk on the beach with Gulliver and a skimpy perusal of the *Sunday Telegraph*, she called the number they had been given by the new owner of the Newtons' house.

When Giles answered, she said, 'Good morning. My name is Carole Seddon, formerly of the Home Office.' Which was entirely true, but she hoped the words 'Home Office' would have such a strong effect on the man that he would hardly be aware of the 'formerly'.

'Oh yes?' He sounded puzzled, but not as if he was about to put the phone down. Which was already better than the response Jude had got.

'I'm calling in connection with the death of Tadeusz Jankowski.' Again, not untrue, but hopefully misleading about the level of officialness in her enquiry.

'Who?' He sounded genuinely mystified by the name.

'Tadeusz Jankowski. A young man who died in Fethering some ten days ago.'

'I've never heard of him.'

'There's been a lot of media coverage, on national television and in the papers.'

'I wouldn't have seen it. I've been in Dubai the last three months.'

'Oh?'

'I work in oil exploration. I tend to be away for long periods.'

'Ah. Well, in fact, it was your wife I wanted to contact. Melanie . . . is that right?'

'Yes.'

'She wasn't in Dubai with you?'

'No. So far as I know, she was here in England.'

'So far as you know?'

'Yes, as far as I know,' Giles Newton said testily. 'She may have gone travelling. She went abroad last summer, to Holland and Germany, I believe.'

'You *believe*?' Carole echoed again.

'Yes. Look, Mrs . . . I'm sorry, I didn't get your name.'

'Carole Seddon.'

'Well, Mrs Seddon, as you may well have deduced, the fact is that my wife and I are no longer together.'

'I'm so sorry,' said Carole automatically.

'I'm not sure that I am. At least I'm no longer involved in the messes Melanie gets herself into.'

'Messes?'

But echoing his words was not so fruitful this time. 'Look, Mrs Seddon, what do you want? If it's something to do with my wife, you're talking to the wrong person. What she does is her own business. I no longer have any contact with her.'

'But do you know where she's living?'

'No, I don't. We used to live together in a house in Fedborough, but since we sold that, we've gone our separate ways. And may I emphasize that I have no responsibility for her financial affairs. In fact, after some of the things she got me involved in, I hope I never see her again.'

'What kind of things did she get you involved in?'

The question was over-optimistic. 'Mrs Seddon, if my wife has once again got herself into trouble, I suggest you talk to her rather than to me.'

'Well, that's what I want to do, Mr Newton, but I don't have any means of contacting her.'

'I can give you a mobile number.'

'Is it still current?'

'I've no idea. I've made no attempt to contact Melanie since last November.'

And so it was that Carole got hold of Melanie Newton's phone number. The words 'Home Office' did still command a measure of authority.

She knew she should really share her discovery with Jude, but the temptation to present her neighbour with some kind of dramatic coup was too strong. Carole rang the number. It went straight on to voicemail. No identification of the phone's owner, just a terse, 'Leave a message after the tone.'

A pity, but Carole's gratification outweighed her disappointment. She now had a name and a phone number for Melanie Newton. And she had heard the woman's voice.

Zofia Jankowska stayed in her bedroom late on the Sunday morning, but Jude knew the girl was awake because she could hear music. At about half-past eleven she tapped on the door. 'Just wondered what you'd like to do about lunch?'

The girl was dressed and sitting on her bed. She looked as though she might have been crying, her pigtails once again emphasizing her youth and frailty. After a quick look at her watch, she said, 'No, I don't think I have time for lunch. Ted wants me to do a shift at the pub starting at twelve.'

'So you must have done all right last night.' Jude had been in bed before Zofia returned from the Crown and Anchor.

'I think so. Not that you'd have known it from Ted. He watch me all evening like he thought I was about to steal from the cash register.'

'He'll get used to you. He's naturally distrustful.'

'Distrustful of "foreigners", yes.'

'If he's asked you to come back, he can't be too worried.'

'He does not make it sound like he is happy. He

offer me shift today only because he is very busy at Sunday lunchtime, and his other staff let him down. Still he don't say whether there will be more work for me.'

'You'll win him round.'

Zofia grinned. 'Yes, I think I will.'

'Well, look, would you like me to rustle up something quickly for you before you go?'

'No, I'm OK. I'll just have a cup of coffee.'

'How long's the shift?'

'Ted wants me to work till three.'

'I'll have something nice and hot waiting for you when you come back.'

'Please, Jude, you don't have to do this.'

'I want to.'

'You are very kind to me.'

Jude grinned and there was a silence between them. She became aware of the music. Soft acoustic guitar and a gentle voice in a yearning song, some kind of folk tune in a language Jude could not understand. The sound quality was not professional, as though a primitive microphone had just been placed in front of the singer in an ordinary room.

'This is your brother, Zosia?' The girl nodded and once again tears welled in her eyes. 'He's very good. Is it one of his own songs?'

The girl gave another nod, not daring to speak lest it start her weeping. Jude sat down on the bed and put her ample arms around the thin shoulders. 'We will find out what happened to him. Don't worry. I promise we will.'

'Yes.' Zofia's hazel eyes sought Jude's. 'That will not bring Tadek back, will it?'

'No, I'm afraid it won't. Nothing will do that.'

'But finding out who killed him, is that supposed to bring me . . . closure?'

'I hate the word. American psychological claptrap. But I think knowing how and why Tadek was killed may make it easier for you to live with what has happened. I'm not stupid or simplistic enough to tell you that the grief will ever go away.' Another silence. Jude could feel in the tension of the girl's shoulders how hard she was trying not to cry. 'I'm sorry, not knowing any Polish, I've no idea what this song is about.'

'What does it sound as if it's about?'

Jude listened to the music for a moment. 'Love. Yearning. A love that is doomed.'

'Then Tadek has written a good song, if you can understand the feeling without understanding the words. Yes, it is about a love that is doomed. He wrote songs for all of the women he loved.' She let out a wry little laugh. 'And with every woman he loved, I'm afraid the relationship was doomed.'

'You said most of them were older women?'

'Yes, this song was for one of his music teachers at the university. She was married with two small children.'

'So did they have an affair?'

'No, no. A lot of his relationships were not . . . what do you say? Hands on?'

'He worshipped from afar?'

'That is a good way of saying it, yes. The love was

mostly in his head. He put the women on . . . what was that word you told me . . .?'

'A pedestal.'

'That is correct.'

'What do the words of the song say?'

'I can't translate exactly, but Tadek is saying that, though he and the woman can never be together, this does not stop his love from being beautiful.'

Jude nodded. 'That explains it. Because, although the song is yearning, it doesn't actually sound sad. It isn't a miserable song.'

'No, sometimes I think Tadek likes it that his love affairs never work out. Perhaps he finds it is easier to write about an imagined woman than a real woman.'

'Typical romantic. It's much easier to remain romantic about an imagined woman than a real one.' There was a moment of stillness as Jude listened to the song. 'He was very talented.'

'I don't know. I like his music, but he is my brother. And he writes old-fashioned songs. If he could be successful in the commercial world, that I do not know.'

'Did he write songs about all the women who he . . . put on a pedestal?'

'Yes, I think so. I think it is these hopeless loves that make him able to write songs. Perhaps if he had had a real love affair that really worked, he would not have felt he needed to write songs.'

'So if, and I suppose it's possible, he came to England because of a woman . . . then you might have expected him to have written songs about her?'

'I am sure he would have done. I am sure Tadek

could not have been in England as long as he had without writing songs.'

'And yet there was no evidence of any in the belongings you collected from the police?'

'No, not only his guitar is missing. Also there are no notebooks, no CDs, no tapes.'

'So, if we could find those . . .?'

'If we could find those, where we found them might be a good clue to what happened to him.'

'Yes, and if the songs were written to another older woman here in England, finding that older woman would be another very good clue.'

At that moment Carole rang, to tell Jude the good news that she'd now got a mobile number for Melanie Newton.

Chapter Twenty-two

'The police could do it,' said Carole gloomily.

'Do what?'

'Track down where a person is by their mobile phone. The technology's there. It's just not yet available to amateurs.'

'Just as well for some.'

'Hm?'

'If you could always tell where someone was phoning from on their mobile, it would considerably slow down the activities of certain philanderers. "Oh, darling, I'm in the office," when in fact the speaker is in a Travelodge bedroom – and not unaccompanied. Would spell the death of adultery as we know it.'

Carole couldn't stop her face from looking disapproving at that. Though she was fully aware that adultery existed – indeed, even thrived – something in her background prompted a knee-jerk reaction of censure.

'So we're really no further on,' she continued in gloomy vein.

'How can you say that? We've not only got a name for the woman Tadek spoke to in the betting shop, we've now also got her mobile number. That's a huge advance.'

'Yes, but she's not answering the phone.'

'True.'

'So how on earth are we going to track her down?'

'I could try the internet. If she's in a phonebook, wherever she happens to be . . .'

'But if she only moved out of the Fedborough house in November, she isn't likely to be in a phonebook yet.'

'Maybe not, but there are other things I could try on the laptop. Just googling her name, see if that brings anything up.'

Carole was silent. She was still a bit of a dinosaur when it came to computers. Which she knew was silly, because she had the kind of brain that would respond well to that sort of technology. And indeed, had computers played much of a part in her work at the Home Office, she would have embraced them and developed her skills. But they hadn't, and as always when faced by something new, Carole Seddon didn't want to expose her ignorance.

'Well, you can try,' she said, her voice full of resentful scepticism.

'I will,' Jude responded, her optimism, as ever in such circumstances, even stronger than usual.

Carole looked at her watch. 'Is Zofia at the Crown and Anchor?'

'No, she's having a lie-down. We had some lunch together. She's exhausted. I think the reality of what's happened to her is beginning to hit home.'

'Yes. I'm surprised to hear that Ted would take on a

foreigner. He seems to be getting more right-wing with every passing day.'

'I kind of put him in a position where it was difficult for him to refuse. Give him a few days with Zosia and I bet he'll come round.'

'Zosia? I thought her name was Zofia.'

'Her friends call her Zosia. Apparently most people in Poland have kind of pet names. Like Tadek.'

'Ah.' A sudden thought came to Carole. 'I say, you don't think that what you heard the boy say, that "Fifi" . . . could be a reference to his sister? Zofia?'

'I asked her. No. He'd only ever called her Zosia.'

'Well, maybe "Fifi" means something in Polish?'

'I asked her that too. She said it could be the beginning of certain Polish words, you know, that he was trying to get out, but she couldn't think of any that had any potential relevance.'

'Ah,' said Carole, disappointed.

Her disappointment, however, was short-lived, as Zofia came rushing down the stairs, holding her mobile phone.

'Jude! Oh, hello, Carole. Listen, I have just had a call from Marek!'

'Is he back in Brighton?'

'No, not yet, but they did give him the message to call me when he rang the restaurant.'

'And had he seen Tadek since he'd been in England?'

'Oh yes. They were in contact, but Marek did not know about what happened to my brother.'

'How could he avoid knowing?' asked Carole. 'It's

been all over the national newspapers and on television.'

'Marek has been off travelling with a girlfriend the last week. He does not see any television.'

'When did he last see Tadek?' asked Jude.

'Round Christmas they meet and drink, but – and this is the interesting part – he fix to see Tadek on the day he die.'

'But he didn't see him?'

'No.'

'Where were they going to meet?'

'At Tadek's room in Littlehampton. The door is left open, in case Tadek is not there when Marek arrive. They are both not good with being on time. Marek gets to the room, he waits an hour, two hours, Tadek does not come. Marek goes back to Brighton. He has a shift to be at work.'

'So he was probably in your brother's room,' asked Carole, 'at the time the murder took place?'

'Yes, I think so.'

'Did he say what he did while he was waiting?'

'He sat around, being bored, he tell me. Then he find Tadek has a bottle of vodka, so he drinks some. He wants to play music, but there is nothing there.'

'No CDs, no nothing?'

Zofia shook her head so vigorously that the pigtails slapped against her face. 'No. And that is not like Tadek. Wherever Tadek is, he always has his music.'

'And his guitar.'

'Yes, and his guitar. So someone must have been

into the room to steal those things. And I do not know why anyone would do that.'

Jude pieced her thoughts together slowly. 'You said your brother always wrote songs about the women he was in love with . . .?'

'Yes.'

'So his songs, if he'd recorded them, would probably have identified the woman he was in love with?' Zofia nodded. 'And if that person had something to do with his murder, then she would try to remove anything in his room that might make the connection between them?'

'Certainly.'

'Then I think that must be the explanation. It becomes even more imperative that we find the woman your brother was in love with.'

'We may be closer to that than we were before,' Carole interposed with renewed pride. And she told Zofia of the advances they had made in tracking down Melanie Newton.

'This is good. There must be a way we can contact the woman.'

'I've tried the number a few more times. Still just get the voicemail.'

'But you will keep trying?'

'Yes, of course,' replied Carole, slightly affronted by Zofia's question.

'Mind you,' said Jude, uncharacteristically sceptical, 'we don't know for sure that a woman was the reason why your brother came over here.'

Zofia beamed. 'Yes, this we do know. This is another

thing Marek tell me. When Tadek first contact him, he say that he has come to England because he has met a woman with whom he has fallen in love and she lives in England.'

'He didn't volunteer her name?'

'No. He say no more than that he is madly in love, and that this is different from every other time he has been in love. Mind you,' Zofia concluded sadly, 'that is what he say every time he meet a new woman.'

'And your brother hadn't been to England before last summer? He couldn't have met the woman over here?' asked Carole.

The girl shook her head firmly. 'Tadek has travelled a lot in Europe. But this is the first time he come to England.'

'So we're looking for a woman who has been to Europe relatively recently.'

'Giles Newton told me his wife had been travelling in Europe,' said Carole with some satisfaction.

'Yes, we must talk to her.' Jude had another thought. 'Have the police spoken to Marek? Have they been in touch with him?'

'I ask him this and he tell me no. But the police might not know the connection between my brother and Marek. It is a long time ago they play in Twarz together.'

Carole looked bemused, but then had the name of the band explained to her. 'Well,' she announced, full of Home Office sternness, 'what you must do immediately is ring Marek back and tell him to phone the police in charge of the investigation.'

'But I cannot do that. As Marek was talking to me, the power on his phone run out. The battery needs recharging. And Marek tell me he will not be able to do this recharging until he is back in Brighton.'

'Oh, good,' said Jude.

Later that Sunday the phone rang in Woodside Cottage. Jude answered it, and was not wholly surprised to hear Andy Constant's voice.

'Listen, I'm sorry, I was a bit churlish on Friday.' Though this was undoubtedly true, she made no comment. 'Sorry, I was preoccupied with the show. You know, I get like that when I'm in production. A kind of creative tunnel vision, if you know what I mean.' Oh yes, I know what you mean, thought Jude. You're full of pretentious self-importance. 'Anyway, now the show's finished . . .'

'Did last night go well?'

'Bloody brilliant. Though I say it myself. Wish you'd seen last night, in fact, rather than Friday. It really gelled. The kids made me bloody proud of them, they kind of realized my vision.'

'I thought it was *their* vision that was meant to be realized.'

'Well, yeah, but, you know, *Rumours of Wars* was meant to be, kind of, an ensemble piece. A mutual vision, if you like.'

'OK.'

'But the reason I was ringing was . . . I wonder if my churlishness put you off too much . . .' He paused, but she wasn't about to put him out of his suspense '. . . or if maybe we could meet up again?'

'What are you suggesting?'

'Just a drink. I mean, not some heavy date or anything like that. I just thought, we got on all right, be nice to, you know, chat further about this and that.' His voice was by now so laid-back as almost to be comatose.

'When had you in mind?'

'After work tomorrow? Sixish?'

'I might not be able to do tomorrow.' Caution dictated that she shouldn't sound too available.

'Tuesday then, same sort of time . . .?'

'Might be possible. Where were you thinking of? As you know, I live in Fethering.'

'Yeah. Bit difficult for me to get down there . . . you know, what with my commitments at the college. But we could meet up in the Bull again. At least you know where that is . . .'

'Yes.' The lazy, arrogant, mean bastard, not prepared to make the effort to stray off his own patch, not even inviting her out to dinner.

'So, what do you say? Shall we meet up at the Bull at six on Tuesday?'

Against her better judgement, Jude said, 'Yes.' And once again she tried, without much success, to convince herself she'd only agreed to the meeting to further her murder investigation.

Chapter Twenty-three

'Is that Carole Seddon?'

'Yes.'

'Are you feeling lucky?'

'I'm sorry, who is this speaking?'

'It's Gerald. Gerald Hume.'

'Oh, I'm so sorry. I didn't recognize your voice.' She should have done. Those precise, clipped tones were very distinctive. 'How nice to hear from you.'

'Have you finished the *Times* crossword?'

'I did most of it over breakfast. About three clues left. But please don't—'

'Carole.' He sounded aggrieved by the imputation. 'There is honour among crossword-solvers. I would never give away an answer to a fellow cruciverbalist, unless specifically asked to do so. And if someone did ask me for an answer, I have to confess that I wouldn't regard that person as a proper cruciverbalist.'

'Good. We understand each other.'

'So I revert to my original question. Are you feeling lucky?'

'I don't think I ever feel lucky,' Carole responded with rather dispiriting honesty.

'I was referring to the likelihood of your being successful on the horses today.'

'I don't think I'm ever likely to be successful on the horses.'

'Why not? You have a keen analytical mind.'

'That's as may be. The fact remains that the only way of being successful on the horses is by putting bets on them, and since I never put bets on them, my chances of success in that arena are correspondingly diminished.' Strange, she thought, how whenever she spoke to Gerald, her locutions became as mandarin as his own.

'But if you were to come down to the betting shop and make some investments, your chances would be correspondingly increased.'

'But why should I come down to the betting shop?'

'Because you might enjoy it.'

'I don't think that's a good enough reason.' For anything, her puritan upbringing might have added.

'Then a better reason might be that I have some information regarding the woman about whom you questioned me during our last encounter.'

'Melanie Newton?'

'The very same.'

'I'll be down there straight away.'

He was sitting in his usual seat, in pin-striped suit and tie, his briefcase at his side and ledger open on the table in front of him. 'Ah, Carole,' he said, rising politely to greet her. 'I am so glad you could make it.'

The environment still felt alien to her. The walls covered with newspaper spreads, the banks of television screens, the eternal pinging of the games machines, Chinese waiters chattering in one corner. The only other women in the place were the girl behind the counter and the woman Jude had identified as Pauline.

'Well, what is it you have to tell me?' she asked, rather brusquely.

'Before we do that, I would appreciate your input into the knotty problem of the two-ten at Towcester.'

'Toaster?' Carole echoed in bewilderment, thinking of a kitchen appliance.

'Towcester as in the Northamptonshire town, whose racecourse is set in the Easton Neston Estate. Towcester being one of those English place names which so charmingly befuddle foreign visitors. In the same way that Leominster and Bicester can confuse the unwary. And indeed with British surnames there are many whose pronunciation is similarly at odds with their spelling. One need only mention "Chumley" spelt "Cholmondley", "Dee-ell" spelt "Dalziel" and "Fanshaw" spelt "Fetherstonehaugh" . . . though there is further confusion with the last, because some owners of that surname do insist on pronouncing it "Feather-stone-haugh".'

Carole couldn't help smiling. 'Yes, Gerald, I think I've got your point.'

'I am delighted to hear it. So, the two-ten at Towcester . . . a treat for lovers of alliteration everywhere.'

'I'd really rather you'd just told me—'

He raised a hand that was at once deferential and commanding. 'After the two-ten at Towcester.' He held out a copy of *The Times*, folded back to show the relevant runners and riders. 'Because of the recent frost, the going will be quite hard, which factor I am sure will affect your assessment of the race, Carole.'

'Gerald, I know nothing about horse racing.'

'Perhaps you don't have a great deal of education in the matter of horse racing, but you do have an instinct for the sport.'

'I don't. It doesn't interest me.'

'Carole, would you do me the kindness of approaching this race as if it were a crossword puzzle?'

'I would, if a horse race had any features in common with a crossword puzzle.'

'It has many. In a horse race there are many variables, but only one answer.'

'Yes, but—'

'And one reaches that answer by a process of deduction and elimination.'

She couldn't help being intrigued as well as amused. 'Could you spell that out to me a little?'

'Very well.' He pointed down to the list of runners. 'Here we have twelve horses, only one of whom is going to win the race.'

'Yes.'

'So, before we commence on the process of deduction, let us deploy our skills of elimination.'

'Remove from consideration the ones that have no chance?'

'Exactly. And to do this we look at the recent form.'

'Where is that?'

'In front of the horse's name. The position in which they finished in their previous races. You see, that list of numbers.'

'So that one with "4–6–5–6–0" . . .?'

'In its last race it was unplaced – that's the nought. In the previous one it came sixth, the one before that fifth, the one before that sixth again, the one before that fourth.'

'Not much of a prospect then?'

'No.'

'And what about this one? This has got letters too. Look . . .' She spelt them out. '"0-F-F-P-0-P".'

'That, Carole, is an even worse prospect. The zeros, as you know, mean that the horse was unplaced. And "F" stands for "fell".'

'The horse fell?'

'Yes. And "P" means "pulled up".'

'Sorry, I don't know what that means.'

'The horse was doing so badly that the jockey pulled it up. In other words, it didn't complete the course.'

'Ah. So in the form, letters are bad news?'

'Yes. "0FFP0P" . . .' He spoke the word as an acronym '. . . is not the horse to back. And there's another letter to watch out for, which is "U".'

'What does that mean?'

'"Unseated rider".'

'Again bad news?'

'Very.'

'So this one, Conjuror's Rabbit, whose form is "33211", is a much better bet.'

'Which is why it's the odds-on favourite. Look, it's down to thirteen to eight on.'

'All right, well, looking at the form, I would say there are seven of these horses that can be ruled out completely.'

'Excellent. You're catching on to the idea.'

'In fact, I'd say that Conjuror's Rabbit is definitely going to win.'

'Maybe.'

'Why maybe? It's obvious, Gerald. Look at the form.'

'Ah, but because of that form, because of those two recent wins in particular, the handicapper is making the horse carry more weight.'

'What, a heavier jockey?'

'More likely weights put into the saddle.'

'That seems rather a dirty trick. It's punishing success, isn't it? A horse wins and immediately something's done to make it less likely to win next time.'

'That's how it works, yes. But if one didn't have some compensatory system of that kind, the same horses would win all the time.'

'Well, that'd be fairer.'

'It might be fairer, but it would remove the excitement from the racing. The thrill of the unpredictable.'

'Generally speaking, I don't find unpredictability thrilling.'

'Oh, Carole, I'm sure you do.'

'I don't. So, anyway, this poor Conjuror's Rabbit is

now carrying too much weight to have a chance of winning?'

'No, no, it has a very good chance of winning. That's why it's favourite. And the ground's in its favour.'

'I'm sorry?'

'Back to what I was saying about the going. The overnight frost has made the ground hard, so it's easier for a heavy horse to move over it. If it were muddy, the weight would make a bigger difference.'

'Oh. I see what you mean about variables. Having to think not just about the horse's recent form, but also the weight it's carrying, not to mention the weather.'

Gerald Hume chuckled. 'And that's just the start of it. There's also to be considered the horse's breeding, the length of the race, which jockey's up on him, the horse's state of health, how well the trainer's yard is currently doing . . . I could go on.'

'I think I get the point. But I'm not sure that your crossword analogy is quite valid. There the only real variables are the number of words in the English language.'

'Yes, but you narrow those down in the same way. No, it can't be this word because the second letter's got to be an "m". No, it can't be that one, because the seventh letter isn't a "j". And so you go on till you reach the one, inevitable solution.'

Carole smiled at her new friend. 'I can see why it appeals to you, Gerald. And I can see why photography appeals too.'

'Ah, do you want me to start on the variables that

have to be considered when taking the perfect photograph? There's the shutter speed, the light, the—'

She held her hand up to stem the anticipated deluge. 'No need. I'll take your word for it.'

'So, after all that exegesis of the form book, it is now two eight and fifty-three seconds. Are you going to make an investment on the two-ten at Towcester?'

'Well, I'm sure Conjuror's Rabbit is going to win.'

'And are you going to put your money where your mouth is?'

'Why not?' She opened her handbag, took out her purse and held up a two-pound piece.

'Last of the big spenders,' said Gerald Hume.

'Would you mind putting it on for me when you put your bet on?'

'Very well.' He went to the counter. Carole tried not to look self-conscious. She needn't have worried. Nobody was interested in what she looked like.

'So,' she asked, as Gerald returned, 'have you done the favourite too?'

'No.'

'So what have you done?'

'Ssh. They're under orders. I'll tell you when the race is over.'

They watched, along with the rest of the crowd, including Pauline, the Chinese waiters and Wes and Vic. The decorators were noisy with 'Go on, my son!'s. Conjuror's Rabbit showed his class from the start, easing himself into third early on and holding that position until they turned into the straight with two fences to jump. Finding another gear, he moved smoothly forward to overtake the two ahead of him and sailed over the penultimate obstacle. Then, six lengths ahead, with the race at his mercy, he approached the last. Carole began to get a distant inkling of what the attraction of gambling might be about.

But the calculation of her modest winnings was interrupted. Suddenly Conjuror's Rabbit seemed to break his stride. He crashed into the top of the last fence, stumbled on landing and neatly deposited his jockey on to the ground. The second horse, a twenty-to-one outsider called Draggle Tail, clumsily crossed the last fence and had enough momentum to reach the winning post first.

'Well, that's stupid,' said Carole. 'You can't apply any logic to something like that. What a very unsatisfactory exercise – two pounds straight down the drain.'

'Not unsatisfactory for everyone,' said Gerald slyly.

'What do you mean?'

'I had a fiver on Draggle Tail.'

'What? But why? What possible logic could there be in that? No, I'm afraid your analogy with crosswords is completely destroyed by what's just happened.'

'No, it isn't.'

'How so?'

'I backed Draggle Tail because "Draggle" is, all but for one letter, an anagram of "Gerald".'

'And you call that logic? So much for all your talk of "mathematical probabilities".'

Carole was still fuming when Gerald Hume returned from the counter with his winnings. 'Having dragged me down here,' she said sniffily, 'to squander my hard-earned pension, you will now perhaps have the goodness to give me the information that you have about the betting shop's mystery woman.'

'Oh yes,' he said, with a twinkle. 'That would only be fair, wouldn't it?' He sat down on a blue plastic seat beside her. 'The woman you refer to is Melanie Newton, who has an address in Fedborough.'

'Yes, except that she has moved from that address, and has apparently split up with her husband and could be anywhere.'

'So you've no other means of contacting her?'

'I got a mobile number for her, but she doesn't answer it.'

'Have you left a message?'

'No. I don't want to put her off. If she thinks we're on the trail, that might be a prompt for her to make herself scarce.'

'Yes. Assuming she has something to hide. Which is rather a big assumption. You have no real reason to think Melanie Newton is involved with wrong-doing of any kind.'

'No,' Carole agreed. Though in her mind the scale of Melanie Newton's wrong-doing had been increasing disproportionately. 'The trouble is, with only a mobile number as a means of contact, she could be anywhere in the world.'

'Well, Carole, I am glad to be able to say that I can narrow the focus down a bit from the whole world.'

'I'm glad to hear that.'

'Melanie Newton is in Fethering – or at least was in Fethering yesterday.'

'How do you know?'

'Because I saw her.'

'Not in here? Is the betting shop open on Sundays?'

'It is, but it wasn't in here that I saw her. As I believe I mentioned at our first meeting, I live in River Road. And I am fortunate in that I live in one of the houses with a sea view. For this reason, to maximize that view, my sitting room is upstairs, and I was sitting there yesterday afternoon setting up some shots with my camera. I never tire of taking pictures of the view from my window at different times of year.

'While I was engaged in this activity, I noticed hurrying towards me from the direction of the river a woman whom I thought I recognized as Melanie Newton. She looked somewhat unkempt, and I could not be sure that it was her until she was virtually opposite my house. But when I saw her that close, there was no doubt. Thinking of your eagerness to identify her, I regretted that I had not had the presence of mind to take a picture of her. But still, the chance was gone, so I returned to my own photography.'

He paused, relishing the hold he had over her attention. Carole had to use great control not to ask what happened next.

'Well,' Gerald Hume continued in his own time, 'luck was on my side . . . as I must say it appears to have been this afternoon with the triumph of Draggle Tail . . !' Carole could have done without such excursions in his narrative, but again kept her calm and her silence. 'Because a mere quarter of an hour later, I saw Melanie Newton returning the way she had come, this time bearing two loaded carrier bags from Allinstore, which I'm sure you know to be the—'

This time Carole cracked. 'I know what Allinstore is!'

She spoke with such vehemence that Gerald Hume picked up speed. 'Anyway, I saw her coming towards me, I had time, and the outcome is: that I took a photograph of her.'

'Do you . . .?' she asked tentatively.

'Of course I do.' Gerald Hume reached down for his briefcase, lifted it up on to the table and opened it. He took out an envelope containing a colour print.

Carole had not seen the woman before. But at least she now knew what Melanie Newton looked like.

Chapter Twenty-four

'But surely, Jude, it suggests that she lives down by the river.'

'It could do.'

Carole found herself infuriated by her neighbour's reaction. 'It must do. Look, she walks up River Road to the High Street, does her shopping in Allinstore, then walks back down towards the river. She must live down there.'

'I agree, she might do, but we don't know that for certain. She could have just parked her car down by the river.'

'Why would she do that? She could have parked a lot nearer to Allinstore. And Gerald said she was weighed down by two quite heavy bags. She wouldn't have done that, unless she lived down by the river. If you've got heavy bags, you take the shortest route between where you've been shopping and where you want to get to.'

'Yes, usually.'

'Jude, why are you being like this? Normally I'm the one who's the wet blanket on everything.'

'I just thought I'd see what it felt like.'

'Oh, now you're being tiresome.'

'No, I'm not. I'm playing devil's advocate.'

'Well, it isn't a role that suits you,' said Carole grumpily and flopped back on one of Jude's draped sofas. She felt something hard through the bedspread that covered it, and pulled out a plastic potato masher.

'Oh, I wondered where that had got to,' said Jude.

Which didn't improve Carole's mood. As she looked round the soft curves of the Woodside Cottage sitting room, she longed for the antiseptic right angles of High Tor. But even as she had the thought, she knew that Jude's home had a warmth and welcome hers would never achieve.

'I think you're feeling grumpy because you're still not over that flu.'

'I am quite over that flu, thank you very much. And I am not feeling grumpy,' said Carole grumpily.

'Look, I agree with you that it is most likely that Melanie Newton lives somewhere down by the river.'

'She must do, because if she lived further along, you know, near Marine Villas, that area, then her quickest route to Allinstore wouldn't be along River Road.'

'Carole, I've said I agree with you. The question is how we find out exactly where she lives.'

Carole looked shame-faced, 'I did sort of . . . lurk about a bit down there this afternoon, just to see if there was any sign of her.'

'"Lurk about"?' Jude was intrigued and amused by the image. 'Were you in disguise?'

'Don't be silly, of course I wasn't. I just . . . well,

I took Gulliver down by the river for his walk. And I . . . made the walk rather longer and slower than I normally would. You know, I let Gulliver sniff at anything along the towpath that he wanted to. And then later . . .'

'What did you do later, Carole?' asked Jude, trying to keep the smile off her face.

'I drove down in the Renault and . . . parked there for a while.'

'You mean you did a "stake-out"?'

'I don't think there's any need to call it that, but I did kind of . . . well, look out to see who was coming and going.'

'How long did you stay there?'

'Till it got dark. Then I came back home.'

'Good. Because I wouldn't like to think of you being arrested for kerb-crawling.'

'Jude, I don't know why you're being so childish this evening.'

'No, nor do I. Sorry.'

'You may have lost interest in this murder investigation, but I haven't.'

'Nor have I. I promise, I promise.'

'Good.' Carole sighed. 'Oh, it's so frustrating! We've got this woman's name, we've got her mobile number, we know what she looks like, we have strong reason to believe she lives in Fethering, but we can't find her.'

'I'm sure, if we worked out the right thing to say, we could leave a message on her mobile that would make her ring us back.'

'What? "Hello, we're from the *Reader's Digest* and

we're ringing to tell you you've won a quarter of a million pounds in our prize draw."'

'No, it's got to be something she'll believe. Nobody believes it when the *Reader's Digest* says they're going to win a quarter of a million pounds – they know they're just being sold some rubbish CD. Maybe, if we just leave a message saying it's in connection with the death of Tadeusz Jankowski . . .?'

'If Melanie Newton's got anything to do with that, then there's nothing that would frighten her off quicker.'

'No, I take your point. Well, we can ask around in Fethering, about new people who've just moved in.'

'Let's be logical about it, Jude. If Melanie Newton only moved out of the Fedborough house in November and she moved into a new house of her own, surely her husband would have known about that. He'd have to, unless she's got a lot of money of her own, which he implied she hadn't. So that probably means she's currently renting. We don't have an in with any of the local estate agents, do we?'

'Well, perhaps we do. I was given a lift back here on Friday by Ewan Urquhart. Yes, I could give them a call.'

'I don't think estate agents are meant to give out details of their clients, but I suppose he might respond to your "feminine wiles".' Carole knew that Jude had these. She suspected that she herself didn't.

'I'll see how I go. And I think that's probably all we can do at the moment. Are you going to continue your stake-out of the towpath of the River Fether tomorrow, Carole?'

'No, of course I'm not.'

'Well, Zosia should be able to contact Tadek's friend Marek tomorrow. I'm pretty sure it was Tuesday he was due back. Let's hope he knows something.'

The Polish girl did indeed speak to her brother's friend the following morning. He was working in a café/bar/restaurant in Hove. His shift started at twelve, but if they could be there by eleven, he could spare time for them. He wanted to talk to Zofia; he still hadn't taken in the news of his friend's death.

'If we leave Brighton by twelve, can we be back in Fethering by one o'clock?' she had asked Jude.

'Certainly if we go by car. I'm sure Carole would be happy to drive us. But why do you need to be back by one?'

The girl had grinned. 'Ted wants me to do another shift.'

'Ah, coming round to the idea of employing *foreigners*, is he?'

'You would not think so, the way he speak. It is only short term, he tell me, just till he gets his proper staff back. He has not said anything yet that he is pleased with me, with how I work for him.'

'The fact that he keeps asking you back means he must be.'

'But he do not say so.'

'God, Ted can sometimes be so curmudgeonly.'

'I'm sorry? I do not know this word.'

'I'm not surprised. Well, it means . . .' Jude had been

perplexed as to how to explain it. 'It means the way it sounds, really. Think of Ted, think of any other grumpy old man and yes, you know what curmudgeonly means.'

'Oh, thank you.'

That morning Jude put into practice a plan that she had been nursing for a while. Remembering the circular letter she'd had from Urquhart & Pease, she rang the office and asked to have her home valued. She spoke to Hamish Urquhart, who sounded surprisingly efficient, and they made an appointment for him to come to the house on the Thursday morning at ten. Jude thought, with the young man actually on her premises, she could easily question him about rentals in the area. And maybe get a lead to Melanie Newton.

Carole readily agreed to take on the role of driving to Hove, because that meant she would be part of the next stage of the investigation. And so at a quarter to ten on the Tuesday morning (Carole always left more time than was needed and she knew that parking in the Brighton conurbation was notoriously hard to find) the three women set off in her immaculate Renault. As it turned out, they found an empty meter easily and so reached their destination nearer half-past ten than eleven.

The place where Marek Wisniewski worked was in Church Road, Hove, which ran parallel to and up the hill from the sea front. Virtually every business there seemed to be a restaurant of one ethnicity or another. Hove had always had the image of being more staid and geriatric than its louche neighbour Brighton, but that was changing and its plethora of restaurants and clubs suggested that young people could thrive there too.

The ethnicity of Marek's place of work had nothing to do with Poland. A glance at the menu suggested a more Mediterranean flavour, a mix of Italian, Greek and Turkish cuisine. But it was very much open for business at that hour in the morning – and indeed had been since seven-thirty – serving a variety of breakfasts and coffees to a predominantly youthful clientele, none of whom seemed in a great hurry to leave their conversation and newspapers to engage in the world of work. It felt a bit *young* to Carole, the kind of place she might have thought twice about entering on her own; she was glad to have Jude and Zofia with her.

The girl ordered for them, because she recognized the waitress also to be Polish and had a quick incomprehensible exchange with her. She would have a latte, Jude a cappuccino and Carole a 'just ordinary coffee, black, thank you'. Zofia also established from the waitress that Marek was not in yet. Another exchange in Polish followed, which left both the girls laughing.

'She says,' Zofia explained, 'it is good we fix to meet Marek at eleven. That means he will be in time for his twelve o'clock shift. He is not a good . . . what do you call it?'

'Time-keeper?' suggested Jude.

'Yes, that is it. So I know Marek has not changed. Always when Twarz are going to play some place, the other ones in the band are waiting for Marek.'

He finally put in an appearance round twenty past eleven. When he took off his anorak, he was wearing black trousers and a black shirt with the logo of the café embroidered on its short sleeves. Tall with a shaven head and mischievous blue eyes, Marek Wisniewski was greeted by Zofia with a kiss, immediately followed by what was clearly a dressing-down. Neither Carole nor Jude could understand a word of it, but the tone of voice and the body language made the nature of what the girl said absolutely clear.

When she had finished, Marek looked sheepish but not really cowed. 'I tell him,' said Zofia, 'it is bad to not be good time-keeper. It is bad for the image of Polish people here in England. Already people worry about us taking jobs. They call us "spongers". We must show we are efficient and hard workers, so people cannot criticize us for that.'

Then Marek, completely unsubdued by his carpeting, was introduced to Carole and Jude. He smiled, shook hands and greeted them in English which was adequate, though his accent was much thicker than Zofia's. He said how desolated he had been to hear of Tadek's death. 'He was good friend of me. I not really good musician, but he support me when I in band with him.'

Zofia had got out her blue notebook and was poised to record any information they got from Marek. Carole, too, was eager to get on with the business of investigation. 'Did you see a lot of Tadek since he came to England?' she asked.

'A few times I see him. We are both busy with work. It is not always easy to meet. But we stay in touch . . . messages, texts on phone.'

'That's a thought,' said Jude. 'What happened to

Tadek's mobile phone? It wasn't among the possessions that the police gave you, was it, Zosia?'

The girl shook her head. 'Perhaps the police keep it still? To check the phone calls my brother make?'

'I should think that's quite likely,' said Carole.

'Or perhaps,' suggested Marek, 'the phone is taken from his room by the person who take his other things.'

'You're certain that other things were taken from his room?'

'Yes. I go there to meet with Tadek at end of December. His room is like his room always is in Warsaw. Cassettes, CDs all over the place. And of course his guitar. When I go there two weeks ago none of these things is there.'

'So it does sound like someone cleaned them out,' said Jude.

'To avoid incriminating themselves,' added Carole. Then she fixed the focus of her pale blue eyes on the young Pole. 'Zofia told us that you had said her brother definitely came over here because of a woman.'

'This is what he tell me, yes. With Tadek it is always a woman.' He and the girl exchanged wistful grins. 'Always it is the big romance.'

'Which is not how you treat women, Marek,' said Zofia knowingly.

He grinned with shamefaced cockiness. 'No, with me it is always the big sex.'

'So this girl you have just been away with for a week . . .?'

'It is very good, Zosia. Good sex.' He grinned again. 'Now I think over. Time to move on.'

'You do not change, Marek.'

'I hope not. I like women very much, but not one woman,' he explained for the benefit of Carole and Jude.

Carole didn't think tales of his philandering were really germane to the current discussion. 'This woman,' she said, firmly redirecting the conversation, 'did you know her name?'

'Tadek do not tell me. But he say she is very beautiful, he has never felt like this before, she is the one.' Again he and Zofia exchanged rueful smiles.

'Did he say where he'd met her?'

'Yes. It was at a music festival last summer. In Leipzig.'

'Ah,' said Jude, pleased to have at least one of her conjectures confirmed. Zofia wrote down the new fact in her notebook.

'Did he say whether the woman was older or younger than him?' asked Carole.

'No, he do not say.' Marek looked at Zofia for endorsement as he went on. 'But with Tadek it is always older woman, no?'

The girl nodded. 'Well,' said Carole, 'there seems a strong likelihood that it was this woman . . . this older woman who cleared out his room of all his music stuff.'

The boy shrugged. 'Perhaps. Do you know who this woman is?'

'We may do.' But Jude didn't give any more information about Melanie Newton.

'I think,' said Zofia, 'that Tadek would have written songs for this woman.'

'Oh yes,' Marek agreed. 'Always if he is in love, he write songs.'

'But he didn't play you any?' asked Jude.

'No. Tadek knows I not very good with music. Only a drummer. When he was asked about the line-up for his band, he always say old joke: "Three musicians and a drummer." I join Twarz because I like other people, not because I have musical talent. Which is why,' he added philosophically, 'the others ask me to leave. So no, Tadek does not play me any songs. If he want to discuss songs, it is always with Pavel.'

'I told you about him, Jude,' said Zofia. Then she explained for Carole's benefit, 'Pavel is the other songwriter in the band. Very close friend of my brother. They write songs together sometimes. If Tadek write a song, he probably show it to Pavel.'

'What, he'd post a copy to him?' asked Carole.

She had turned on her the young person's stare that is reserved for Luddites and other dinosaurs. 'No, he'd email the MP3.'

'Oh. Right,' Carole responded, as though she had a clue what was being said.

'Why didn't I think of that before?' exclaimed Zofia.

'You speak to Pavel since Tadek die?' asked Marek.

'No, he is playing music in Krakow. But I will email him, ask if he has received anything from Tadek. If my brother had written new songs, I am sure he would have sent them to Pavel.'

'Aren't the police likely to have been in touch with him?' asked Jude. 'They would know the connection between the two of them.'

'Perhaps. The police in Poland maybe are following this up.'

'Speaking of the police,' said Carole severely. 'I think you, Marek, should be in touch with them.'

'Oh?' Immediately he looked defensive, guilty even.

'The fact that you had been in Tadek's room on the afternoon he was killed is something of which they should be informed,' she went on in her best Home Office manner.

'You think so?' the young man pleaded.

'Certainly. It's your duty to do it. You will, won't you?'

'Yes,' said Marek wretchedly.

As she drove the Renault demurely along the coast road towards Fethering, Carole announced, 'I'm very glad that Marek's going to tell the police what he knows. It may be relevant to their enquiries.'

'Yes,' said Zofia. 'I do not think he will do it, though.'

'What?'

'Marek does not want dealings with the police.'

'Why? Is there something wrong with his immigration status?'

'No. He just does not want dealings with the police.'

'You mean you don't think he will get in touch with them?'

'No. I am sure he won't.'

Carole snorted with exasperation. Jude didn't say anything, but she was delighted.

Chapter Twenty-five

Before she started her shift at the Crown and Anchor, Zofia just had time to send an email to Pavel from the Woodside Cottage laptop. She didn't know when she was likely to get a response. It would depend on how long he stayed in Krakow.

Jude's afternoon was committed to a client whose whiplash injuries after a car accident needed massage and healing. Carole said she was going to spend a quiet few hours reading. But in fact she had other plans.

Jude knew she had other plans. Why else would Carole have asked to borrow her mobile? But, as she handed it across, she didn't ask for any explanation.

The *Times* crossword was there as an ostensible reason for sitting in the Renault by the towpath at the end of River Road, but Carole had to admit she felt cold. Whenever she'd seen cops doing a stake-out on television, they seemed to have supplied themselves with bottomless hipflasks and a copious supply of cigarettes, and now she could understand why. Surveillance was very boring and unrewarding work.

Nor did her distracted concentration allow her to make much headway on the crossword. She knew

Tuesday's could sometimes be tricky, but her mind that afternoon was not dissecting and analysing words as it should have been. A few clues made sense, and she got them so quickly that she suspected the others were equally easy. But her brain couldn't see through the verbal obfuscation to the patent truth. She knew if she failed to complete the puzzle, the answers in the next morning's paper would make her kick herself for her ineptitude.

There was a phone number that could be rung to get answers to the day's crossword, but Carole Seddon would never resort to that. For a start, calls were priced at the exorbitant rate of seventy-five pence per minute, and then again . . . well, it just wasn't the sort of thing she'd do. She felt sure that Gerald Hume would be as much of a purist in such matters as she was.

The road by the River Fether was not busy on a chilly February afternoon. The few people out walking their dogs were what Carole thought of dismissively as 'pensioners' (until she realized that she and Gulliver would also fit the description). Between half-past three and four a few schoolchildren, defiantly coatless in the cold weather, returned to their homes. But as the shadows of the encroaching evening closed together and lights came on in the houses before their curtains were closed, the area was deserted.

It was nearly five o'clock and Carole could hardly even see the crossword, though she knew that two corners of clues remained intractable. There was a fifteen-letter word straight down the middle of the grid. She knew if she could get that, all the other answers would fall into place. She also knew that the solution was quite easy, but she could not for the life of her see what it was.

Stuff this for a game of soldiers, thought Carole. It was not an expression that she would ever have spoken out loud, but it was one she had learnt from her father and cherished. Time to get back to High Tor.

Before she turned the key in the ignition, however, movement from one of the houses along the road drew her attention. A woman was coming out of the front door. She moved, in a manner which to Carole's imagination looked furtive, towards the turning into River Road. In the deepening gloom, Carole couldn't make out the woman's face well, nor could she see Gerald Hume's photograph clearly enough to make comparisons. But the stranger was about the right age.

When the woman was close to her, Carole put the next part of her plan into action. On Jude's phone she keyed in the number given her by Giles Newton, and pressed the 'call' button.

The woman reacted. She didn't answer the phone, but she definitely reacted to its ringing.

She was Melanie Newton.

Chapter Twenty-six

Jude felt empowered after her session with the whiplash sufferer. There were times when her healing really worked and, though she might be drained by the transfer of energy entailed, she felt the peace of knowing she had actually done someone some good.

But her contentment was not total. There was something else that was making her feel bad. Her agreement to meet Andy Constant at the Bull that evening. She tried to convince herself that she'd only made the arrangement because he might be able to give her some useful information about the murder case, but she knew that was casuistry. She was going to see Andy Constant because she wanted to see him. And she knew he was seriously bad news.

Jude rather despised herself for the aromatic bath she took before her excursion. Also for the care she took with what she wore.

Andy Constant was an arrogant, selfish boor. He hadn't even had the decency to invite her on a proper date, just a drink in a location which involved her in either a train journey and a long walk or an expensive cab ride. He didn't deserve her attention.

But she still wanted to see him. Some instincts were stronger than logic.

Carole really did feel like something out of a television cop show. She waited till Melanie Newton was halfway up River Road before driving the Renault slowly along and parking again a little behind her. Then, when her quarry turned right into the High Street, she edged the car further up till she could just see round the corner. Melanie Newton's errand appeared to be the same as when Gerald Hume had seen her. She disappeared into Allinstore.

While the woman was in the shop, Carole turned the Renault round and parked at the top of River Road, facing towards the Fether. Sure enough, Melanie Newton soon passed by, carrying two loaded carrier bags, and retraced her steps. Carole waited till the woman was about to turn at the end of River Road and then drove the Renault back to where she had originally been parked. She was just in time to see Melanie Newton use a key to let herself into the house whence she had emerged some ten minutes earlier.

Carole hadn't really planned her next step. Having found where the woman lived was perhaps achievement enough for that afternoon, but not for the first time she wanted to present Jude with a more tangible advance in their investigation. Also she recalled that Jude had a client that afternoon and was then going out somewhere for the evening. Either Carole would have to wait till the following morning to tell her neighbour of their quarry's whereabouts, or she should try to consolidate her achievement straight away. She got out of the car.

It had felt cold inside, but that was as nothing compared to the freezing blast that hit her when she emerged. That cold evening in Fethering worries about global warming seemed seriously exaggerated.

She crossed resolutely to the house into which her suspect had disappeared. It was a semi, probably with three bedrooms. Before she had time for second thoughts, Carole rang the doorbell. A moment passed before it opened, and she found herself face to face with a young teenage girl in school uniform.

'Good afternoon, I'm looking for Melanie Newton.'

'She's in her room at the top of the house.'

'Could I see her?'

The response was one of those 'no skin off my nose' shrugs which only teenage girls can really do properly. After it, the shrugger seemed to lose interest in the proceedings and disappeared into the kitchen from which she'd presumably come.

Carole closed the front door behind her, and set off up the stairs. She found herself on a landing with four doors leading off, presumably to three bedrooms and a bathroom. But the girl had said 'the top of the house'. That must mean up the uncarpeted wooden staircase which led up to what must be a loft conversion.

Carole went on up. The final step at the top of the flight was not much wider than the others. She stood there for a moment, gathering her thoughts, and then knocked on the door.

There was a gasp from inside, then silence. She knocked again. This time she heard movement from the room, footsteps approaching, and the door was opened a fraction. In the narrow gap Carole could see the frightened face of the woman Gerald Hume had photographed.

'Melanie Newton?' Carole asked, although she knew the answer.

'How did you find me?' The voice was cultured but taut almost to breaking point. 'Who let you in?'

'A girl in school uniform.'

'She's not supposed to. The fact that I'm renting this room is supposed to be a secret. Her mother swore they wouldn't let anyone in.'

'Well, she let me in.'

'Who are you?'

'My name's Carole Seddon.'

'And which one of them do you come from? Who do you represent?'

Carole couldn't really supply an answer to that rather strange question, so she just said, 'I want to talk to you about Tadeusz Jankowski.'

The woman's reaction was mixed. Her face still showed fear and suspicion, but there was also something in it that looked like relief.

Andy Constant wasn't there when Jude arrived in the Bull. It was loud with University of Clincham students, taking advantage of the 'Happy Hour' offers and, in the time-honoured student fashion, converting their grants into alcohol. They looked very young, and completely harmless.

She was annoyed with herself for ordering a pint of Stella for Andy along with her glass of Chardonnay, but given the scrum at the bar it was once again the sensible thing to do. Sitting down at a table for two, she wondered again why the hell she was there. She had no illusions about the kind of man Andy Constant was, and she ought to be too old to go deliberately looking for trouble. And yet there she was.

Jude didn't recognize any of the students, but she saw again the poster for Magic Dragon with the blurred photograph of Sophia Urquhart. It reminded her that she wanted to ask the girl about Joan, the other Drama Studies student, and Joan's relationship with Andy Constant.

When he came in, though, sweeping back his long grey hair, she couldn't curb a little kick of excitement. It wasn't just his similarity to Laurence Hawker that got to her; Andy Constant affected her viscerally in a way that few men had. And the men who did trigger that response had always been bad news. Jude made a pact with herself to be extremely sensible that evening. No joining him in a guided tour of the Drama Studio.

He brushed his lips against her cheek, and slumped down into the chair opposite. He reached for the pint of Stella and took a long swig. 'God, that's good,' he said as he put the glass down. No thanks for the drink, just 'God, that's good.'

'Ooh, am I knackered?' he continued. He was one of those men, Jude felt sure, who were always more tired than anyone else, the implication being that they put so much more energy into their creative lives than mere mortals could even contemplate.

'What have you been doing – lecturing?'

'Why should I be doing that?'

'I thought that was your job description. When you first introduced yourself, you said you were a lecturer.'

'Yes, but in my discipline that doesn't mean giving many lectures. In Drama it's more role-playing, work-shopping, you know the kind of thing.'

'Which is what you've been doing today?'

'Kind of.' He said it in a way that implied she wasn't bright enough to understand a fuller explanation. 'The trouble is,' he went on, 'these kids are full of ideas, but their ideas are all so derivative. Based on the latest movies, based on what they've seen on television. It's a real effort trying to get them to think outside the box.'

'And that's what you've been doing with them today?'

'Sure.' He took another long draught of lager. 'Tough, tough, tough.'

'Was Joan one of your group?'

'Who?' he asked. But she felt sure he knew who she meant.

Jude spelt it out for him. 'The Joan whom Sophia Urquhart mentioned on Friday.'

'Ah, that Joan.' The idea seemed to amuse him. 'Yes, Joan was in the group.'

'But had to go home?'

'What do you mean?'

'When we were in here last Friday, Sophia Urquhart

241

apologized that Joan couldn't go back with you, she had to get a lift back with her father.'

Andy Constant's brow wrinkled with aggrieved innocence. 'I'm sorry, I don't know what you're talking about.'

'I am suggesting that there is some kind of relationship between you and this Joan.'

'Hey, whoa, whoa,' he said sardonically. 'Aren't we getting a bit ahead of ourselves here? We're meeting for a drink for only the second time, and already you're telling me who I should and shouldn't see.'

'I'm not doing that, Andy. I'm just trying to clarify your personal situation. You told me about your defunct marriage . . . I assume that still is defunct?'

'Dead as a dodo. Has been for years.'

'Right, so that's the marriage dealt with. I was wondering if you were going to tell me about Joan too.'

'Nothing to tell.' He shrugged ingenuously. 'You have just got the wrong end of the stick in a very major way, Jude. Apart from anything else, it would be totally inappropriate for someone in my position to be messing about with one of my students. Maybe it's a long time since you've been in an educational establishment, but let me tell you, these days they're very hot on what's appropriate and what's inappropriate behaviour. And me having anything to do with a student would be a very big no-no.'

'I know what I heard on Friday,' Jude insisted.

'No. You know what you *think* you heard on Friday. Different matter altogether.'

He sounded so convincing that for a moment Jude

almost believed him. Perhaps she had misheard, or misinterpreted what she heard. She was aware of his hooded eyes lazily watching her, appraising, wondering what she'd do next. And she was aware of the power those eyes could exert over her.

But she resisted them. 'I think you're lying,' she said.

He spread his hands wide in a gesture of harmless self-depreciation. 'Do I look like a liar?'

'Oh yes. And if you're prepared to lie to me about this Joan, then it's quite possible you lied to me about Tadeusz Jankowski.'

'About who? Ah, the Pole. The one you came enquiring about. The one without whose existence we wouldn't have met.'

'Yes. Can I ask you again whether you know of any connection between him and Clincham College?'

'You can, my sweet Jude,' he said, 'but I'm afraid you'll get the same answer you got before.' A new idea seemed to come to him. 'Though just a minute . . . I have thought of some other admission files we can check . . . then we'll know if he ever did make any application to the college.'

'Where are the files?'

'Over there.' He jerked his head towards the university campus. 'Do you want to come with me and look through them, Jude?'

She should at least have thought about her answer, but immediately, instinctively, she said 'Yes.'

Chapter Twenty-seven

The room into which Carole was ushered was indeed a loft conversion. One wall was a large gable window, which must have provided a wonderful view over the River Fether to the English Channel beyond. But the glass was covered by thick curtains and the stuffiness in the room suggested they had been closed for most of the day.

There was very little light, only what spilled from an Anglepoise whose shade had been pushed down low to a table on which stood an open laptop, its screen idle. But Carole could see enough to recognize that the room was in a mess. As was the woman who faced her. If the descriptions the betting shop regulars had given on how well dressed Melanie Newton was were anything like true, then she'd certainly let herself go.

She was wearing jogging bottoms and a shapeless grey cardigan. There was no make-up on her haggard face and white showed at the centre of her roughly parted hair where the roots were growing out.

'What do you want from me?' she asked, half defiant, half frightened.

Carole reminded herself that she must be cautious.

She had succeeded in her primary objective, of finding Melanie Newton. Now she mustn't scare the woman off by clumsy interrogation.

But fortunately, before she could make a gaffe, the woman asked her another question. 'Are you from one of the agencies?'

'Agencies?'

'Debt collectors. Because I can pay it all back and—'

'No, no. Good heavens, no. I'm not a debt collector.' Carole Seddon's middle-class soul was shaken by the very suggestion.

'Really?' There was anguished pleading in Melanie Newton's voice.

'Really. I'm a retired civil servant from the Home Office.'

'Home Office?' The idea of contact with any authority seemed to upset the woman.

'Retired, I said. Retired. I don't mean you any harm at all, Mrs Newton. As I said, all I'm interested in is what you can tell me about Tadeusz Jankowski.'

'You mean the young Polish boy who was killed?'

'Yes.'

She looked puzzled. 'Well, I don't think I can tell you anything about him. Please sit down.' Now her anxieties about debt collection had been allayed, Melanie Newton remembered her manners. But she didn't make any move to put more lights on in the gloom. Carole noticed one of the Allinstore carrier bags on the table. A sandwich had been torn from its packet and half-eaten, as though its consumer needed fuel rather than food.

She sat on an armchair whose covers felt thread-bare under her hands. 'But you're not denying that you met him?' she asked.

'No, I'm not denying that. He came to see me.'

'Here in England?'

'Yes.'

'When you were living in your house in Fed-borough?'

Melanie Newton looked suspicious again. 'You seem to know rather a lot about me. Are you sure it's nothing to do with the debts?'

'I can absolutely assure you of that. I didn't know that you had any debts. The only thing I do know about you is that you used to be a regular in the betting shop here in Fethering and that early last October you were seen to speak to Tadeusz Jankowski in there.'

'Then how did you find me here?'

This was a potentially difficult question to answer. For Carole to describe her surveillance techniques might raise the woman's paranoia once again. So all she said was, 'Somebody told me you lived in Fedborough. I consulted the telephone directory and spoke to the new owner of your house.'

'She didn't know where I lived, did she?' asked Melanie Newton, once again alarmed. Maybe some of her creditors might go in person to her old address.

'No, she didn't. But she gave me your husband's mobile number.'

'I didn't know Giles knew I was here.' But it didn't seem to worry her that much. 'Not that he's likely to come looking for me.'

'No, I gathered there had been some . . . estrange-
ment between you.' Which was an odd word to use, but
the one that rose to Carole's lips at that particular
moment.

Melanie Newton let out a bark of contemptuous
laughter. 'You could say that. I've come to the conclu-
sion that for a marriage to have any hope of success a
degree of proximity between the participants is
required. That's what Giles and I never had. His work
takes him off on contracts for considerable lengths of
time. Three months, four months, sometimes six
months at a time. Not the best recipe for connubial
bliss. Months of loneliness when they're away, interrupted by weeks of disappointment when they're
home.'

She seemed to be in confessional mode, so Carole
made no attempt to interrupt the flow. 'I think there
were probably things wrong with the marriage from
the start, if we could but have recognized them. But the
separations certainly didn't make it any easier. God
knows what Giles got up to while he was away. I think
there may have been other women. In fact, I found
proof that there was at least one other woman when he
was out in Mexico. And when I did find out, do you
know . . . it hardly worried me at all. I think that was
when I realized that the marriage was dead in the
water.'

Melanie Newton, who had been standing up until
that point, slumped into a chair, drained by her
revelations. Her movement must have jolted the laptop, because the screen came to life, displaying a highly

coloured roulette wheel and board. The woman's eyes could not help but look at it, and her hand moved involuntarily towards the keyboard.

'Your husband implied,' said Carole tentatively, 'when I spoke to him on the phone, that you had got into financial problems.'

'That was an understatement,' came the listless reply.

'And is it the gambling?'

Melanie Newton sighed a huge sigh, which seemed to encompass a whole world of troubles. 'Yes. I started . . . I don't know, a couple of years ago. It was at a time when Giles was away on one of his really extended trips, and I was feeling low. I think I'd just found out about the woman in Mexico, and that hadn't done a lot for my self-esteem. Then I went for a day's racing at Ascot. It was a corporate freebie. I work for a PR agency, get offered lots of stuff like that. Well,' she corrected herself, 'I say I work for them. What I mean is, I *did* work for them. Anyway, up until that point I'd never thought much about horse racing. Might put a small bet on the Derby or Grand National, join in the office sweepstake, you know . . . like most people, I could take it or leave it.

'But that day at Ascot I really enjoyed myself. I had a good day, I was with nice people. There was even a man there who made me think I might not be a totally unattractive has-been as a woman. And also, when it came to backing horses that day, I couldn't do anything wrong. First horse that won I remember was called Mel's Melon. And I backed it for purely sentimental reasons, because my friends call me "Mel" . . . well, used to call me "Mel". That romped home at twelve to one. And for the rest of that day it didn't matter what method I used, the form book, a horse's name that appealed to me, just sticking a pin in the paper . . . I was invincible. Came home more than five hundred pounds to the good.

'I didn't think any more about it for a few weeks, but then I had a rather upsetting phone conversation with Giles, who told me his contract had been extended by two months and he basically couldn't be bothered to come home for a break which he could easily have arranged. A bit of a slap in the face for me, as you can imagine . . . and I was feeling bad again. So at lunchtime that day I went out to the betting shop near where I used to work and . . . well, I had some good days and some bad days and . .' She seemed to run out of words.

'It became a habit?' suggested Carole.

'Yes. Very good way of putting it. It became a habit. Though I think "habit" is too mild a word. "Obsession" might be nearer the mark. "Obsession" as in "love". I came to love the thrill of gambling. It replaced ordinary love for me. Giles was out of my life, so far as I was concerned. Whether he was abroad or at home, he wasn't part of me or anything to do with me. He had stopped loving me. Perhaps he never loved me. But I could close my mind to that. Gambling gave me hope, offered me the chance of making a new life for myself.'

'How?' asked Carole, incredulous.

'Because I'd win!' replied Melanie Newton, as if

speaking to an idiot. 'I'd win a lot of money and then have the freedom to do what I wanted.'

'But did you win a lot of money?'

'Sometimes,' came the defiant reply.

'Did you need a lot of money, though? If you had a good job in PR, and your husband must have been earning quite a bit in oil exploration . . .'

'I didn't need money then. And soon I won't need it again.'

'Why not?'

'Because,' she explained patiently, 'I'll soon have a big win. Soon I'll pay off all the debts, on all the credit cards. And then I'll get my life back on track.'

Carole indicated the computer screen. 'Through roulette?'

'I'm playing roulette at the moment. I'm on a winning streak on the roulette. You have to be sensible, you know. When you're on a losing streak, you must change games. Then your luck will change.'

'And does your luck often change?'

All that got was another recalcitrant 'Sometimes.'

'Melanie, have you ever asked for help?'

'Help? I don't need help. I can gamble perfectly adequately on my own, thank you.'

'I meant help with stopping gambling.'

This sparked another paranoia of suspicion. 'Has someone sent you? Is Giles behind this?'

'No, I have come completely of my own accord. I'm nothing to do with your debts or your gambling problem. I'm—'

'I don't have a gambling problem,' Melanie Newton

insisted. 'When I get the big win, everything'll be sorted out.'

'All right.' Carole held her hands out in a pacifying gesture. 'Then I'll just ask you what I came to ask you.'

'What was that?' The woman sounded distracted now. Her eyes kept darting to the laptop screen and her hand was itching for the keyboard.

'About Tadeusz Jankowski . . .'

'The boy. Oh yes.'

'How did you come to meet him?'

'He came to the house in Fedborough last autumn.'

'Just out of the blue?'

'No.'

'By arrangement then?'

'Yes.'

'So, after your first meeting in Leipzig you kept—?'

'What?' Melanie Newton asked curiously.

'Your husband told me that you went travelling in Holland and Germany last summer.'

'I wanted to get away. I wanted a clean break. Giles was abroad, as ever. I thought going off on my own might be the answer. It wasn't. I'd booked a fortnight and I came back after five days.'

'But during those five days you met Tadeusz Jankowski?'

'I don't know what you're talking about. He came to see me in Fedborough in answer to an advertisement.'

'An advertisement for what?'

'I put a card in the newsagent's window. Advertising a room in the house. I . . . Well, the fact is . . . I was rather hard up. Giles was going to be away for four months. He would never know if I got in a lodger – not that I'd have cared much if he did find out. We'd already decided to split up and sell the place. I thought a bit of income would help the interest payments on the credit cards, so I advertised. Tadeusz Jankowski was about the only response I got.'

'But he didn't take the room?'

'No. He didn't think he could afford what I was asking. He said he'd look around and get back to me. But he never did.'

'Though you did see him again in the betting shop?'

'Yes. That was while I still used to go in there.'

'Why did you stop going?'

The woman gestured to her laptop as if it were something of exotic and unparalleled value. 'Why bother making the effort to go into a betting shop when I can get all this at home?'

Carole found it sad to see how narrow the focus of the woman's life had become. 'So what did you say to Tadeusz Jankowski in the betting shop?'

'I can't remember. We're talking about last October. I don't know. I suppose I said hello, how are you, asked him about how his girlfriend was.'

'His girlfriend?' Carole, who had been about to question Melanie Newton about her affair with the boy, was completely wrong-footed.

'Yes. He mentioned a girlfriend when he came to see the room. He said she was why he had come to England. But that he just wanted the room for himself, they wouldn't be cohabiting.'

'Did he tell you her name?'

252

'No.'

'Anything about her?'

'Just that she went to the University of Clincham. He asked me how to get there. I didn't know where it was, so he asked somebody else. '

'Ah,' said Carole. 'Thank you.'

Chapter Twenty-eight

Andy Constant strode through the University of Clincham campus as though he owned the place. And the proprietorial manner was increased when he pulled out a large bunch of keys to open the block marked 'DRAMA STUDIO AND REHEARSAL ROOMS'.

'Is this where the admissions records are kept?' asked Jude, with some scepticism.

'I keep everything to do with me here.'

'A little empire?'

'Yes, one that has declared UDI from the rest of the university and its policies.' He pushed open the glass door and ushered her into the unlit lobby. As Jude knew he would, he put his arm around her ample waist as he propelled her into the darkness.

He opened another heavy door and she found herself in a space which felt larger, but was totally black. Andy released his hold on her and said, 'Just get some light on the situation.'

He seemed to know the way around his empire blindfold. There was a click of another door, then after a few seconds, the space was filled with light. Not bright light, but subtle warming light which seemed to focus on the edges and corners of the room. Jude looked up and saw the source, stage lights hanging from a gantry in the ceiling, their harshness muted by gels of pink and orange.

The space they revealed was painted matt black, a functional studio for drama workshops or even small-scale productions. Folding audience chairs were stacked against the walls. On the floor were large blocks, a free-standing door in a frame, other chairs, all painted matt black. Against the wall were a couple of crestfallen sofas and – surprise, surprise – a double bed mattress covered with black sheets.

Andy Constant appeared from the lighting box, a bottle of whisky and two not very clean glasses in one hand. 'Drink?' he asked.

Jude nodded. 'You seem to have got yourself very nicely set up here.'

He shrugged as he poured the drinks and gestured to one of the sofas. 'Need a versatile space for the kind of stuff I do.'

Jude wondered if the ambiguity was deliberate, and decided it probably was. She sat down on the sofa and he slumped beside her, passing across a glass of Scotch.

'Cheers.'

She echoed the toast and took a long swallow. The whisky burned its comfort down her throat. 'So . . . are you going to have a look through the admissions files . . . to see if Tadeusz Jankowski ever applied for a place here?'

'I'll do that in a little while,' he replied. 'Let's just enjoy a drink first. I've had a hard day. I need a break.'

They both took a long swallow.

'Workshopping, were you?'

'Yes. Right here. We were doing some role-playing about broken relationships.'

'Which no doubt involved a lot of rolling about on the bed over there?'

'A certain amount, yes.' He read the potential censure in her eye. 'Nothing inappropriate, I can assure you. This generation of kids are very hot on what's appropriate and inappropriate. What they get up to in their own time is not my problem; here on the campus they're quite sophisticated in their approach to gender politics.'

'And you have a position of trust with them?'

'Very definitely. A duty of responsibility. Which I take very seriously. I wouldn't last long here if I didn't.'

'Which could bring us back to the mysterious Joan.'

'It could, but it needn't.' His hand was now resting gently on Jude's shoulder. She could have told him to remove it, but she didn't want a scene. Not yet, not before she'd got some more information out of him. Besides, she was a grown woman. She could look after herself. And having his hand on her shoulder was not a wholly unpleasant sensation.

'So you deny that you're having a relationship with her?'

'I've told you. It'd be more than my job's worth. And it'd be far too public for me to do such a thing. A campus like this is a breeding ground for gossip. Everyone

256

would immediately know all the details. How could I possibly manage it?'

'This place seems quite private. We didn't see anyone when we came in here this evening, did we?'

'The CCTV cameras would have clocked us.'

'Yes, and the security people might be interested in me. Because I have nothing to do with the university. But you . . . it's part of your job to come and go as you please. And presumably Joan's enrolled as a student here, so there's nothing odd about her wandering around. If she's studying Drama, why shouldn't she come into the Drama Studio?'

'Jude, might I say that you do have rather a one-track mind?'

'Maybe.'

His hand was now holding her shoulder rather than just resting on it. And he was moving his face closer, as if to kiss her.

Jude, tempted but strong, held up a hand. 'I came here because you said you kept the admission files here.'

'Yes, they're on my laptop.' Recognizing that he wasn't going to get anywhere with her at that moment, he raised himself out of the sofa's depths. 'I'll get it.' He went back to the lighting box.

Jude swallowed the rest of her whisky. She topped up her grubby glass from the bottle on the floor. She looked around the room. Andy Constant's convenient little seduction venue. Against the walls were racks of costumes, rifles, banners, swords, kitchen equipment, stepladders. All the impedimenta of the fantasies worked out by the students in the space. The fantasies which were engendered and controlled by Andy Constant during workshop sessions. And others that he realized out of academic hours.

He returned, holding his laptop open and already keying instructions into it. 'What period were you talking about?'

'He came over to England round the end of last September. Any time since then, I imagine.'

'University term starts at the end of September. He'd have had to apply much earlier than that if he wanted to enrol as a full-time student . . .'

'Are there part-time courses?'

'Some.'

'Could you check those too, please?'

'Jude, I would be within my rights to ask you why the hell you want to know all this stuff?'

'If you did, I'd reply that I want to know why Tadeusz Jankowski was murdered.'

'Whatever the reason for his death, I can assure you it had nothing to do with Clincham College.'

'The information I'm asking you to check could maybe prove that. You do have it there, don't you?'

'Yes,' he replied tartly. 'The main records are over in the Admin block, but I keep copies of everything here. It is my job, you know.' He seemed to resent Jude's insinuation that he might be less than diligent in his duties. Looking at the laptop screen, he said, 'No, the name's not here.'

'May I have a look?'

He sighed at her suspicion, but obediently sat down

and placed the laptop on her plump knees. 'OK, we're in the file "ALLAPP", short for "All Applications". As you see, the dates are on different tabs. Check along the period you are interested in. The applicants' names, you'll see, are in alphabetical order.'

Jude went through the files for the previous nine months. The name "Tadeusz Jankowski" did not appear. She handed the laptop back.

'So now do you believe me?'

'About that,' said Jude, 'yes.'

He deliberately closed the laptop and placed it down on the floor. Then he put his hand on her shoulder and moved it quickly round to her neck. He drew her face towards his.

He had cleaned his teeth. He had at least made that effort to meet her. She could smell the fresh mint from his mouth. She could feel the strength of his eyes as they locked with hers. And he did have very kissable lips.

Jude had no puritan instincts in sexual matters. She tended to let her actions be dictated by the promptings of instinct. Such an attitude had frequently led to disaster, but the way to that disaster had sometimes been a pretty one.

Their mouths engaged. It was pleasant. He seemed in no hurry. His lips teased and nibbled at hers, his tongue flicking against her teeth.

Their eyes had disengaged, and over Andy's shoulder Jude could see the contours of the room, the black walls washed by honey-coloured light, the jumble of stage equipment against the wall. She felt his hand slip

259

over the curves of her shoulder towards the more rewarding curves of her breast. She liked the feeling. She didn't like the man, but she liked what he was doing to her.

Suddenly her eye was caught by a flash of colour amongst the black of the props. She saw the outline of a face, red, with two black and white eyes over a circular mouth.

Propped up against the wall of the Drama Studio was a red-painted guitar.

Chapter Twenty-nine

'He said he had no idea where it came from,' Jude announced. 'He'd asked the students to bring in musical instruments for some workshop they were doing. One of them brought in that guitar.'

'Which one?'

'He claimed he couldn't remember, Carole. He didn't notice. A lot of them brought stuff in.'

'Do you think he was telling the truth?'

'From what I know of Andy Constant, I'd think it was unlikely.'

'Hm.' Carole looked at her neighbour curiously. 'And how did you actually come to be in the Drama Studio with him?'

For the first time in their acquaintance, she saw Jude look embarrassed. 'Oh, I was just checking out with him whether Tadek had ever applied to the university.'

'And Andy Constant kept those records in the Drama Studio?'

'Yes, he did.' Although she was speaking absolute truth, Jude found herself blushing like the biggest liar on earth.

'I see,' said Carole witheringly. 'Anyway, that ties in with what I found out from Melanie Newton. About the connection with the University of Clincham.'

'Yes, I haven't congratulated you properly yet on tracking her down. That was a brilliant bit of detective work.'

Carole glowed in the beam of the compliment, which also, as Jude had intended, took the focus off her own discomfiture. 'Oh, it was Gerald Hume who gave me the lead. Once I'd got the photo from him, the rest was straightforward.'

'I'm still impressed.'

'Well, thank you.' Now it was Carole's turn to blush.

'So I don't think it would be too great a leap of logic to conclude that the girl from the University of Clincham with whom Tadek fell in love was the one who had taken the guitar from his room. And who then handed it over when Andy Constant asked them to bring instruments.'

'So who would that be? One of his Drama set, obviously. And the only one we know about of those is Sophia Urquhart.'

'There's also the mysterious Joan. The one I said he was having an affair with.'

'I thought you said he denied having an affair with her.'

'Yes, but Andy Constant is not the kind of man whose truthfulness I'd trust very far in matters of relationships. He's a born liar.'

'So you haven't even met this Joan?'

'Well, I wonder . . . You remember that day when

we went to see Andy up at the college, and he took us for coffee?'

'Yes.'

'The girl who came to fetch him . . . do you remember her?'

'Dark-haired? Looked a bit Spanish?'

Jude nodded. 'I saw her with him again just before that show I went to see. And she was in the pub afterwards, but then I didn't notice her there when Sophia gave Andy the message about Joan not being able to make it. I reckon there's a strong chance she's the one.'

'So how do we contact her?'

'Through the college – or university or whatever it wants to call itself.'

'We didn't have much luck there when we were trying to find out about Tadek.'

'No, but he'd never been enrolled. We've got more to go on with this girl. We know what she looks like, we know she's studying Drama with Andy Constant and we know her first name's Joan.'

'Any idea of her second name?'

'No . . .' Jude suddenly remembered. 'But I've got the programme for *Rumours of Wars* upstairs. I know she wasn't performing in the show, but I'll bet her name's there in the backstage crew!'

She rose excitedly from her sofa, but in the hall met an equally excited Zofia running downstairs, clutching Jude's laptop. 'I've heard from Pavel!' the girl shouted.

'What, about the songs?'

'Yes. He's back from Krakow, he reply to my email.

And we were correct. Tadek did write a song to his English girl. He sent a copy to Pavel.'

'Do you have the lyrics for it?'

'Better. I have a recording.' Zofia bustled into the sitting room and, after a quick greeting to Carole, placed the laptop on a pile of books on one of Jude's cluttered coffee tables. 'You are ready to hear it?'

'Yes, please,' said both women eagerly.

Zofia pressed a key and from the laptop's tiny speakers came the strumming of an acoustic guitar. Then followed a voice, an innocent light tenor, singing in heavily accented English.

> *You're my love and I love you like hell,*
> *Though I don't speak your language so well.*
> *You're the best in all the whole world,*
> *You are all that I want in a girl.*
> *I love you in good or bad weather,*
> *I love things that we do together –*
> *Sing, make love, talk on the phone.*
> *All the time you're just like Joan.*

Carole and Jude exchanged satisfied looks as their suspicions were confirmed. Tadek's song went into its chorus.

> *Just like Joan,*
> *I'm overthrown*
> *By the power of your love.*
> *Just like Joan,*
> *You're in my zone,*
> *Like an angel from above.*

Oh, how big my love has grown.
It's because you're . . . just like Joan.

There was a silence as the song ended. Tears glinted in Zofia's eyes. Hearing her brother's voice sounding so close and real brought home to her once again the hard fact of her loss. To fight off sentiment, she said in matter-of-fact tones, 'I think that is Tadek's first attempt to write a song in English.'

'Then it's pretty good,' Jude assured her.

'And,' said Carole, 'it also confirms the suspicion we've had about who his mystery woman is.' They quickly brought the girl up to speed with their thinking, and told her about the pretty dark-haired girl they had seen at the University of Clincham.

'Then I must see her,' said Zofia immediately. 'I must go to the university and talk to her.'

'Exactly what we were thinking.'

'But we must be careful,' Carole cautioned. 'If she has something to hide, she's going to be on the lookout.'

'Yes, she doesn't want anyone to make the connection between her and your brother,' said Jude. 'I think she has already gone some way to cover her tracks.'

The girl looked puzzled. 'I'm sorry. I do not understand.'

'Look, you say your brother was devoted to his guitar?'

'Yes.'

'So, however much he loved a girl, he'd never give it to her, would he?'

'No.'

'Which means that if – as seems likely – this Joan was the one who gave the guitar to Andy Constant, she must have got it without your brother's knowledge. Marek said, when he waited in Tadek's room on the day he died there were no signs of his music, no guitar, no CDs, no tapes. I think Joan must have gone into the room and cleared it all out.'

'Because it would link him to her?' Carole nodded. 'Yes, that makes sense. And if she did do that, it means she must have known that he was dead . . . or about to die. So she either killed him herself or at least knows who did.'

'I think, Zosia,' said Jude, 'that you should get back to your brother's friend Pavel again. He might know more about this Joan. After all, if, as we think, they got together at the music festival in Leipzig, then Pavel might well have met her.'

'Yes, that is good idea. But we must see her as soon as possible,' said Zofia urgently. 'We know she is called Joan. Do we have her other name?'

'Actually I was just on my way to check that when you came downstairs. I think her full name is likely to be in the programme for the show I saw at Clincham College.'

Jude hurried back up to her bedroom to fetch the printed sheet she had been given at the university theatre, but she came down more slowly, studying the text.

Back in the sitting room, the two women looked up at her expectantly.

'Well, that's very odd,' said Jude. 'There's no one on this programme whose first name's Joan.'

Chapter Thirty

'You're the expert in surveillance work.'

'Don't be ridiculous, Jude.'

'Come on, who was it who did that very successful stake-out to find Melanie Newton?'

'Well . . .' Carole couldn't help being flattered.

'And what we're trying to do here is much easier.'

'Is it?'

'Of course it is. We know the girl is a student at the University of Clincham, we know she's doing Drama, and we know her name's Joan. Much more information than you had when you tracked down Melanie.'

'Yes, but we didn't get much cooperation when we went to the university reception asking about Tadek, did we?'

'No. That's why I'm talking about surveillance. Look, there's only one entrance to the university. Which means all the students have to go through it every day.'

'Don't they have halls of residence? For the minority of students who don't live at home? If they do, a student could stay inside on the campus as long as he or she wanted to.'

'They do have halls of residence, but they're not right on the campus. Andy Constant told me. So all the students do have to go in and out through the main gates.'

'So, Jude, are you suggesting I spend the next few days sitting in the Renault outside the university's main gates until I get a sighting of this Joan?'

'No. I'm suggesting we go and have a drink in the Bull. It's right opposite those gates.'

'You mean now?'

'Yes.'

'But Zofia wanted to come too. And she's gone down to do another shift at the Crown and Anchor.'

'Carole, I don't think she'll mind, so long as we actually track the girl down.'

'No, I suppose not.'

'So off to the Bull, in we go. And you never know, we might get lucky.'

They did get lucky. Luckier than they had any right to expect. It was about five when they reached Clincham and the Bull was empty enough for them to get a table in the bay window, which commanded a perfect view of the university's main entrance. Darkness had fallen during their drive from Fethering, but the area was well lit and they could see the comings and goings of the students.

Mostly goings. Clearly many lectures or classes or seminars finished at five and a lot of the students were on their way home. They gathered in little knots, draped round each other, looking even younger in their muffled anoraks and hoodies. As always, they gestured flamboyantly, as though they were taking part in some adult performance of a play to which they did not quite yet know the words. Some were busy texting on mobile phones, some waving elaborately dramatic farewells to friends they would undoubtedly see the next day.

Carole and Jude had only been in their surveillance point for about twenty minutes when their luck kicked in. A bunch of students emerged from the campus, behaving even more flamboyantly than the others, and Jude was quick to recognize some of them from the cast of *Rumours of Wars*. She couldn't see Sophia Urquhart amongst them, but it was definitely the Drama set. Even better, it included the girl whose pretty dark face was framed by long black hair. Better still, she was one of the group who decided to have a drink to start off whatever entertainment the evening might hold.

The Bull's 'Happy Hour' seemed more or less permanent. The management recognized the value of their location and used low prices to encourage the students' alcoholic consumption (not that many of them needed much encouragement). The Drama lot equipped themselves with pints of lager for both genders and commandeered a large table over the other side of the bar. Their presence doubled the decibel level in the pub.

'Well, there she is,' said Carole. 'How do you propose that we start talking to her?'

'Not a problem,' said Jude, rising to her feet. 'If you

want to start a conversation with anyone involved in the theatre, all you have to do is to tell them how good their last show was. And fortunately I had the dubious pleasure of witnessing this lot's last show.'

Carole, as someone who hadn't seen *Rumours of Wars*, thought she should stay put, while her friend sashayed across the bar towards the loud assemblage of students.

Two of the boys were just coming to the end of some routine in cod French accents and Jude timed her entrance so that she rode in on a wave of laughter. 'Sorry to interrupt,' she said, 'but you lot were in *Rumours of Wars*, weren't you?'

Their attention was duly grabbed. Someone actually wanted to talk to them about their work. They confirmed that they had been in the show. One or two of them put on the faces they had practised in their mirrors for the moment when they would be interviewed on television about their professional lives.

Time for the tactical half-truth. 'I thought the show was terrific. Saw it on Friday. Really packed a punch.'

A couple of the girls agreed that it was powerful stuff. 'We felt, like, absolutely *drained* at the end of it,' said one.

'Yeah, like, the director really made us get into our parts. Even if it's only a couple of lines, he said, I want to *feel*, like, the energy you're transmitting to that person.'

Yes, I bet he said that, thought Jude. And a lot more garbage along the same lines.

Their eyes were gleaming, pathetically hungry for

praise. 'Well, I thought you were all terrific. I mean, I used to act and I do know what I'm talking about.' They lapped it up. 'And the staging, too. It was a real ensemble piece.'

'Yeah, that's what Andy – he's, like, the director – he said he wanted us to be an ensemble.'

'Yeah, he said we should be like the . . . Berlin Ensemble . . .?' the girl hazarded.

'Berliner Ensemble.'

'Right, whatever.'

'A lot of backstage effort went into that show too.' She looked at the dark-haired girl. 'I didn't see you in it. Were you part of the stage management?'

'No,' the girl said, in an accent that sounded very slightly Spanish. 'I was the assistant director.'

'Ooh yes. Like, working *very closely* with the director,' insinuated one of the boys.

'Shut up!'

But he'd got the others going. 'You sound guilty to me,' said one.

'Teacher's pet,' crowed another. 'Or teacher's heavy petting, maybe?'

'Just shut up!' the girl said again. But there was no vindictiveness in their banter.

'I wonder, actually,' said Jude to the girl, 'if I could just have a quick word with you . . .' Time for another tactical lie '. . . I'd love to ask you about how the improvisation element worked out.'

'Sure.' The girl seemed quite ready to detach herself from the teasing boys around her. Picking up her pint, she sidled out of her seat.

'Let's go and join my friend.'

'Is she interested in the theatre too?'

'Oh yes. Very,' Jude lied. Then, as they approached Carole, she continued, 'I was just saying how interested you are in the theatre.'

'Really?' Carole's pale blue eyes looked daggers at her neighbour.

'What was it you wanted to ask about?' said the girl as she sat down easily between them.

'Well, I know Andy Constant, and I just wondered how closely you worked with him on the production? You know, as his assistant?'

She grimaced. 'Not very closely at all, really. I mean, like, I had this title of assistant director, but really Andy did everything himself. I don't think he's very good at delegating.' No, I can believe that, thought Jude. 'Andy had all the ideas, he wasn't really interested in what I had to say.'

'But did you work with him on the improvisations?'

'Well, yes, but they were pretty useless. I mean, we all did improvisations, but Andy didn't use much of our stuff. It was like he had the whole thing planned from the start, almost like he was working from a script that was already written.'

'Something he'd done before?'

'It felt like that at times.' Which didn't surprise Jude one bit. She could imagine Andy Constant bringing out some long-written script, dusting it down, slotting in a few contemporary references and making his students think that they had worked it out through their own improvisation. That would be typical of his control-freak approach to his work. And would also explain why *Rumours of Wars* had felt so old-fashioned.

'You imply that being assistant director to Andy Constant wasn't the most rewarding creative experience of your life.'

'No way. He just used me as cheap labour. Photocopying, typing up rehearsal schedules – that was the extent of my creative input.'

'So was that why you didn't let them put your name on the programme?'

The girl's forehead wrinkled with bewilderment. 'My name was on the programme.'

'But I thought your first name was Joan.'

The bewilderment increased. 'I'm not called Joan.'

Her name, it turned out, was Ines Ribeiro. Her parents were part of the Portuguese community in Littlehampton. She had never been nicknamed 'Joan' by anyone. She didn't know anyone in the Drama set who was called or nicknamed 'Joan'. She had never met Tadeusz Jankowski. And, in spite of the insinuations of her friends, the suggestion that she might have been having an affair with Andy Constant shocked her to the core of her Portuguese Catholic being.

It was not Carole and Jude's finest hour. After a very offended Ines Ribeiro had left them, they hastily finished their drinks and beat an ignominious retreat back to Fethering.

Chapter Thirty-one

That evening Jude was getting ready for bed when Zofia returned from her shift at the Crown and Anchor. 'Please, I am sorry for intrusion,' said the girl. 'May I just check the email on the laptop?'

'Of course you can. But actually it's not here. I took it downstairs, so that you'd be able to get at it. It's on the kitchen table.'

'Oh, I am sorry. I did not look down there.'

'No reason why you should have done.' Jude belted her dressing-gown around her substantial waist. 'I'll come down and see if anything's come through.'

'I just wish to see if there is anything more from Pavel,' said Zofia, as they made their way down to the kitchen. 'I asked him if he knew about Tadek's Joan.'

'Well, let's hope he knows more than I thought I did.' And, while Zofia got to work on the keyboard, Jude spelt out the failure of her trip with Carole to the Bull.

'Ah yes, there is a reply from Pavel,' said the girl excitedly. 'Quite a long one. And look – he has attached another song as well.'

Jude looked at the lines of incomprehensible words on the screen. 'So what does it mean? What does he say?'

'I'll tell you. First I get out my notebook, make some notes.' She opened the blue book on the kitchen table. Then, as her eyes scanned down the text, the girl translated from the Polish. 'He say yes, Tadek did meet the English woman at the festival in Leipzig last summer. He say Tadek did call her "Joan", but he think perhaps it is a nickname. The girl come up on stage and sing with the band one evening when they are in a club. That is how my brother meet her. And Tadek is in love . . . yes, yes, like he has never been in love before. Always the same with my brother. And Pavel says the woman is very beautiful.'

'What does she look like?'

'He does not say. Maybe later. It is a long email, and Pavel writes like he talks, all out of order, just thoughts as they come to him. Ah, and then he says the songs he is attaching are ones Tadek recorded in Leipzig with the girl, her singing to his accompaniment . . . Now he says why Tadek call her "Joan". He think her voice like one of his favourite singers, Joan Baez.'

'Of course. His other song was called "Just Like Joan". We got it wrong. The girl's name wasn't Joan, she was *like* Joan.' Jude was pretty sure now that she knew the mystery woman's identity. 'Can we hear the song?'

Zofia's nimble fingers set up the playback. Again it was an amateur recording. 'The Night They Drove Old Dixie Down'. Another Joan Baez standard. With Tadek's acoustic guitar accompanying the pure soprano that Jude had last heard in the theatre at Clincham College singing 'Where Have All the Flowers Gone?'

Chapter Thirty-two

Jude grinned with satisfaction. 'I think we're looking at an old-fashioned love triangle,' she told Zofia. 'Sophia Urquhart is loved by two men. Your brother Tadek who we now know met her in Leipzig during her gap year, and Andy Constant who came on to her once she became enrolled in his Drama course.'

'OK, let me write this down,' the girl responded excitedly. She took a biro, opened a clean page of her notebook and drew three separate crosses. 'Here are the corners of our triangle. We have Sophia Urquhart . . .' She wrote the names as she spoke them. 'Tadek . . . and Andy Constant . . . We draw a line here . . . Tadek to Sophia . . .' She scribbled down, 'He loves her.' 'And the same thing from Andy Constant to Sophia . . .' She wrote that down too, and nodded with satisfaction. 'It's beginning to make sense.'

'Yes. Of course, the one side of the triangle you haven't filled in is the relationship between Andy Constant and your brother.'

'You think . . . it is hatred perhaps? Hatred enough to kill someone?'

'It's possible, Zosia. At last we're getting somewhere.' Jude beamed. 'I think this deserves a celebration. How about a glass of wine before we go to bed?'

'I would like that very much.'

The buoyant certainty Jude had felt the night before received a predictable inundation of cold water the next morning. 'I don't see how you can be sure she'd even been to Leipzig,' said Carole, reverting to her customary wet blanket role.

'Carole, of course she was there. She was the woman Tadek talked to his friend Pavel about, the one he followed to England.'

'I don't understand how you can make that assumption.'

'I can make it because I heard Sophia sing in *Rumours of Wars*, and now I've heard the song she recorded with Tadek in Leipzig. I'd put money on the fact that it's the same voice.'

'You'd put money on anything.'

Jude grinned. She reckoned her neighbour was behaving like this because it was not she who had made this latest leap of logic. Carole could be very competitive at times and that quality, coupled with her recurrent paranoia, could make her a difficult companion.

'I'm not so sure,' Carole went on sniffily. 'Anyway, if what you say is true, who's our murderer?'

'Well, having seen the kind of anger Andy's capable of when he's thwarted, I think he has to be way up the top of the list.'

277

'You think he killed the boy?'

'Two rivals for the love of the same woman. Wouldn't be the first middle-aged man who's felt his virility challenged by a young upstart.'

'But . . . But, Jude, there's so much we don't know. Tadek came to England to follow Sophia Urquhart . . . all right, it sounds from what his friend Pavel said that that's true. So he was in love with her. But was she in love with him? And what did she think about her Drama teacher? Or him about her? It all seems terribly vague. You don't know Sophia was having an affair with her teacher.'

'I've told you, Carole. I overheard Sophia apologizing to Andy that "Joan" could not go back with him, because she was getting a lift home with her father. And that made him angry because he "wanted" her. We now know "Joan" didn't exist, but was a nickname for Sophia. And I actually travelled in the car from the university with Sophia, so it was her father who was giving "Joan" a lift home. It can't be plainer than that.'

'I don't know,' said Carole, infuriatingly unconvinced.

'Anyway,' Jude looked at her watch, 'I'll soon be able to find out about whether Sophia went to Leipzig or not.'

'How?'

'Because her brother Hamish is due here in ten minutes.'

'Why's he coming?'

'To value the house.'

'Oh.' Carole also looked at her watch. She had

already exercised her dog on Fethering Beach that morning, but she said curtly, 'I must go. Gulliver needs a walk.'

There was something of the play-actor about Hamish Urquhart. His manner was studied rather than spontaneous. Maybe, Jude reflected, being an estate agent was similar to the professions of lawyer, doctor and teacher, where young recruits took on the manners of people much older than themselves. In Hamish's case, of course, he took on the manners of his father, becoming a hearty facsimile of Ewan Urquhart.

He was dressed in a gold-buttoned blazer and mustard-yellow cords. Under his arm was a brown leather briefcase, from which he produced a clipboard, some forms and a pocket-sized laser distance measure. He also handed Jude his business card and some stapled sheets of details from houses Urquhart & Pease had recently sold.

'The property market's still very buoyant at the moment, I'm pleased to say. Particularly down here in the south-east. We could sell every house that comes on to the market three times over. Just not enough product, that's the problem. No, we'd have no problem in getting you a very good price for this.' He looked without total conviction around the clutter of the Woodside Cottage sitting room. Jude reckoned he was thinking, 'even in this condition'. But he was too courteous to vocalize the thought.

'Now, if you don't mind, I'd just like to go around

the property, take some details, make some notes. You may accompany me if you like, or . . .'

'No, you just wander round at your own pace. The place is empty apart from me. I do have a friend staying, but she's out this morning. Anyway, I've got some stuff to put in the washing machine.'

'Fine. Well, I'll have a look at the kitchen first, and then be out of your way doing the rest of the house.'

'Yes. Would you like a cup of coffee or something?'

'No, thanks. Just had some at the office.'

He quickly checked out the dimensions of the back garden and the kitchen, then said, 'It's not pivotal at this juncture, but when you do sell, you'll have to decide whether you'd want to take or leave your kitchen equipment. Oven, washing machine, what-have-you . . .'

'Oh, I'm not definitely thinking of selling. Just sort of . . . testing the water, trying to find out where I stand financially.'

'Yes, of course, Mrs . . . er, Miss . . .'

'Just call me Jude.'

'Right. Jude.'

She had decided that she'd question him about his sister after he'd finished the valuation, so she set her load of washing going while he surveyed the house. It didn't take long. Soon he was downstairs again, tapping at the kitchen door. They sat down either side of the kitchen table for him to give his verdict. Jude told him to push aside some of the clutter so that he would have room for his clipboard. She noticed that Zofia had left her notebook open on the table from the night before.

'Well, to be quite honest, Jude,' said Hamish cheerily, 'Urquhart & Pease could get you a buyer for this property tomorrow. No problems at all. Fethering is quite a property hot-spot, a much sought-after area, because it's still one of those villages which has kept its . . . Englishness.'

'I'm sorry? What do you mean?'

'Well, I mean, most of the people . . . Not to put to fine a point on it, you don't see too many coloured faces in Fethering . . . and you don't hear too many Eastern European accents when you're shopping in Allinstore.' The guffaw which followed this, not to mention the sentiments expressed, made him sound exactly like his father.

Jude didn't approve of what Hamish had said, but made no comment and let him continue. 'So, as I say, very much sought-after. And you'd be surprised how many wealthy city folk are looking for that ideal of a country retreat. Woodside Cottage would tick all the boxes for them. So far as I can tell, the structure's very sound, though . . .' A blush spread across his face and down to his thick neck '. . . not everyone might share your taste in decor. Some of the windows are getting a bit shabby, and the exterior paintwork needs to be done. So I think any potential purchaser would be looking to spend a bit of money on the place. Or you could have some of the work done yourself before you put the place on the market. Mind you, having a house redecorated with a view to selling doesn't always work, either. In a lot of cases, the new owners are going to want to redo everything, anyway.'

'Yes, it's supposed to be a natural human instinct. Marking one's territory. Like dogs peeing at lamp-posts.'

'Really?' The young man looked puzzled. 'I hadn't heard that.'

'So what sort of price would we be looking at?' Although she'd had an ulterior motive in asking for the valuation, Jude was still intrigued to know how much her property was worth.

After a bit of professional hedging and prevarication, Hamish Urquhart named a figure. It was considerably in excess of what Jude had been expecting. Of course she'd read the constant newspaper reports about the inexorable rise in house prices, but was still shocked to hear the sum spelt out for Woodside Cottage. She was sitting on a little gold-mine.

'That's very gratifying,' she said.

'Yes. As you say, you're not looking to sell at right this moment, but, you know, when you do make the decision, I hope you'll remember Urquhart & Pease. There are, of course, other estate agents around, the area's bristling with them, but many are branches of big chains, and I think you're guaranteed a more sympathetic experience dealing with a family firm like Urquhart & Pease.' He reached once again into his briefcase. 'I do have a sheet here, spelling out the terms of our business transactions, fee structure and so on, and I think you'll find Urquhart & Pease are competitive with . . .' He looked, puzzled, into the recesses of his case. 'Damn, I don't seem to have brought it with me.'

'Never mind, Hamish. I'm sure we can take those details as read. I've just put the kettle on. Are you sure I can't tempt you to a coffee?'

'Oh, well . . .' He looked at his watch. 'I've got a bit of time before my next appointment. Why not?'

Making the coffee gave Jude a good excuse to change the subject. 'Very interesting seeing that play your sister was in last week . . .'

'Yes. Pretty damned odd, I found it. I mean, I don't pretend to know much about the theatre. Like a good musical . . . you know, Lloyd Webber, that kind of thing. Something where you don't have to think too much. But that thing of Soph's . . . can't say I got all of it. I mean, she was very good, but . . . Also, the message it seemed to be putting across . . . I'm not sure I went along with it.'

'In what way, Hamish?' asked Jude as she put the coffee cup in front of him.

'Thanks. Well, the show seemed to be saying that war is always a bad thing.'

'And you don't agree with that?'

'Good God, no. I mean, I'm not recommending that countries should go around invading and bombing other countries whenever the fancy strikes them, but sometimes action has to be taken. Every country needs to have an army, and I reckon we've got one of the best in the world. So I don't like it when I hear our brave boys being mocked. They do a damned fine job in extraordinarily difficult conditions. And they're bloody necessary. Always have been. I mean, if Mr Hitler had been allowed to go his merry way in 1939 without anyone trying to stop him . . . well, we'd probably now be conducting this conversation in bloody German!' Again he sounded as if he was quoting his father verbatim.

'Talking of Germany . . .' said Jude, snatching at the most tenuous of links, 'your sister was saying she'd been there in her gap year.'

'Yes. Lucky old Soph, actually getting a gap year. I didn't have one. Straight out of school into the family business. None of that university nonsense for me.' Hamish made it sound as if he had made a choice in the matter, but Jude remembered Ewan Urquhart saying it was lack of academic ability that had kept his son out of university.

'And she's such a good singer,' Jude went on, worming her way round to what she really wanted to ask. 'Do you know if Sophia did any singing while she was in Europe?'

'I think she did, actually. I know she went to some music festivals and things. She kept sending Dad postcards.'

'Where from?' Hamish seemed so innocent and unsuspicious in his answers that Jude didn't worry about pressing him.

'Berlin, certainly. I remember she was there. And Frankfurt, I think . . . and Leipzig. I remember that, because Dad made some comment about my sister being in the land of the Commie Krauts!' He guffawed once again at his father's wit.

Still, Jude had got what she wanted. Proof positive that Sophia Urquhart, in spite of her denial when asked

284

about it, had actually been to Leipzig. So now Jude had a solid fact to underpin her conjectures.

'Are you musical too, Hamish?' she asked.

'God, no. Can maybe join in the chorus of some filthy song down the rugby club, but that's the extent of it. No, Soph's the one in the family with talent.' He spoke this as an accepted fact, one that he had been told about so many times that it caused him no resentment.

'And she's very pretty too,' said Jude, still angling the conversation in the direction she wanted it to go. 'She must be surrounded by boyfriends.'

'She hasn't had that many, actually.'

'Seems strange. I'd have thought the boys'd be after her like bees round a honey-pot.'

'Maybe some'd like to be, but they don't get far.' He let out another hearty laugh. 'You see, none of them can pass Dad's quality control.'

'You don't know whether she met anyone on her gap year?'

'No,' Hamish replied shortly. Then he clammed up. For the first time, he looked suspicious of Jude.

'Or what about at college? Drama students traditionally are supposed to have colourful love lives.'

'No, I don't think . . . I don't know . . .' He looked confused. 'I don't think she'd got anyone special, but . . . Why, have you heard anything?'

Jude shrugged, in part at the incongruity of the question. So far as Hamish knew, she had nothing to do with Clincham College, and yet here he was asking her for information about his sister's relationships there.

'Just rumours,' she replied airily. 'As you know, the main product of this entire area is gossip.'

'Yes,' said Hamish thoughtfully.

At that moment the doorbell rang. Jude went through to the hall to let in Ewan Urquhart, who with unctuous smoothness held her hand for slightly longer than was necessary and asked, 'Sorry? Is my idiot boy still with you?'

'Hamish is here. Through in the kitchen.'

Ewan Urquhart marched through, brandishing a couple of stapled printed sheets. 'Only forgot to bring the terms and conditions, didn't you, Hamish?'

His son admitted his error, looking like a guilty schoolboy. But once again he didn't seem genuinely shamed. His incompetence was an essential part of his personality. Perhaps within the family it was what made him lovable.

Ewan handed the sheet to Jude. 'Sorry. The old adage that if you want something done, you'd better do it yourself has never been more true than when it comes to dealing with Hamish. As I have learnt, to my cost, over the years. Anyway, I hope he's done a proper valuation for you.'

'Yes, he's been excellent,' said Jude, who was getting sick of hearing the young man constantly diminished.

'What price did he give you?'

Jude told him. The older man rubbed his chin sceptically. 'I think he may have overstated it. Exuberance of youth, eh? To be on the safe side, I'd say five thousand less.'

'Well, it's still a huge amount more than I paid for it.'

'I bet. Oh, you can't go wrong with property. Just sit at home and watch the money grow around you.' He let out a guffaw, exactly like the one Hamish had copied from him. Then he turned to his son. 'Come on. We've got a business to run. Can't sit around drinking coffee all day.'

The young man was on his feet before his father had finished speaking. Ewan Urquhart focused on Jude again. 'Just whenever you decide you want to sell, remember Urquhart & Pease. There are, of course, other estate agents around . . . the area's bristling with them, but many are branches of big chains, and I think you're guaranteed a more sympathetic experience deal-ing with a family firm like Urquhart & Pease.'

So Hamish had actually learnt the spiel word for word from his father.

Before he left the kitchen, Ewan Urquhart paused for a moment, looking at the clutter on the table. Jude couldn't be certain, but it looked as though he had seen the open notebook on whose page Zofia had spelt out his daughter's love triangle. Something certainly seemed to have changed his manner. As he said good-bye, there was a new beadiness in the older estate agent's eyes.

Next door at High Tor, Carole Seddon sat in a state of bleak desolation. Her lifelong instinct had been never to trust anyone, and once again it had been proved right.

Drop your defences, allow another person inside your comfort zone, and you're just inviting them to betray you. Only a matter of time before it happens.

Jude was selling Woodside Cottage. She hadn't thought it necessary to impart that decision to her neighbour. And Carole, who didn't have many, had thought they were friends.

Chapter Thirty-three

Jude would have gone straight round and told Carole about the confirmation of Sophia Urquhart's presence in Leipzig, but her friend had said she was going to take Gulliver out for a walk. So Jude rang Andy Constant's mobile.

'I wondered if we could get together.'

'I don't see why not.' His voice was full of lazy self-congratulation. The parting from their last encounter had not been harmonious. When she'd seen Tadek's guitar in the Drama Studio, Jude had broken from their kiss to question Andy about it. The interruption had destroyed the mood between them and certainly thwarted the plans he had been nursing for the rest of the evening. In his frustration he had become very childish and refused to answer her questions.

But there was still information Jude needed that she could only get from him, so another meeting was imperative.

Of course, Andy Constant, being the kind of man he was, interpreted her getting in touch with him as the action of a woman who had seen the error of her ways. Yes, she must have known she had behaved badly when they last met, but she obviously couldn't stop thinking about him. He reckoned the old Andy Constant animal magnetism was once again exerting its irresistible pull.

Jude didn't mind what he thought her motives were, so long as he agreed to see her again. Which he readily did. 'Don't let's bother with meeting in the pub,' he said, his voice low in a way that he knew to be sexy. 'Come straight to the Drama Studio.'

'Will I be able to get in?'

'I'll leave the building unlocked.'

'I meant – will I be able to get past security on the main gate?'

'There's another way in. There's a small door into the campus in Maiden Avenue. It's meant to be locked, but some of the staff have keys and it very rarely is. A lot of the students come and go through it.' There was something unappealing about the practised ease with which he went through these details. Jude wondered how many other women had been given these instructions before an assignation with Andy Constant.

'All right. I'll come in that way.'

'Good, Jude.' He sounded patronizing, as if speaking to a recalcitrant child. 'Let's say six o'clock. I'll really enjoy seeing you.'

I wouldn't be so sure about that, thought Jude as she finished the call.

She rang to see if Carole was back, but there was no reply. In the afternoon she had a couple of clients for her healing services, a man with a stomach complaint for which the doctors could find no explanation, and a woman who suffered from panic attacks. In both cases Jude felt she made some progress.

Just before she left for Clincham, she tried ringing her neighbour again. Still no reply. Must be out.

Inside High Tor, Carole looked at the Caller Display and did not pick up the phone.

The door in Maiden Avenue was, as Andy Constant had promised, unlocked. The road fringed Clincham's main park and there was no street lighting. The February night was dark. Jude slipped into the campus, reflecting on the laxness of the security. No doubt an alternative means of access was convenient for the staff, but it would only take one incident of violence by an outsider against a student for them to realize their foolishness in leaving the door unlocked.

Jude hadn't yet worked out the best approach to use with Andy Constant. Her suspicion was growing that the lecturer had killed Tadeusz Jankowski. Replaying the scene she had overheard between him and Sophia Urquhart in the Bull made her more certain than ever that they were lovers. He was having an affair with 'Joan' and 'Joan' was Sophia's nickname, at least for Tadek. Maybe she had told her Drama tutor that and he had relished the idea of using it as well.

Andy Constant was a spoilt and petulant man, used to getting his own way. He wouldn't have taken kindly to having a rival for his beautiful student's affections. Quite how he'd come to be in Fethering to meet and kill the young Pole, Jude didn't know, but she felt sure she could find out.

As she pushed open the door into the unlit Drama Studio block, she felt a little stab of fear. If Andy was the murderer and she threatened to reveal that fact to the world, he might not think twice about killing again. Pauline's late husband's view that the prime motive for murder was to keep people quiet came into her mind. She needed to be very circumspect in her approach.

There were no lights on in the lobby, but memory guided her towards the door of the studio itself. She pushed open its heavy mass. The only light inside came from an illuminated 'Exit' sign.

It wasn't a lot, but sufficient for her to see the body of a man lying on the double mattress. And sufficient to be reflected in the glistening of wet redness on his chest.

Jude heard a sound behind her in the lobby. She reached for her mobile and pressed the buttons to dial Carole's number.

In High Tor, as soon as the caller was identified, the phone remained untouched.

Chapter Thirty-four

There was a call that Carole did take later that evening, and selfishly she almost wished she hadn't. It was from Gaby, at her wit's end because Lily had developed a high temperature and would not be comforted. The doctor had been called and was going to come again in the morning. If the little mite wasn't better then, she'd be taken into hospital for observation.

For Carole, already desolated by Jude's betrayal, that was all she needed. She knew she wouldn't sleep a wink that night, expecting every minute a phone call with terrible news from Stephen or Gaby.

She had forgotten that awful panic that can be instantly summoned up by the sickness of a child. Lily was so perfect, but so tiny. The lightest puff of illness could blow her away, it seemed to Carole as she faced the long agony of the night. Everything in her life felt suddenly threatened and fragile.

Jude heard only the clattering of the external door of the Drama block. She shivered as she realized she must have passed within inches of whoever it was in the lobby. She must have been within touching distance of someone who was probably the murderer of Tadeusz Jankowski.

But her first priority was the man lying on the bed. She felt along the walls for light switches, but in vain. She remembered that Andy Constant had achieved his lighting effects from the box, but she didn't know how to get in there.

Still, if she concentrated . . . Her eyes slowly adjusted to the gloom. The light from the 'Exit' sign seemed to grow stronger.

Soon she could see clearly enough to recognize that the man on the bed was Andy Constant himself. Blood was pouring from his chest, but he was still breathing.

Jude rang the police.

They were much tougher with her this time than they had been after Tadek's death. To discover one stabbing victim might be considered bad luck; discover two and the authorities are bound to get suspicious. It took Jude most of the evening to convince the detectives that she had no responsibility for either crime. Their questioning remained polite, but they were very persistent.

Andy Constant, she was told, had been taken to hospital and was in intensive care. They promised to let her know when they heard anything about his condition. And meanwhile they kept going over the same ground, asking about her relationship with the lecturer, on and wearily on. She was suitably cagey on the subject, admitting that they had met for a drink a couple of times, but denying things had gone any further than that. Which was pretty much the truth.

In fact, Jude answered all the detectives' questions as honestly as she could, but she didn't volunteer any information they didn't ask her about. Above all, she didn't mention that she and Carole had been trying to solve the murder mystery themselves. She knew the derision with which professional policemen would greet that news.

To her surprise, in what the detectives said to her they did not seem to be linking the two attacks. Or maybe they were, but did not want her speculations going down that route. As an amateur, she had the usual difficulty in knowing how far the official investigation had proceeded. And she wasn't about to be enlightened on the subject. Jude was a witness and a possible suspect. The police weren't about to tell her their secrets.

Finally, around ten-thirty, the detectives seemed to decide that there really was nothing more she could tell them. They said that they were trying to keep what had happened secret for as long as possible and firmly forbade Jude to have any contact with the media about the stabbing. It was their hope to make some headway with their investigation before they had to deal with the intrusions of press and television. Then they thanked her politely for her cooperation and asked if she wanted a lift home, an offer of which she took grateful advantage.

It was an unmarked police car that dropped her outside Woodside Cottage. She looked up at High Tor, but the curtains of Carole's bedroom were closed. Oh well, she could bring her neighbour up to date in the morning.

Inside, she found that Zofia Jankowska was not yet back from the Crown and Anchor (where, though Ted Crisp would never admit it, she seemed to be becoming an essential member of staff). Jude didn't wait up for her. She was totally exhausted by the events of the day, so got to bed as quickly as she could and passed out.

Chapter Thirty-five

Gaby rang back at eight-thirty. Lily had slept well and, though a bit grizzly, no longer had such a high temperature. The doctor's return visit had been put off. Stephen had gone off to work. They were all right.

She hadn't rung her mother-in-law earlier because she hadn't wanted to wake her. To Carole, who'd been sleeplessly entertaining the most ghastly speculations all night, this was an unhelpful thing to say. But she didn't mention the fact, just said how relieved she was about Lily's improvement and asked for regular updates on the tiny girl's progress.

At least one cause of her perturbation was diminished. The other, she thought, might never be resolved.

Waiting for the call from Gaby had kept her at home when she would normally have been taking Gulliver down to Fethering Beach, so her next priority was giving the dog his walk.

As she opened the front door, dressed in her smart Burberry, thick scarf and hat, Carole found herself face to face with Jude, who had been on the verge of lifting the knocker.

'Good morning,' said Carole coldly. 'I'm just taking Gulliver for his walk.'

'Well, I'll come with you. Just give me a moment to get a coat.'

'I don't think it'll be necessary for you to come. I'll be fine on my own.'

And with that, Carole Seddon, with Gulliver in tow, stalked off down Fethering High Street in the direction of the beach.

Open-mouthed, her neighbour watched her go. But it wasn't in Jude's nature to let wounds fester. If something had come up between her and Carole, then she had to find out immediately what it was. She got her coat and set off after the figures of woman and dog dwindling into the distance.

Though not overtly looking back, Carole was aware of the pursuit. When she reached the edge of the beach, rather than going left towards the estuary of the River Fether, she turned right and strode firmly away, Gulliver off his lead and performing eccentric circles around her. That way the beach stretched on for miles. Carole's long stride took her ever further away from her pursuer, who not only had shorter legs but also had a lot more weight to carry.

After walking about a quarter of a mile and not making any inroad into her neighbour's lead, Jude stopped and sat on the end of a wooden breakwater where it nuzzled into the high shingle of the beach. There was no alternative route; Carole would have to come back the way she had gone. It was just a matter of waiting.

Jude sat there for over an hour. Carole must have known that she was making a fool of herself, but when she finally did come to where her neighbour sat, she looked all set to walk by without acknowledging her.

Jude wasn't having any of that. She stood up and blocked Carole's way. 'Look, will you please tell me what's going on.'

'Nothing's going on,' replied Carole icily.

Gulliver very much let the side down by going up to Jude and enthusiastically licking her hand.

'Carole, I have done something to offend you. I don't know what it is, but I can assure you it wasn't deliberate.'

'Don't worry about it. It's not a problem.'

Carole once again tried to manoeuvre herself past, but found her arm grabbed. 'Look, we're friends. And it's stupid for friends to split up over something trivial.'

'People have different definitions of trivial,' came the sniffy reply.

'Listen, Carole, I have actually got a lot of new information on the murder case. You won't believe what has happened.'

Though clearly tempted, Carole wasn't going to succumb to curiosity. 'I'm sorry. I must be on my way.'

'No.' Jude kept her neighbour's arm firmly in her grasp. 'I am not going to let you go until you tell me what's bugging you.'

'All right,' said Carole with exasperation. 'You've just said we're friends. Well, I would have thought it was a rather strange person who moves house without telling her friend about it.'

'Moves house?' Jude looked at Carole with incomprehension. Then slowly the penny dropped. 'Oh, no . . . the valuation? You didn't think . . .? That was not because I was really selling the house. I set it up just to get some information out of Hamish Urquhart. And it worked. He confirmed that Sophia had been in Leipzig last summer, which is where she must have met Tadek.'

'Oh,' said Carole, suddenly feeling rather small.

'You idiot!' said Jude affectionately. 'You absolute idiot! Now will you please let me tell you what has happened in the last twenty-four hours?'

As the two women walked back up the beach, Carole heard everything, about the second stabbing and Jude's uncomfortable evening with the police. By the time they got back to Woodside Cottage, her bad mood had dissipated and she was once again totally caught up in the murder investigation.

'You haven't had any news as to how Andy Constant is?'

Jude shook her head. 'There was a lot of blood. I don't have the medical knowledge to assess how serious it was. The police said they'd keep me informed, but I doubt if they'll bother.'

'I'll put on the radio when I get in – and check the television . . . see if there's anything about the attack.'

'Yes, well, if I hear anything, obviously I'll let you know as soon as possible. And, Carole,' Jude went on as her friend moved towards High Tor, 'don't ever imagine that I would sell my house without telling you.'

'But are you thinking of selling it?'

'Not today,' said Jude enigmatically. And Carole had to be content with that.

The phone in Woodside Cottage rang at about five that afternoon. 'Is that Jude?' asked a well-spoken woman's voice she did not recognize.

'Yes.'

'You don't know me. I'm Esther Constant. Andy's wife.'

'Ah,' said Jude, fearing the worst. 'How is he?'

'Surprisingly good, actually. He's out of intensive care.'

'Wow, that was quick.'

'Yes, although there was a lot of bleeding, the wound itself wasn't very deep. He's still quite weak because he lost so much blood, but no, he's basically on the mend.'

'I'm delighted to hear it.'

'Yes.' Esther Constant was silent for a moment, as though uncertain how to phrase the next bit. 'Andy . . . he . . . he said he'd like to see you . . .'

'Oh. Really?' Jude was thrown. Was Andy's wife aware of his interest in her? 'Why is that?' she asked.

'He said so that he could say thank you.'

'Thank me for what?'

'Andy reckons it was your arrival which frightened his attacker off. He thinks you may have saved his life.'

*

The wounded lecturer was in a private hospital not far from the University of Clincham campus. Whether he had been put in there for reasons of security or because he had a good private health insurance, Jude didn't know. She'd gone by train along the coastal line to Clincham and got to the hospital's reception round seven-thirty. They were expecting her and when she asked for Andy Constant, a smartly suited woman directed her to a suite of rooms on the fourth floor. The decor of the hospital was all soothing pastel blues and greens. There were tasteful photographic prints on the walls and gratuitous reproduction coffee tables on the landings.

A nurse sitting behind a reception desk on the fourth-floor landing led her to a door which had a card marked 'Mr A. Constant' fitted into a plastic slot. She tapped on the door and Esther Constant's voice said, 'Come in.'

The scene that greeted Jude was one of long-standing connubial bliss. Andy was propped up on a lot of pillows, with an edge of bandages visible at the neck of his pyjamas. Esther, a pretty woman with short dark hair, was seated at his bedside, holding his hand. She rose and said, 'You must be Jude.'

'Yes.'

'I'm so grateful to you for coming. Andy really wanted to see you.'

The patient smiled weakly and gave a feeble wave. Jude felt the knee-jerk suspicion that she had in all dealings with Andy Constant. He wasn't as badly hurt as he was pretending. Once again he was milking a situation for all it was worth.

'As I said on the phone,' Esther Constant went on, 'he really thinks you may have saved his life. His attacker would have gone on stabbing him if you hadn't arrived. Andy reckons the attacker must have heard you coming in through the main door of the Drama block, and that's what made him do a runner.'

'Maybe. I didn't see anything, but I think I must have passed him – or her – in the lobby.'

'Anyway, Andy says thank God you arrived.'

Jude's conjecture that the whole conversation might be conducted with Esther verbalizing her husband's thoughts ended, as Andy himself said, 'Yes, I can't thank you enough.'

Jude shrugged. 'I'm glad if that is what happened, but it was pure luck. A serendipitous accident of timing.' But in spite of his injured state, she couldn't help moving instantly into investigative mode. 'Did you see who it was who attacked you?'

'No. He – or she – was waiting for me in the lighting box. Must have known I switch on the studio lights from there. Leapt on me as soon as I got through the door.' His voice sounded pretty robust, considering he had just emerged from intensive care.

'Have you been questioned by the police yet?'

'Just basic stuff.'

'They're coming again tomorrow morning,' Esther Constant interposed. 'Assuming he's stronger by then.'

Andy Constant showed a brave smile. 'Which I'll hope to be.' Then he reached out and took his wife's hand. 'Esther love . . . I just want to ask Jude a few details about what she saw . . . and I don't want to make you go through the whole thing again. Maybe you'd like to ask the nurse to get you a cup of coffee?'

His wife, obedient to his every whim, took the hint and made for the door. 'I'll give you five minutes.' Then, explaining to Jude, she said, 'Important that he doesn't get too tired. He's very weak.'

Weak he may have been, but the minute Esther was out of the door, he sat up in bed and said urgently, 'Have the police talked to you yet, Jude?'

'Yes. At some length.'

'And did you tell them anything?'

'About what?'

'About you and me.'

'There isn't much to say about you and me, is there?'

'Come on. We've met a few times. But for . . . external events, we'd be lovers by now.'

Jude wondered how accurate that was. Any attraction she might have felt for Andy Constant had melted away in the last couple of days. But, looking back and being honest with herself, she had a nasty feeling his words might be true.

'Well, I certainly didn't tell the police that.'

'What did you tell them?'

'Just that we'd met for drinks a couple of times, that you'd asked me to go and see *Rumours of Wars* . . .'

'And what about last night?'

'I said that you'd asked me to join you for a drink in the Drama Studio.'

'Just that?'

'Pretty much, yes.'

'Hm.' He looked troubled. 'The thing is, it's very important that Esther doesn't find out anything about us.'

Jude saw him then for what he was. Just another cheap philandering husband. All his talk of the moribund nature of his marriage was so much guff. At home he was the dutiful husband, but he used those elastic moments between work and home to conduct his affairs. His favourite time for an assignation was not a dinner, not a whole evening. No, six o'clock in his own convenient little knocking-shop, the Drama Studio. Time for a furtive glass of Scotch and a quick sexual encounter. Then, no doubt, back home to Esther with an airy, 'Oh, met up with some people for a drink after work.'

Jude shuddered inwardly to think how nearly she had become involved with a man like that.

'Andy, I've said what I told the police. What they make of the information, how much further they want to go with it, that's not up to me.'

'I just don't want Esther to get hurt. She's quite fragile emotionally. I don't want her getting hold of the wrong end of the stick.'

Getting hold of the right end of the stick, thought Jude. Being made to realize what a bastard her husband really was. Yes, it was quite possible that Esther was completely unaware of Andy's finely practised seduction technique. As the saying went, the wife was always the last to know.

'I won't do anything to make the situation worse,' said Jude. Then, suddenly she asked, 'And what about you and Sophia?'

She wouldn't have thought it possible for his face to have gone paler, but it did. 'Me and Sophia? The police didn't ask about that, did they?'

It was the nearest she was likely to get to an admission that he had been having an affair with the girl, so Jude pressed home her advantage. 'No, they haven't asked me about that, but what do you want me to say if they do?'

'Do you think that's likely?'

She shrugged. 'I don't know which way the police investigation is going, do I?'

'Oh, God.' He looked really bad.

'So you're not denying that you were having an affair with her?'

'Look, these things happen.' He was trying to sound disingenuous, but it wasn't cutting any ice with Jude. 'Two attractive people who're attracted to each other, sometimes the emotion can just get too strong to cope with. Even with the difference in ages. I think in fact the difference in ages made it even more powerful. We could learn so much from each other. Come on, haven't you ever been in a situation like that, Jude?'

She had, but she wasn't about to tell him so. 'How long had it been going on?'

'I suppose the attraction was there since the beginning of the academic year, when we first met . . .'

That made sense. Sophia had met Tadek in Leipzig in the summer, he had followed her to England in late

September. Maybe they had begun or continued an affair. But round the same time Sophia had started her university career, and found the archetypal lecherous lecturer coming on to her. As Jude had deduced before, it was a classic love triangle.

'And when did you become lovers?' she asked implacably.

'I suppose it must have been in the run-up to Christmas. You know, there were lots of parties and things on the campus. And I was working closely with Sophia on some one-to-one role-playing exercises.' Yes, I bet you were, thought Jude. He shrugged helplessly, as he went on, 'And, you know, one thing led to another. We both admitted how much we fancied each other and . . .'

Jude suppressed her fury. Andy Constant had shamelessly abused his position of responsibility and was now trying to get sympathy for himself as a plaything of the gods, a man incapable of resisting the surging power of a *grand amour*. All she said, though, was, 'And are you and Joan still love's young dream?'

'Joan? How do you know about—?'

'I know it was Sophia's nickname. One given to her by her other boyfriend.'

'Other boyfriend?'

'Didn't she mention that she had another boyfriend?'

'Oh, yes,' he recalled. 'There had been someone, apparently. But she implied that that had been over for a long time.'

Taking a leaf out of your book then, thought Jude. 'No more details?'

'No, she said she'd got rid of him.'

'Hm.' Jude took in the implications of this for a moment, then said, 'I actually asked whether your affair with Sophia was still going on.'

'Well, no.' He screwed up his face wryly. 'We had had a bit of a falling-out, during the last week, really. I mean, often the really powerful loves have only a limited duration. "So quick bright things come to confusion", and all that. I had to tell her that it wasn't working. And, you know, I was beginning to feel guilty about Esther.'

Oh yes, very handy – the married man's time-honoured way of getting out of an extramarital entanglement: he's worried about his wife.

'How did Sophia take the news?'

He grimaced. 'Not very well, I'm afraid. She was terribly upset, talk of suicide, all kinds of things.' He smiled a put-upon smile. 'Clearly, the whole thing meant much more to her than it did to me.'

Once again Jude was struck by Andy's arrogance. He saw himself doomed to go through life as a babe-magnet, powerless against the devastating strength of his own attractiveness.

'So thoughts of Esther were the only reason you said your affair with Sophia must end?'

'Well . . .' He smiled winningly. 'There was another reason.'

'What was that?'

'I thought maybe things were going to work out with you.'

This time Jude had great difficulty containing her anger. Even from his hospital bed the sleaze-bag was coming on to her. One moment he was talking of breaking off one relationship out of consideration for his wife, the next he was proposing to start a new one. She calmed herself, and said, 'Going back to what happened to you last night, you didn't get any sight of your attacker, did you?'

He shook his head. 'It was pitch dark. And it happened so quickly. The whole thing was over in a matter of seconds.'

'So nothing? No glimpse of a face? No touch of a body?'

'Well, as a matter of fact, as I tried to defend myself, I got hold of his or her coat. And it felt like waxed fabric.'

'A Barbour?'

'That kind of thing, yes.'

Jude nodded thoughtfully. 'Oh, well, no doubt the police will catch the culprit.'

'I doubt it.'

'Why not?'

'Well, it was probably a drifter, who just broke into the Drama Studio in hope of finding some equipment he could sell to buy drugs.'

'That's nonsense, Andy. Too much of a coincidence. My view would be that your attacker was very definitely targeting you. You said as much yourself. It was someone who knew your habits very well, knew that you frequently went into the Drama Studio without switching on the working lights.'

'I'm sure it wasn't.'

This was said with such intensity that Jude suddenly understood. Andy Constant thought he knew precisely who had attacked him. And at that moment Jude reckoned she did too.

'Andy, was it Sophia who stabbed you last night?'

'No. Of course it wasn't.'

But he didn't sound convincing, so Jude pressed on. 'I think it was. And I think that's why you're going to push your theory about the perpetrator being some nameless drifter. You're afraid that if the police get on to Sophia, Esther will find out about the affair you've been having with her.'

'No, Jude. I'm sure it wasn't Sophia. It wouldn't be in her nature to do something like that.'

'You don't think so? "Hell hath no fury" . . . et cetera.'

'I'm sure it wasn't her.' But now he sounded as though he were trying to convince himself.

'It could have been, though,' Jude persisted. His silence was more eloquent than an admission. 'Come on, Andy, tell me what it was made you think it was Sophia?'

'Well,' he said feebly, 'it's just an impression I got, split-second thing. But there's a very distinctive scent she wears. I thought I got a whiff of that last night.'

Chapter Thirty-six

It was nearly nine o'clock when Jude left the hospital. Her route back to Clincham Station took her past the university campus. Which meant that she also passed by the Bull, from which emanated the sound of music and weak applause.

Of course. Friday night. She had witnessed the workings of synchronicity too often to be surprised by its magic. Friday night was the night the Bull hosted 'Clincham Uni's Number One Folk/Rock Band.' Magic Dragon, the band fronted by Sophia Urquhart. Who were actually playing in the pub at that moment. Now that was magic.

She called Carole on the mobile. 'Look, I haven't got time to explain the details, but could you come to Clincham straight away? Meet me in the Bull. And could you check at Woodside Cottage to see if Zofia's there? If so, could you bring her too?'

Magic Dragon didn't seem to be much of a Friday night draw. Maybe the University of Clincham students went further afield for their weekend entertainment, to the clubs of Brighton or Portsmouth. Or maybe they wanted a more up-to-date musical repertoire than the band provided.

There had been so many sixties revivals, but Jude was still surprised to hear the songs that Magic Dragon had chosen. It was mostly the Joan Baez back catalogue. Given Sophia Urquhart's voice, this made sense. The songs suited her pure soprano. But they seemed an odd choice for a student group in the early twenty-first century.

'Farewell Angelina', 'Banks of the Ohio', 'Go 'Way from My Window', 'There But for Fortune', 'With God on Our Side' . . . they all brought back Jude's youth and she loved hearing them, but she wondered who had made the selection. Was one of the band members an enthusiastic researcher of the period? Had there been some influence from Tadek, with his love of sixties music? Or from Andy Constant, who seemed never to have left the sixties? Maybe Jude would find out when she finally spoke to Sophia. Though she had more serious things to discuss with the girl than her musical tastes.

Carole and Zofia arrived in the pub at about twenty to ten. Which was good timing – more synchronicity, thought Jude – as Magic Dragon took a break, after their first set, at nine forty-five. So she was up at the bar buying drinks when the thirsty band approached.

'Sophia!' she cried. She was aware once again of the girl's expensive perfume, the smell that Andy Constant had detected on his attacker. 'I'm Jude – remember?'

'Yes, of course.'

'Wanted to hear your band. Your father was telling

me how good you were. Wonderful stuff! Can I get you a drink by way of congratulation?'

'Well, erm . . .'

'Go on, what would you like?'

Like most students, the girl didn't prevaricate long over the offer of a free drink. 'Pint of Stella, please. I get very thirsty singing.'

'I'm sure you do.' Jude added it to her order. 'Do come and join us. I've got a couple of friends who'd love to meet you.'

'Well, I . . .' She didn't want to, she wanted to be with her mates, but Sophia Urquhart was a well-brought-up girl and knew that accepting a drink from someone did involve certain social responsibilities. 'Yes, fine. But I'd better not be long, because we don't get much of a break before the next set.'

Sophia helped Jude carry the drinks across to her table, where she was introduced to Carole and Zofia. By first names only.

'Excellent music.' Carole had only heard one number, but she knew it was the appropriate thing to say.

'Not much of a turn-out tonight, though.' Sophia Urquhart looked round the room with disappointment. Now she had a chance to study the girl, Jude could see that she looked stressed and tired. The gold-red hair didn't quite have its usual lustre, and there was a redness around the eyes.

'Our type of music's not very popular, I'm afraid. Most of the people at uni want stuff they can dance to. Think this could be the last gig we do here.'

'Oh?'

'Landlord said, if we didn't pull in a bigger crowd, that'd be it.'

'Well, hopefully you'll be able to get booked in somewhere else.'

'Maybe.' The girl sounded listless, as though the fate of Magic Dragon didn't matter one way or the other.

Jude decided it was time to move into investigation mode. 'Sophia, Zofia is the sister of Tadeusz Jankowski.'

The shock took their suspect's breath away. She looked at the Polish girl with a mixture of incredulity and fear.

'I think you knew him,' said Jude.

'No. I . . . don't know what you're talking about.' Sophia Urquhart's hastily scrambled-together defence didn't sound convincing.

'You met at a music festival in Leipzig last summer.'

In the face of the facts, her resistance crumbled. 'Yes,' she admitted apathetically.

Zofia took over the interrogation. 'We know you play music together. Pavel has sent me recordings.'

'Pavel,' came the echo.

'I have come from Warsaw to England to find out what happened to Tadek . . . to my brother.'

'He was killed.'

'I know that. I want to know why he was killed. And who killed him.'

The English girl slumped like a rag doll. Her spirit was broken. 'Everyone wants to know that. Everyone always asks the same questions.'

'When you say everyone,' asked Carole, 'do you mean the police as well?'

Sophia looked puzzled. 'Presumably the police will be asking questions, if they're investigating Tadek's death.' She was now making no pretence of not having known the murder victim.

'But have the police questioned you?'

'About Tadek's death? Why should they?'

'Didn't they know about him being in love with you?'

'I don't think so. Nobody knew.'

'We managed to find out about it,' said Carole. 'It's pretty difficult to keep a love affair a complete secret. The participants may think nobody knows, but that's very rarely true.'

'Where did you meet after he came to England?' asked Jude more gently.

'We went to his room in Littlehampton. First he found me at the college. He had been texting and calling me and sending me songs ever since we met in Leipzig. He kept saying that he would come to England, and I didn't believe him. Then one day, early in the term, there he was on the campus. And he's telling me he loves me.'

'Were you pleased?'

'Yes. But it was difficult. I didn't want people to know about him.'

Zofia was offended by this apparent slight on her brother. 'Why you not want people to know about him?'

'Because . . .' The English girl looked confused. 'Because things were more complicated than he thought. Tadek thought if we loved each other, everything would be fine. That was all that mattered. We wouldn't have to think about practical things. He wanted me to drop out of uni, travel Europe with him, play music. I told him life could not be as simple as that. You have to get qualifications, make a living, get on with things. You can't just drift.'

As her brother had, Sophia Urquhart sounded as though she were parroting her father's sentiments. No relationship between the idealistic Pole and this conventional product of the Home Counties could ever have had a long-term future. But would Sophia have regarded the young man as enough of an inconvenience to murder him?

'Tadek thought that was possible,' responded Zofia sadly. 'All he wanted to do was just drift. Write his songs, play music and drift.'

'Well, that's no way to go through life.' Sophia Urquhart was once again her father's daughter.

'Did you love him?' asked Jude.

'Maybe for a while. I liked him, certainly. In Leipzig it was very romantic. Yes, I think I was in love with him then. It was a kind of unreal time, I was away from home and . . . yes. But that was an exotic dream, and it's difficult to recapture that kind of dream in somewhere like Fethering or Clincham. So the relationship had to end.'

'But he still loved you?'

'Probably.' She spoke as though the boy's continuing adoration had been a minor irritant. 'He kept phoning and texting me, and writing the songs. I got sick of it. Every time I heard his voice, saying, "Fee this, Fee that".'

'"Fee"?'

'It was his nickname for me. He could never pronounce "So-fie-ah". He always said "So-fee-ah". So he called me "Fee".'

'Ah.' Finally Jude had her explanation for Tadeusz Jankowski's dying words. But she didn't pursue it at that moment. Who knew how the girl might react on hearing that the boy had died with her name on his lips? Anyway, there were more urgent questions to be asked. 'You say you didn't want anyone to know about the connection between you. Is that why all of his music had to be taken from his room?'

Sophia Urquhart hesitated before replying, as though she needed to prepare her answer. 'Yes. Once he'd died, there was bound to be a police investigation. I didn't want to get involved in anything like that.'

'So what did you do with the CDs and things?'

'I put them in a litter bin on the street.'

'But not the guitar?'

'No, it wouldn't fit. I was looking for a skip to dump it in on my way to uni the day after Tadek died. But then I met one of my friends from the Drama set and she asked me what I was doing with the guitar. I remembered that Andy had asked us to bring instruments in, so that's how I explained it away. I thought it would be safely hidden in the Drama Studio. The police investigation wouldn't go as far as uni.'

'You mentioned Andy Constant,' said Jude.

'So?' The girl looked defiant, but a blush was spreading up from her neck.

'Might he have been another reason why your relationship with Tadek had to end?'

'I don't know what you're talking about.'

'I've just come from the hospital where Andy Constant is recovering from being stabbed.'

There was a silence around the table. The raucousness of a small group of students round the bar was suddenly loud.

'Andy told me about the affair that you and he had been having,' Jude went on. 'He told me about using the nickname "Joan" for you.'

'Which is the name Tadek used,' said Zofia.

'I didn't know . . . Andy . . . had been stabbed.' Sophia spoke haltingly, with great difficulty.

'No?' asked Carole sceptically.

'I thought it possible that someone might have attacked him . . . but I didn't know he had been . . . stabbed,' she said again. 'You say he's in hospital. Is he badly hurt?'

'He'll survive. Though he was lucky that his attacker was frightened off before more damage could be done.'

'Good,' said Sophia Urquhart softly.

'Andy also said,' Jude went on inexorably, 'that he recognized the perfume his attacker was wearing.'

'Perfume?' Sophia mouthed, uncomprehending.

'Yes. Andy Constant said his attacker smelt of the perfume that you use.'

The girl looked bewildered, but whether her bewilderment was genuine Carole and Jude could not guess.

Then suddenly a memory came to her, and her hand went up to her mouth. 'Oh, my God. My Barbour!'

'What?'

'My Barbour jacket. I couldn't find it last night. That would smell of my perfume.'

Carole thought this sudden recollection was too neat. She felt sure the girl was just play-acting. 'And what time did you go out last night?'

'About eight. I went to meet Daddy in a restaurant for dinner.' Sophia Urquhart caught sight of the other members of Magic Dragon, who were gesturing that they should start playing again. She half-rose from her seat.

'No, you can't go yet.' Carole said this so fiercely that the girl sat back down again. 'Tell me, were you at home before you went out to meet your father?'

'Yes, I'd left uni early. I wasn't feeling too good. So I got back to Fethering at about four.'

'And didn't go out again till eight?'

'No, I didn't.' If that were true, then Sophia Urquhart couldn't have been in the Drama Studio at the University of Clincham at six, stabbing her lecturer and former lover. 'It was when I went out to meet Daddy that I couldn't find my Barbour.'

'I don't suppose,' asked Carole cynically, 'that anyone could vouch for the fact that you were at home yesterday at the times you say you were?'

'As a matter of fact,' the girl replied almost smugly, 'there's someone who can. It was fairly slack in the office yesterday, so my brother Hamish was home by five. And he was still there when I left.'

With that and a curt nod, Sophia Urquhart went across to join the rest of Magic Dragon. The moment she arrived, the guitars and fiddle started the intro to 'All My Trials', and, whatever emotions were going through her mind, they were suppressed as her pure voice took up the song.

> *Hush little baby don't you cry,*
> *You know your mama was born to die.*
> *All my trials, Lord, soon be over.*

Just like Joan.

Carole and Jude looked at each other. And the identical logical progress was going through both their minds.

Chapter Thirty-seven

There was no difficulty the next morning in making an appointment with Ewan Urquhart. Though it was a Saturday, business in the offices of Urquhart & Pease remained slack. 'Won't really pick up again till the spring, when the sun comes out,' he had told Jude when she rang through. He sounded, as ever, urbane, the Old Carthusian to the last polished vowel.

If he thought it strange that Jude arrived with a friend to discuss the valuation of Woodside Cottage, he was too well bred to articulate his feelings. He and Hamish were both in the outer office when the women arrived. The younger man sat at a desk, looking blank. Despite the potential seriousness of the situation, Jude couldn't help being reminded of the old joke:

Why don't estate agents look out of the window in the morning?

Because it gives them nothing to do in the afternoon.

There appeared to be no other staff on duty that morning. Maybe 'in the spring, when the sun comes out', there would be more. Ewan Urquhart offered them coffee, but Carole and Jude said they'd just had some. He then invited them to join him in his back office. 'You hold the fort out here, Hamish. Fight off the hordes of eager purchasers, eh?'

His office gave the impression of the library of a gentlemen's club. There were shelves showing the leather spines of unopened books, and the intervening areas of wall were dark green, with a couple of framed sporting prints. In pride of place was an etching of the neo-Gothic splendour of Charterhouse school. The desk was reproduction mahogany, the chairs were reproduction leather. And Ewan Urquhart's vowels were reproduction upper-class.

He gestured them to chairs and said, 'Now do tell me what I can do for you, ladies? I didn't gather, Mrs Seddon, do you actually live at Woodside Cottage with, er . . . Jude?'

'Good heavens, no.' She didn't know whether he actually was making a suggestion of lesbianism, but it was a notion she wanted to dispel as quickly as possible. 'I live next door. High Tor.'

'I know it well. Part of my business to know the names of all the houses in the immediate vicinity. Never know when one might come up for sale, and one likes to keep a step ahead of the opposition. A highly competitive business, ours, you know.'

'I'm sure it is.' There was a silence. Having built themselves up to the confrontation, neither of the women was sure how next to proceed. They should have planned what to say.

'So, Mrs Seddon, am I to gather that you are also thinking of putting High Tor on the market? I would be more than happy to arrange a valuation for you too if—'

'No, no. I'm quite settled there at the moment, thank you.'

'Good.' As another silence extended itself, Ewan Urquhart pushed his fingers through the greying hair of his temples. 'So, please tell me. What can I do for you?'

Jude had had enough of prevarication.

'We've come to talk to you about Tadeusz Jankowski.' He looked surprised. 'Don't pretend you don't know the name.'

'I am making no such pretence. I read the newspapers and watch television. I know that Tadeusz Jankowski was the name of the young man stabbed here in Fethering a couple of weeks ago. But I don't know what he has to do with me.'

'He has to do with you the fact that he was in love with your daughter Sophia.'

Ewan Urquhart chuckled lightly. 'My dear Jude, I'm sure there are a lot of young men who have been in love with my daughter. She is an exceptionally beautiful and talented young woman. It is inevitable that she attracts the interest of the opposite sex. Whether she would give any encouragement to a Polish immigrant, though, is another matter.'

'Your daughter met Tadeusz Jankowski at a music festival in Leipzig last summer,' Carole announced. 'While she was InterRailing in Europe.'

He did look shaken by this revelation, but they couldn't tell why. It could have been new information to him, or he could have been surprised by how much detail they knew of his daughter's life.

'They had an affair out in Germany,' Carole went on, 'and then Tadeusz Jankowski came over to England to look for her.'

For the first time Ewan Urquhart began to lose his cool. 'My daughter would not have a relationship with a foreigner!'

'What you mean, Ewan,' said Jude, 'is that you wouldn't like your daughter to have a relationship with a foreigner. I don't have children, but I've seen often enough that they do not always turn out as their parents want them to.'

'Sophia is an intelligent girl. She wouldn't mix with people who're unworthy of her.'

'And what makes you think Tadeusz Jankowski was unworthy of her?'

'His nationality, apart from anything else. All right, I know we have reason to thank some Polish airmen for the help they gave us against Hitler, but as a race they're not to be trusted. Sophia has been brought up to keep foreigners at a healthy distance.'

'Didn't it occur to you,' asked Carole, 'that if she went InterRailing round Europe, she might meet some foreigners?'

'Yes. I wasn't keen on the whole idea of a gap year, but Sophia managed to persuade me. She went against my better judgement. But I can assure you you've got the wrong end of the stick if you think she's been having affairs with foreigners. When Sophia does get to the point of having affairs, I'm sure she will be very selective in her choice of men.'

'"When she gets to the point of having affairs"?' Jude echoed. 'How old is your daughter, Ewan?'

'Nineteen, nearly twenty.'

'Well, surely you know from the media that these days most young women of nearly twenty have been sexually active for some years.'

'Most young women, maybe,' he snapped. 'Not Sophia!'

For the first time they realized the depth of his obsession with his daughter, and his obsession with her purity. In her father's eyes, no man would ever be good enough for Sophia Urquhart. He had built up an image of her as untouchable, and what he might do to anyone who threatened that image was terrifying.

'If you claim not to know about her affair with Tadeusz Jankowski, then presumably the same goes for her relationship with Andy Constant.'

'Andy Constant?'

'You know the name?'

'Of course. I've met the man. He's Sophia's Drama tutor at the university.' He was now very angry. 'Look, what is this? What are you two up to? I don't have to listen to malicious slander of my daughter from small-town gossips.'

'It is not malicious slander. It is the truth. Andy Constant was, until recently, your daughter's lover.'

'No! He couldn't . . . Sophia wouldn't . . . Not with a man of that age . . . She's not like her mother. Her mother was little better than a tart, who'd open her legs for any man who offered her a smile and a kind word.' Gifts of which, both women imagined, she hadn't received many at home. 'Sophia's not like that. She wouldn't . . . She hasn't been brought up like that!' Now he was really losing control. His face was growing red and congested. 'God, if I thought a man like that Andy Constant had touched my daughter, I'd kill him!'

He seemed then to realize what he'd said, and opened and closed his mouth, as if trying to take the words back.

'Which,' said Carole calmly, 'is what you failed to do last night.'

'What?'

'You stabbed Andy Constant,' said Jude, 'but you didn't kill him.'

'I'm sorry? Where is this supposed to have happened?'

'In the Drama Studio at Clincham College. You waited for Andy Constant in the lighting box. When he came in, you stabbed him. You would have stabbed him more than once, but you heard someone arriving. It was me, actually. You passed me in the lobby, I think, when you made your escape.'

'You're saying I stabbed Andy Constant?' His eyes were wild now, darting about from one of the women to the other.

'Yes. For some reason – maybe to disguise yourself – you wore your daughter's Barbour when you committed the crime. You couldn't stand the thought of anyone touching Sophia, so you tried to kill Andy Constant – just as you had killed Tadeusz Jankowski.'

He shook his head wordlessly, a pathetic figure now. His urbanity had deserted him, leaving a shell of a man, a husk wearing an Old Carthusian tie.

'Maybe you stabbed the young man here in this office,' said Carole. 'It was somewhere near the betting shop, somewhere along this parade probably. Or maybe the attack took place in your car. You'd managed to get him into it on some pretext.'

'I can't stand this,' Ewan Urquhart moaned feebly. 'What on earth is going on?'

'Don't worry, Dad. I'll deal with it.'

They hadn't heard the door from the outer office open. Carole and Jude both looked round at the same time to the source of the new voice.

And saw Hamish Urquhart standing in the doorway. With a long kitchen knife in his hand.

Chapter Thirty-eight

'Hamish, call the police,' said Ewan Urquhart. 'These two women are mad and dangerous.'

'They're certainly dangerous,' his son agreed, 'but I don't think the police are the right people to deal with them.'

'I don't understand. I've hardly understood anything that's happened for the last half-hour.'

'Don't worry about it, Dad. I'm in control of the situation.' And, for the first time in Jude's dealings with him, Hamish Urquhart did seem to be in control. There was now a dignity about him which she had not seen before. She was aware of the power in his stocky body and the cold menace in his eyes.

Both women made as if to stand up, but were stilled by a wave of the knife.

'I'll sort this out, Dad,' said Hamish. 'Just as I sorted out your other problems.'

'What other problems?'

'I know how you feel about Soph, Dad. I know how you'd feel about her getting into the wrong company. Particularly the wrong male company. So I sorted things out for you.'

'What do you mean, Hamish? I don't know what you've been doing.'

'No, I know you don't.' There was a quiet smile of pride on the young man's face. 'You didn't need to know. I did things the way you've always said they should be done. The British way. No fuss. No showing off. Not standing up and saying "Aren't I wonderful?" But that quiet British pride of doing the right thing without crowing about it.'

It was chilling to hear the young man echoing his father's words. Ewan Urquhart cleared his throat uneasily and said, 'What do you mean by doing the right thing, Hamish?'

'Getting rid of the wrong sort of people. People who threaten us Urquharts. I knew what you'd think about Soph going around with a foreigner, so I . . . dealt with the problem. Never wanted you to know anything about it, but these two busybodies have told you, so you may as well have the details. Soph told me about this chap she was seeing, this Pole, and I knew you'd disapprove. So I thought, "No need to get the old man worried about this. Time for me to show a bit of Urquhart initiative and sort the problem out for him."

'So I got his address from Soph and went round to see him. He wasn't in, but the door to his room was open. Inside I found . . . He had written songs about her, songs about Soph. There were tapes, CDs, a guitar. I took them all. I didn't want any connection ever to be made between my sister and . . . *that foreigner*!'

'Sophia implied that *she*'d taken the guitar and things,' said Carole.

'Did she? No, I got them, then I gave them to her to dispose of as she thought fit.'

'So your sister knew what you had done?' asked Jude. 'She knew it was you who stabbed Tadek?'

Hamish Urquhart smiled a patronizing smile. 'I didn't tell her. There was no need for her to be involved in anything distasteful. I've always tried to protect Sophia from the nasty things in life.'

Just as your father has, thought Jude. She looked across at Ewan Urquhart, whose face registered growing shock and disbelief as Hamish continued to describe his actions.

'Anyway I had just started driving back here, when I saw the Pole walking back to his room. I stopped the car, told him that I was Sophia's brother and that she was back at the office and wanted to see him. He was over the moon about that and got into the car without a hint of suspicion. So I drove him back here. Knew you'd be off for a couple of hours doing a valuation, Dad, knew it was unlikely there'd be much trade on a Thursday afternoon.

'Anyway, soon as we get back here, his first question is: where's Sophia? I tell him she must have just slipped out for a minute. Said she was probably shopping along the parade.'

Finally Carole and Jude had the explanation for Tadek's appearance in the betting shop on the afternoon of his death. He had been looking for Sophia. His last moments of life had been spent looking for the woman he loved. Though whether they would ever be able to pass the information on to anyone else looked, at that moment, unlikely.

Hamish smiled in self-congratulation. 'I thought that was rather clever. Thinking she was nearby and would be back in a minute, he relaxed. I asked him to take his coat off, and then revealed the real purpose of his visit. I told the sneaky bastard we took a pretty dim view of his interest in Soph and . . .' He made an eloquent gesture with his knife.

Ewan Urquhart was having difficulty in believing what he was hearing. 'You stabbed him?'

'Yes. In the chest.' Hamish grinned with self-satisfaction. 'Worked out rather well, really. I hadn't decided what I was going to do with the body, but then he put his coat on and went out. Luck was on my side, of course – it always is for people who dare to be bold. The weather suddenly turned, and that hailstorm meant nobody saw him leaving the office. Then he went to the betting shop and . . .' He spread his hands wide. They all knew what had happened next. 'I think I can be said to have used the Urquhart initiative.'

'And Sophia's lecturer?' asked Ewan Urquhart, his eyes wide with terror.

'Yes. Andy Constant,' said Hamish in a self-congratulatory tone. 'Soph had mentioned him to me, but I didn't know until recently that he'd been coming on to her.' He grinned triumphantly at Jude. 'In fact I had my suspicions confirmed when I was doing the valuation of your cottage. There was some writing in a notebook on your kitchen table which linked Andy Constant's name to Soph's.

'Well, I knew what your views would be about that, Dad – the idea of someone nearly your own age messing around with your daughter. And I was right, because I just heard you telling these ladies what you thought about that. So again I thought, no need to bother you about it. I took things into my own hands. Soph had told me a bit about Andy Constant's habits, and I worked out that the Drama Studio would be the best place to get him. I borrowed Soph's Barbour because I thought it'd make me look more like one of the students, you know, pass unnoticed on the campus. And I told Soph, if anyone asked, she should say I was at home with her yesterday evening. Oh, I thought the whole thing through. And I would have killed the lecturer too, if I hadn't been disturbed. By you, I gather,' he said, turning with sudden vindictiveness towards Jude.

She said nothing. The knife was dangerously close, and Hamish Urquhart's eyes showed that he was way beyond responding to logical argument.

'So what are you going to do now?' asked his father, very quietly.

Hamish gestured with the knife. 'Deal with these two,' he said airily. 'I'll put their bodies in the van and dispose of them after dark.'

'Where?'

'I don't need to bother you with the details, Dad. Trust me, it's all in hand.' He still sounded like a parody of Ewan Urquhart. Hamish was relishing the reversal. For once, he was patronizing his father, he was the one making the decisions. 'We need never talk about it again. And don't you worry. If I find any more unsuitable men sniffing round Soph, trust me to deal with them.'

'Are you telling me, Hamish, that you killed Tadeusz Jankowski and nearly killed Andy Constant because you didn't think they were suitable men to mix with your sister?'

'Yes, Dad. Of course. Come on, you're not usually so slow on the uptake.' The boy guffawed. 'Usually I'm the one in that role.'

'But, Hamish, don't you realize, killing someone because they're having a relationship you disapprove of, well . . . that's no different from an "honour killing", the kind of thing Asian immigrants get involved in?'

'Nonsense. Totally different. I'm just upholding the honour of the Urquharts, that's all.' He looked around the room, then turned to his father and said compassionately, 'Look, I'll sort this out, Dad. No need for you to be involved. Why don't you nip out to Polly's for a coffee and a teacake? Come back in half an hour and the whole thing'll be sorted.'

He spoke so airily that Carole and Jude had to remind themselves that what he was proposing to 'sort' was their deaths. To their dismay, Ewan Urquhart rose, zombie-like, from behind his desk and said, 'Yes, Hamish. Maybe that's a good idea.'

When his father reached the door, the son stopped him with an arm on his sleeve. 'One thing you haven't said, Dad . . .'

'What?'

'You haven't said you're proud of me for what I've

done.' The appeal in the young man's face was naked and pathetic.

'No, I haven't,' said his father dully.

'Well, please. Say you're proud of me.'

The two generations looked at each other. In Hamish Urquhart's eyes was abject pleading, asking his father at last to give him a ration of praise. The expression in Ewan Urquhart's eyes was harder to read.

The older man moved very quickly. With his left hand he snatched the knife from his son's grasp. His right, bunched in a fist, crashed up into the young man's chin.

Hamish Urquhart went down like a dead weight, thumping the back of his head on a shelf as he fell. He lay immobile. As ever, his father had proved stronger than he was.

Carole and Jude breathed out, letting the accumulated tension twitch out of their bodies.

Chapter Thirty-nine

Hamish Urquhart was taken in for questioning by the police later that Saturday morning. Their suspicions had been moving towards him for some time, and these were confirmed by their interview with Andy Constant in the hospital. He had also been identified by CCTV camera footage on the campus of the University of Clincham. Soon after, the Maiden Avenue entrance to the campus was bricked up.

In police custody Hamish Urquhart made no attempt to deny his crimes and was quickly charged with the murder of Tadeusz Jankowski and the attempted murder of Andy Constant. His defence team were in a quandary as to whether they should put in a plea of insanity. He showed no remorse about his actions, and kept telling them that he had finally done something that would make his father proud of him.

While he was on remand, his sister Sophia visited him as often as she could. Their father didn't. In Ewan Urquhart's view, his son had always been unsatisfactory. Now he was no longer on the scene, the older man found it easier and more convenient to forget that he had ever had a son.

And, once her brother had been sentenced to life, Sophia's visits to him ceased.

She dropped out of the University of Clincham before the end of that academic year and went to join her father in the offices of Urquhart & Pease. She learnt the business quickly and her good looks went down well with the male clients. There were plenty of admirers around, but none of her relationships lasted for more than a few months. All of the aspiring swains failed for the same reason. They couldn't match the impossibly high standards set by Ewan Urquhart for 'the kind of man worthy of my little Soph'.

Magic Dragon broke up even before Sophia left the university and she didn't sing much after that. The gold of her hair faded and her face and neck thickened out, as she reconciled herself to her fate of looking after her father until he died. Which, of course, suited Ewan Urquhart perfectly. And everyone appreciated the sterling work Sophia put in making teas at Old Carthusian cricket matches. Maybe after her father's death she might be able to carve out a life for herself, but nobody was putting bets on it.

Bets continued, however, to be put on horses at the betting shop (though most of the shop's income continued to come from the fixed-price gaming machines). Sonny 'Perfectly' Frank continued to ask 'Know anything?' to everyone who came in. The waiters from the Golden Palace regularly abandoned serving sweet and sour pork for the quick fix of a bet and kept up their high-pitched wind-chime banter. Pauline continued to enjoy the warm, while Wes and Vic continued to neglect their decorating work. They still shouted at every race, surprised like circling goldfish every time their latest brilliant fancy turned out to be a failure.

One regular ceased to attend. After his flu Harold Peskett had resumed going to the betting shop with his elaborate scribbled permutations of doubles and trebles. Then finally one day the results worked for him, and he won over a thousand pounds. So great was the shock that he died of a heart attack right there in the betting shop. Though it was rather inconvenient for Ryan and Nikki, there was a general view that it would have been the way he wanted to go.

Melanie Newton never went back into a betting shop. She didn't need to. Her laptop offered everything she required. She could play the virtual casinos and roulette wheels twenty-four hours a day. Which she did. And as her credit card debts grew, she kept taking up offers of new credit cards. And kept moving to ever more dingy accommodation, one step ahead of her creditors.

Andy Constant was not the kind of man to change. He recovered completely from his stab-wound, and the scar became another part of his seduction technique. He told wide-eyed female freshers how a woman had once been so desolated by his ending their relationship that she had persuaded her brother to attack him. He continued to entice women into his little kingdom of the Drama Studio. And his wife Esther continued to think that they had a happy marriage, though Andy's workload did mean he often had to stay late at the university.

Whenever Jude thought of Andy Constant, she felt very sheepish and shamefaced. She realized how near she had come to making a complete fool of herself. But she knew that, if the same circumstances were to arise, she might again prove susceptible.

So she continued to do some good by her healing. And to wonder whether she really ought at some point to move on from Fethering.

Zofia Jankowska stayed there, though, moving after a few weeks out of Woodside Cottage to a flat of her own. She enrolled in a journalism course at the University of Clincham, and subsidized her studies by continuing to work at the Crown and Anchor. Ted Crisp grudgingly admitted that she was the best bar manager he'd ever had, 'even though she is foreign'.

Carole Seddon watched the miracle of her granddaughter Lily's development with growing awe. The child's existence brought her closer to Stephen and Gaby, but she resisted their ongoing attempts to include David in family encounters.

And she appreciated increasingly the sedate friendship of Gerald Hume. They didn't often go out for meals or anything like that. Such activities would have had too much of the flavour of a 'date' about them. But they did quite often meet in the betting shop.

Carole became very quickly convinced that Gerald's 'system' for applying his accountancy skills to gambling was just as ineffectual as every other 'system' that had been invented since mankind had first bet on horses. But logic did occasionally work, and she drew satisfaction from her own infrequent wins (though the largest sum she ever bet was two pounds).

Her attitude had changed, though. She could begin to see the appeal of gambling. In fact, one rainy day some weeks after Hamish's arrest when she was sitting in the betting shop with Gerald Hume, she surprised herself. Looking at the wet window, Gerald had turned to her with a grin. 'Two quid says the raindrop on the left reaches the bottom of the window frame before the one on the right.'

Carole assessed the relative size of the two rain-drops. She knew a good thing when she saw it. 'You're on,' she said.

THE POISONING IN THE PUB

What's your poison?

Fethering residents Jude and Carole get more than they bargained for when a lunchtime meal in their local pub leaves everyone with food poisoning. The landlord is horrified and when a series of disasters start to befall his business it looks like it could be the end of the road for the Crown and Anchor.

Left with a bad taste in their mouths – and not just from the food – the two amateur detectives wonder if it might just be more than a run of bad luck which is forcing their favourite pub into bankruptcy.

When one of the pub's staff is found in the kitchen of the pub, with a knife through his heart, Carole and Jude swing into action.

There's a killer on the loose in Fethering and our lady sleuths need to uncover who it is before it's last orders for the pub – and themselves.

The Poisoning in the Pub, the delightful new mystery in the Fethering series, is out now.

An extract follows here.

Chapter One

One of the most inauspicious events for any restaurant is to have a customer vomiting on the premises. However distant the cause may be from the establishment's kitchens, whatever rare gastric bug may have triggered the attack, such a happening is never good for business. There is always an assumption on the part of the general public that blame must lie with the food served in the restaurant.

Ted Crisp, landlord of the Crown and Anchor near the sea at Fethering in West Sussex, found that out to his cost one Monday lunchtime in July. His dish of the day was pan-fried scallops with spinach and oriental noodles, and unfortunately it was a choice for which a large number of his customers opted.

Amongst those customers were two women in their fifties. The one whom most people, particularly men, would notice first was called Jude. She had an abundance of blonde hair twisted into an untidy knot on top of her head and a body wobbling between the voluptuous and the plump. She wore a bright cotton skirt and blouse, draped over with a tangle of multicoloured scarves.

Her companion, by contrast, looked as though she wanted to melt into anonymity. Women are said to become invisible when they get into their fifties, and Carole Seddon's appearance suggested that was a tendency of which she strongly approved. She had on a grey Marks & Spencer jumper, beige trousers and shoes so sensible they could have given lectures in civic responsibility. Grey hair was cut into the shape of a helmet; rimless glasses fronted surprisingly shrewd pale blue eyes.

The two were discussing Carole's granddaughter Lily. 'It's down to you,' Jude was saying. 'If you don't feel you're seeing enough of her, then say something to Stephen and Gaby.'

'It's not that I don't feel I'm seeing enough of her,' said Carole. 'It's just I feel I should see more of her if . . .' She petered out.

'If what?'

'Well, if . . .' Carole Seddon was clearly having difficulties with what came next, but Jude's look of innocent quizzicality did eventually begin to elicit an explanation. 'The fact is, Stephen and Gaby have spoken of going away for a long weekend . . . you know, him taking the Friday off and . . .'

'How nice for them.'

'Yes, but . . .' Jude waited patiently. She had the feeling the problem would not be an enormous one. Or at least only enormous to Carole. Her friend and neighbour had a great capacity for getting upset over trifles or, as some of Jude's more New Age friends might put it, 'sweating the small stuff'.

'The thing is,' said Carole in a rush, 'they want to leave Lily with me.'

'Over this long weekend they were talking about?'

'Yes.'

'Well, that'd be lovely for you, wouldn't it?'

'Ye-es.' The length of the vowel betrayed the extent of Carole's anxiety. 'The fact is, Jude, it's years since I've looked after a baby . . . well, since Stephen was born, actually. And I wasn't very good at it then. I don't really think I have much in the way of maternal instinct.'

'Nonsense, you'll be fine. And it's not as if you'll be on your own.'

'How do you mean?'

'I'll be next door at Woodside Cottage. If you have a crisis, you can call on me.'

'Oh, Jude, would you really help?' There was an almost pathetic appeal in the pale blue eyes.

'Of course I would.'

'Thank goodness. Now, please, promise me you'll let me know which weekends you're going to be away, so that I can make sure Stephen and Gaby choose one when you're around.'

'Yes, of course,' said Jude easily. She was continually amazed and slightly puzzled by how seriously her neighbour took things. For Carole Seddon life was a minefield; every step in every direction – particularly a new direction – was full of potential hazards. Jude had always had a more relaxed attitude. There were things which she took seriously, but she really didn't sweat the small stuff. And in this particular instance she couldn't help being amused by the comfort Carole took in her potential as an assistant baby-minder. Jude, despite a varied and exciting love life, had never had any children. The right man for such a commitment had never appeared at the right time.

But Carole Seddon, despite her dauntingly efficient exterior, and despite the fact that she had held down a responsible job at the Home Office with icy control, was totally lacking in confidence when it came to her private life. She had felt even less certainty in such areas since she had divorced Stephen's father David, but she had never really felt at home at home. Her neuroses had made her create a wall of privacy around herself, and Jude was one of the few people who was occasionally let inside that wall.

Carole, embarrassed to have strayed onto such an emotional subject as her granddaughter, looked round the pub for a new topic of conversation, and her eye was caught by one of many identical posters stuck on any available space. DAN POKE COMEDY NIGHT, read the legend. FOR ONE NIGHT ONLY. TV STAR REVEALS ALL HIS NAUGHTY BITS – FANCY A POKE . . . ? The date was the following Sunday evening and the venue – surprisingly to Carole at least – was the Crown and Anchor.

'Know anything about that?' she asked.

Jude shrugged. 'Well, I know about Dan Poke. Was quite a big name on television a few years back.'

'Really? I've never heard of him.'

'One of the first round of alternative comedians.'

The intonation of Carole's 'Oh' suggested that that

was hardly the kind of thing she might be expected to know about. Except for her secret vice of a particular afternoon chatshow, she didn't watch much 'entertainment' television. Carole still had a rather Reithian view of the medium as a purveyor of education and generally watched only news and documentaries. Watching the first was easy – news proliferated from every outlet – but decent documentaries had become an endangered species. Drama, generally speaking, Carole eschewed, though she would watch classic book adaptations featuring Empire-line dresses or crinolines. And, of course, anything with Judi Dench in it.

'Are there people in Fethering who would want to watch someone like that?' she asked Jude, in a tone that very definitely expected the answer no.

'Presumably. Otherwise why would Ted be putting it on?'

Carole's only response was a 'Hm' that was very nearly a 'Hmph' of disapproval. There was a silence while they ate, before she observed, 'These scallops are good.'

'Yes. Ted's new chef is really doing wonders.' Jude looked round the pub. The weather was very hot, so the outside tables were full, and there was very little space in the interior. All the pub's doors and windows were open, but only the slightest breeze drifted lazily in from the sea.

Fethering would always be predominantly a retirement community, so the average age of the clientele was high. The tourists the area attracted tended to be quite mature too. Small children were few, and those that were there were with grandparents rather than parents. Otherwise, a lot of well-heeled people in their sixties and seventies, representatives of the last generation whose pension provisions would be adequate to their needs, sat on the outside benches or in the alcoves of the Crown and Anchor, eating and drinking. As they did most lunchtimes in various pubs along the South Coast. And good luck to them.

'Word of mouth is spreading,' Jude observed. 'Do you remember how gloomy Ted was about the effect he reckoned the smoking ban would have on his business? Looks like he got it wrong. For a Monday lunchtime, the place is heaving.'

Her choice of word was perhaps unfortunate, because at that moment, a pensioner in one of the alcoves rose in panic. Long before he could make it across to the safety of the toilets, his semi-digested lunch spewed in a yellow arc across the floor of the pub.

It is an instinct among the British people to try to pretend unpleasant things have just not happened, but this one was hard to ignore. The Polish bar manager, Zosia, was quick to fetch a bucket and mop from the kitchen behind the bar and Ted Crisp himself followed her out. The landlord was a large man with ragged hair and beard, dressed in his permanent livery of faded T-shirt and equally faded jeans. He gestured for Zosia to get a move on.

But before the clean-up operation could begin, there was another casualty. An impossibly thin little old lady with rigidly permed white hair had risen from her seat in another alcove and tottered forward. She was sick too, though not as profusely as the man had been. Something like mucus spilled from the corner of her wrinkled mouth as she slipped slowly to the floor. And lay ominously still.

Though Jude had no medical qualifications, her work as a healer meant that she knew a lot about the human body and its frailties. So she was quickly crouching beside the stricken pensioner, feeling for a pulse. Ted Crisp looked on in horror as a silence descended on the Crown and Anchor.

A little old man, surely the woman's husband, had tottered out of the alcove after her and was looking down at Jude, his rheumy eyes beseeching her not to bring bad news.

'It's all right,' said Jude. 'Her pulse is weak, but it's definitely there.'

'Thank God,' said the little old man.

'Maybe she just fainted because of the hot weather . . . ?' Ted suggested hopefully.

The husband didn't buy that explanation. 'She was right as rain this morning.'

'What did she have for lunch?' asked Carole.

'The scallops. She insisted on having the scallops.' He was unaware of the communal intake of breath from other customers who had ordered the same. 'Bettina always liked seafood. I could never take it myself. Got one of them allergies to all that stuff.'

Carole and Jude exchanged a look and knew they were both thinking the same. Scallops could all too easily go off in the kind of weather they were having.

The old man's eyes once again appealed to Jude. 'Is Bettina going to be all right?'

'I'm sure she is,' came the brisk reply, 'but I think it might be as well to call an ambulance and get her looked at at the hospital.'

'I'll ring them,' said Ted, relieved to have something positive to do. After the recent excitements, the pub settled back into some kind of normality. Zosia made quick work of cleaning the floor. The man who had vomited first was helped to the Gents to clean himself up, and soon taken home by his friends. Bettina, whose surname Jude discovered from her husband Eric was Smiley, was picked up and settled into a chair. She hadn't fully regained consciousness, but mumbled softly to herself. Eric took her thin liver-spotted hand in his. His grip was so tight that he seemed to fear she might slip away from him.

Gradually, but quite quickly, the Crown and Anchor emptied. Customers who'd ordered other dishes finished them up quickly. Most who had ordered the pan-fried scallops with spinach and oriental noodles just stopped eating. Zosia and her waitresses showed no emotion as they repeatedly asked, 'May I clear that?' In every case the answer was yes.

Carole Seddon had finished her plateful before the vomiting began, and she felt extremely uncomfortable. Her stomach churned. She knew the sensation was probably just psychosomatic, but she still wasn't enjoying it. Carole had always had a terror of disgracing herself in a public place.

The ambulance arrived and its practised crew got

Bettina Smiley wrapped in blankets and onto a stretcher. They had virtually to prise away her husband's hand, then gently led him out to accompany her to the hospital.

An anxious-looking Ted Crisp emerged again from the kitchen just in time to see their departure. Carole and Jude were about the only customers left. Carole looked on edge; Jude's brown eyes beamed sympathy to the troubled landlord.

'Maybe it wasn't the scallops,' she suggested hopefully.

'Bloody shouldn't be. I've used the same supplier for my seafood ever since I've had this place. Never had any trouble before.'

'And everything in the kitchen's OK . . . you know, from the Health and Safety point of view?'

'Yes, it bloody is! Only had our annual inspection last week. Passed with flying colours. They couldn't find a single thing to criticize . . . which always makes them bloody cross. They like to find some little detail to pick you up on.'

'Will you have to report this?'

'Perhaps not, but I'm going to do everything by the book. Since the old girl's gone to hospital, I should report it under RIDDOR.'

'RIDDOR?' Jude looked puzzled. Carole looked increasingly uncomfortable.

'"The Reporting of Injuries, Diseases and Dangerous Occurrences Regulations 1995,"' Ted parroted. 'And I've just called them. Done everything by the bloody book, like I said. Rang through to their

Incident Contact Centre.' He looked even more troubled. 'But when I did, there was something odd . . .'

'Excuse me,' Carole announced suddenly, 'I must go to the ladies' room!' And she rushed off.

Jude passed no comment on her friend's disappearance, but gave the landlord a sympathetic grin. It didn't seem to raise his spirits. 'You said there was something odd . . . ?'

'Yes. When I got through to the Incident Contact Centre . . .'

'Hm?'

'They knew about what'd happened. Someone had rung them only minutes before. Less than twenty minutes after the old girl got sick and the authorities had already heard about it.'

Ted Crisp might have said more, but he was interrupted by the ringing of the phone behind the bar. 'Crown and Anchor, Fethering,' he answered automatically. Under the beard his mouth contorted with anger as he responded, 'No, I bloody haven't got anything to say to you!'

He slammed down the phone and looked at Jude. His face showed a mixture of puzzlement and fury as he said, '*Fethering Observer*. Wanted to know if I had any comment to make about the outbreak of food poisoning in my pub.'

'Good heavens.'

'How did they know?' asked Ted Crisp, almost to himself. 'How did they know so quickly?'

extracts reading groups
competitions books new
discounts extracts
competitions
books
new
events books
extracts
new titles reading groups
interviews
events extracts
discounts
new books events
events new
discounts extracts discounts
www.panmacmillan.com
extracts events reading groups
competitions books extracts new

reading groups

events

reading groups

books

books